Out of the
Girls' Room
and into
the Night

The

John

Simmons

Short

Fiction

Award

University of

Iowa Press

Iowa City

Thisbe
Nissen

Out of the
Girls' Room
and into
the Night

University of Iowa Press, Iowa City 52242

Printed in the United States of America

http://www.uiowa.edu/~uipress

Printed on acid-free paper

"Iowa (Traveling III)" by Dar Williams, copyright © 1996
by Burning Field Music (ASCAP), administered by Bug; see
www.darwilliams.com.

Library of Congress Cataloging-in-Publication Data

Nissen, Thisbe, 1972–

Out of the girls' room and into the night / Thisbe Nissen.

p.   cm.—(The John Simmons short fiction award)

ISBN 0-87745-691-7 (paper)

1. United States—Social life and customs—20th century—
Fiction.   2. Love stories, American.   I. Title.   II. Series.

PS3564.I79O97   1999

813'.54—dc21   99-16672

00   01   02   03   P   5   4   3   2

For my parents, for everything.

I've never had a way with women,

But the hills of Iowa make me wish that I could.

And I've never found a way to say I love you,

But if the chance came by, I would.

—DAR WILLIAMS, "Iowa (Traveling III)"

Contents

The Mushroom Girl / 1

At the No. 1 Phoenix Garden / 18

Apple Pie / 20

When the Rain Washes You Clean
You'll Know / 33

The Rather Unlikely Courtship of Edwin
Anderson and Roz Rosenzweig / 42

Grover, King of Nebraska / 53

29th Street Playground,
September 1968 / 63

What Safety Is / 66

Way Back When in the Now
before Now / 79

Fundamentals of Communication / 91

Flowers in the Dustbin, Poison in the
Human Machine / 95

Mailing Incorrectly / 117

3 1/2 x 5 / 129

819 Walnut / 131

Accidental Love / 148

How Beautifully Resilient the
Human Being / 159

Jono, an Elegy / 171

The Girl at Chichén Itzá / 180

The Estate / 185

A Bungalow, Koh Tao / 196

Grog / 199

After Twenty-Five Years, at the
Palais Royale / 210

Think about if You Want / 212

The Animal's Best Interest / 225

Out of the Girls' Room and into
the Night / 236

ACKNOWLEDGMENTS

Thank-yous of all shapes and kinds to the
teachers, editors, and friends who made this book possible:
Marilynne Robinson and Frank Conroy and Jim McPherson,
Diane Vreuls and David Walker, Katie Hubert, Patricia Law-
rence, Allison Amend, Erin Ergenbright, Peter Orner, Lisa
Miya-Jervis, Ben Schrank, Lois Rosenthal, Eric Simonoff, the
Bread Loaf Writers' Conference, the James Michener Society,
Dar Williams and Charlie Hunter for their generosity in the use
of the epigraph, Sandy Dyas for her haunting cover photograph,
everyone at the University of Iowa Writers' Workshop who
helped these stories through their inception, the journal editors
who gave them homes along the way, and everyone at the
University of Iowa Press for seeing them this far. And for all
their support: Michelle Forman and my parents, Myra and
Tony Nissen.

"At the No. 1 Phoenix Garden" appeared in
Story (spring 1997). "Apple Pie" appeared in *Sycamore Review*
(winter/spring 1998). "After Twenty-Five Years, at the Palais
Royale" appeared in the *Journal* (spring 1999). "Mailing
Incorrectly" appeared in *Reed Magazine* (1998). "Accidental
Love" appeared in *Seventeen* (December 1996). "The Estate"
appeared in *Hampton Shorts* (1997). "Grog" appeared in
Spelunker Flophouse. "A Bungalow, Koh Tao" appeared in
Fourteen Hills (spring/summer 1999). "Think about if You
Want" appeared as "A Brownstone, Park Slope" in the *North
American Review* (May/August 1999). "3 1/2 × 5" appeared
in the *Wisconsin Review* (spring 1999). "The Animal's Best
Interest" appeared in the *New Orleans Review* (fall 1999).
"Fundamentals of Communication" appeared in *Atlantic
Unbound* (September 1999) on the web at www:theatlantic.com.

Out of the
Girls' Room
and into
the Night

The Mushroom Girl

When Drew first sees Maud she is sitting on a stoop across the street. Drew's gone outside for a cigarette and watches her from the shadow of the Movie Place doorframe. She is eating mushrooms from a small carton on her lap. She dusts off the dirt, peels off some of the outer skin. When she puts the stem in her mouth, it looks for a second like she's sucking a pacifier. Popping the cap off, she looks it over closely, nibbling in small, circumnavigating bites. Drew thinks that he has never seen anything so lovely and so sad before in his life. She is skinny, the mushroom girl, with thin, blond hair pulled off her face and a long, crooked nose. He fights the urge to race across the street and tell her that if he could just watch her eat mushrooms like that for the rest of his life he would never need anything else. Everything would be okay if she would just stay there on that stoop forever.

The next time he sees her she is searching the Musicals shelf.

"I'm looking for *South Pacific* and I don't see it out here," she says, irked.

"Someone just rented it," he blurts out. "I'm sorry. Is there something else I can get you?"

"No." An exasperated snort. "There go my big plans for the night."

Drew can think of ten thousand things she could do tonight. Few of them involve *South Pacific*. He can't stand the idea of her leaving the store. She is luminous. He is prepared to offer her anything.

"We just got *Apocalypse Now* back in; that's got a tropical setting too . . . Or you could get a good old one: something classic, trusted entertainment, like . . . Or have you seen *Wings of Desire*? It's in German, but it's beautiful . . ."

She cuts him off. "Subtitles? Look, forget it." She hefts her bag higher on her shoulder. "It's really not a big deal. I'll survive." She heads for the door. Drew grabs the closest video box to him and holds it out to her.

"How about this?" he asks. She turns to look.

"No thanks." She's thoroughly repulsed, he's sure, as he watches her spin away again, toward the door. Drew is left holding onto Carrie in her blood-drenched prom dress, staring after his mushroom girl. Or you could get a love story, he wants to call out, like *West Side Story*, or *The Way We Were*, or *Annie Hall*, or *Love Story* . . .

But Maud is tromping out of the store, a bulging tote bag bouncing against her hip.

"Icy fish," says Mitch, the manager.

"What do you think she has in that bag?" Drew asks him. Mitch is a Jersey Boy, one of those guys who's lifted so many weights in his time that he can't walk right anymore. He swagger-waddles back out onto the floor.

"Lipstick, tampons, those balled-up used tissues that girls always have that go through the laundry and shed all over the place . . ."

"You think she's pretty?" Drew asks.

"Yeesh!" Mitch shudders. "Yeah, if you're into the Miss Auschwitz look. Can you imagine fucking a girl like that? Eeesh." He shudders again.

"Like you're one to talk, Mister I-have-a-poster-of-Heather-Locklear-on-every-exposed-wall-of-my-apartment."

"The difference, my friend? Heather Locklear is hot. That girl," he gestures out the door, "is weird."

"I think I'm in love," Drew says.

Mitch is looking at Drew like he's a lunatic. And maybe he is. But Drew doesn't want what Mitch wants: foxy dates for Saturday nights at cheesy clubs and sexy waitresses to check out at the sports bar. He doesn't even want what he's supposed to want: a partner, compatibility, we-both-like-to-take-long-walks-with-our-dog kind of love. That's yuppie love. Drew wants crazy love: fated, astrological, intense, cosmic, I-saw-you-and-I-knew love. He thinks maybe he could find that with the mushroom girl. He doesn't know why he thinks this, he just does.

"I know," Drew mutters, "I know."

"Don't get all obsessed with some chick you've laid eyes on once, OK?" Mitch says. He is at the computer now, punching keys and scrolling screens.

Twice, Drew wants to tell him. I've seen her twice. First on the stoop eating mushrooms. She was so beautiful and so lonely-looking—"I've seen her twice," he says.

"Oh Jesus, it's too late," Mitch throws up his hands. "He's already gone."

Maud is twenty-four and wishes life worked like musical theater: that people burst into song in the middle of bars and streets, clicking their heels and swinging on lamp posts.

Duct-taped jazz shoes whisk across the studio floor. Zark, the pianist, plunks out a *South Pacific* medley. Bob Starry's cane raps in time to the music, his instructions—"lunge, NOW, pivot pivot UP UP! Where is the life!?!? The LIFE!!!"—rise over the dancers' song—"I'm stuck like a dope with a thing called hope." Maud, at this point, is unable to pant out a chorus, let alone dance and sing at the same time. Barre exercises alone leave her breathless. The studio air is dense with sweat, and the pollen count is soaring. Wheezing, Maud breaks from the group. She grabs her bag from the pile of leg warmers and sweat shirts by the mirrors and heads for the studio door.

"You are leaving us, my dear?" Bob Starry shouts dramatically across the room. Bob calls everyone "my dear." Even Zark.

"I can't breathe," Maud shakes her head, palm to her temple. It's the third class this week she's given up on.

"My dear, my dear, what will we do?" Bob's concern is overblown, as are most of his gestures. He carries on everyday conversation as if he were acting for the last row of the balcony. "When the dancing begins, you flee. Our Cinderella," he says, but already he is turning back to his chorus, the tap of his cane falling in with their steps. "You say you are dancers?" he bellows. "Then dance. Dance!"

Maud looks like a dancer. Looks like the rest of them anyway: jutting jaws, gnarled feet, double-jointed limbs, knobby spines and spiny ribs poking through threadbare leotards. Like them, she has arranged her tiny life around classes at this studio and cattle-call auditions where her shot at dancing on Broadway is about as good as her shot at New York Lotto. *All you need is a dollar and a dream.* But lately this breathing thing has been getting worse, and she knows she's going to have to do something about it. Dancers who can't breathe are dancers who can't dance. And dancers who can't dance aren't dancers.

Weeks pass with no sign of the mushroom girl. When she finally does resurface, Drew doesn't even realize it's her. She calls the video store to place a delivery order, and Drew doesn't recognize her voice. It doesn't even dawn on him until she places her order: *42nd Street, Camelot, Grease, Kiss Me Kate, Pippin, Showboat, West Side Story.* She requests that the movies be charged to her credit card and delivered to Maud Schloss, 16 East 94th, fifth floor. The bell is to be rung once and the movies left in the entrance vestibule. She is ill. "Highly contagious," she tells him. She cannot have contact with anyone.

He knows where she lives! The Red Death couldn't stop him.

When Drew arrives at number 16, he rings the bell marked Schloss and waits in the entranceway. Through the glass-paned door, he can see into a dim lobby area. A staircase begins at the right and veers off behind the wall. He hears scuffling. He thrusts his hands deep in his pockets as if to hide his whole body in them so she will not notice him there. He has no idea what he will say to her. He thinks about running, but his legs won't move. She rounds the bend in the stairs, appears on the landing, starts, and ducks back behind the wall. A congealed voice echoes out into the lobby: "I expressly asked for the movies to be left at the door." There is an edge—desperation? Anger? "Please go away!"

Drew's palms sweat in his pockets. His leg is twitching. He leans in toward the glass. "I'm really sorry, I'm leaving, I'll go . . ." He drops the videos and hurries out the front door onto the street. He feels like a voyeur, a peeper, as though he's invaded her somehow. "I am an asshole. I am an asshole. I am an asshole," he berates himself. He squints into the sun. He wishes he could get high. Generally, he doesn't hate himself as much after a couple of bong hits.

Back behind the desk, in the air-conditioned video store, Drew recalls her face as he saw it for that moment through the door. It was strangely shadowed, puffy. There was a piece of white, like surgical tape, across her nose.

"Hey, Mitch," he says. "You know that girl? The really thin one. *South Pacific*?"

Mitch turns from the VCR he's adjusting. *Casablanca* has no vertical hold. "Icy Girl?"

Drew feels embarrassed. "You know anything about her?" he asks. "Like who she lives with, or anything?"

"What do I look like? The census bureau? How should I know who she lives with?"

"I'm serious, Mitch, really. You've been here longer than me. You haven't seen her come in with someone or anything . . ."

"If you want to know if she's available, why don't you just ask her out and see what she says?"

"No," Drew shakes his head, beckons Mitch closer. Mitch's eyebrows crinkle in as he struts over, thigh muscles packed tight as frozen chicken.

Drew turns away from the customers, speaks under his breath to Mitch. "That delivery? It was hers. And she, I don't know, I mean I didn't see her up close, but she had a bandage on her nose, and, I don't know, but she looked pretty fucked up."

Mitch's eyes widen. His voice drops an octave. "You think someone's knocking her around?" he asks, his hand cupped by his mouth, like 007 in a room he knows is bugged.

"I don't know," Drew says. "Maybe. I mean, maybe she's in a really bad situation."

Mitch is nodding, a look of real concern weighing on his features.

"Maybe that's why she's so thin," Drew says. "Maybe he doesn't let her eat, or tells her she's fat, or something?"

Mitch jumps in. "Maybe that's why she has to get all those musicals. Maybe the guy is older—I mean, have you ever seen anyone her age who watches that crap . . ." Mitch's brain-wheels are churning. "Remember how pissed she was when *South Pacific* was out that one night? And then we didn't see her for like a week or two. And now she turns up all beaten . . . He probably did it when she didn't bring home the movie that night. She knew he would, that's why she got so upset."

Drew doesn't know what he thinks. Mitch is making this all sound like a TV movie. He'd feel like a moron if he was wrong. But what if he's not wrong?

"There's one of those domestic violence center places over near my gym," Mitch offers. "I could check it out tonight."

Sweet, good-hearted Mitch. Drew can just see this lug of a guy bumbling into the domestic violence center, gym bag slung over his shoulder, decked out in a full parachute-cloth outfit, a tuft of chest hair sprouting up from the zipper. Suddenly the whole thing seems so absurd: Mitch and Drew playing Cagney and Lacey during slow season at the Movie Place. "Maybe we should try to find out for sure first," Drew says.

Mitch is nodding vehemently again. "Get some harder evidence. That's probably best. We could really wind up insulting someone if we're wrong . . ."

"Yeah," Drew says. "Maybe let's just wait awhile and see."

Mitch nods once more and then turns back to his adjustments of Bogart. Drew takes up his position at the register. Maybe he should just call a crisis center? Just check to see if this is the right thing to do? He scrounges under the counter and finds a Yellow Pages from three years before. He looks up Abuse, then Hotlines, then Assault. Then a woman comes in asking for *Witness*, which is out, and by the time he's convinced her to take *Steel Magnolias* instead, he's lost his nerve.

"Hey, Beautiful," Zark calls out, slumping down in the chair next to the reception desk. Maud is in back, making coffee. Since her surgery she cannot take class, was even supposed to take a break from office duties—answering the phone, stamping class cards, scheduling rehearsal space, plunging stopped-up toilets in the dressing room—but they're terribly short-staffed, and Maud is coming in a few hours a day to help out.

"Jesus!" Zark balks as Maud comes back from the coffee pot. "I take the 'beautiful' part back. What the fuck happened to you?"

"I told you, Zark." Maud sits. "Wonder of wonders: you didn't listen. The surgery to undeviate my deviated septum . . . ?"

"So you're not deviant anymore?" he asks, fiddling with the pencils in a jar by the phone. He pulls one out and starts to bounce the eraser end on Maud's thigh.

"Nope," she says, "a fine, upstanding citizen."

"Too bad, I liked you deviant," Zark says, grinning. He stops bouncing the pencil and slips it up toward Maud's crotch. She scoots her chair backward. She points to the door.

Zark is a jerk, but he is also the first person Maud met in New York, and she knows that he's not *all* bad. In some remote, warped kind of way she knows that he actually does care about her. And in some sort of obligatory, piteous, I've-slept-with-you-so-I-have-to-find-a-tiny-something-in-you-that-I-can-love-so-I'm-not-utterly-revolted-by-you-and-disgusted-with-myself sort of way, she cares for him too.

Maud Schloss calls the Movie Place to make arrangements for another delivery. She will leave the seven already-viewed videos in the front vestibule of her building in exchange for seven new movies. Drew collects her selections from the shelf: *Singing in the Rain, Meet Me in St. Louis, My Fair Lady, The Sound of Music, Oliver, A Funny Thing Happened on the Way to the Forum, Guys and Dolls*. He walks to 16 E. 94th.

In the entrance vestibule, on the floor, there is a large paper sack of groceries. Drew checks the delivery slip on the bag: *Schloss*. He peeks inside: grapefruits, a bunch of carrots, a box of Irish Breakfast tea, ricecakes, mushrooms, and something cold, melting rapidly at the bottom of the bag. Drew scoops it all up just as someone comes down off the street and pushes into the vestibule with him. It's a young guy about sixteen with a jean jacket on and hair that's trying to be long but is only succeeding in being exceedingly puffy. He starts to dig around in his bookbag.

"Can I help you?" he says to Drew, looking skeptically up at him through a bush of hair.

"Uh, well . . . yeah," says Drew. "I just . . ." Suddenly his brain clicks in and a story unfurls itself. "I just went out for groceries, for my girlfriend, but she's not answering the bell now because she probably decided to take a shower, which probably means I'll be out here all afternoon . . ." He laughs. He looks at the boy, who he sees is smiling too. "See, I've got the key to the apartment." Drew puts the Movie Place bag inside the grocery bag to free up a hand and pulls his key ring from his pocket with renewed confidence. He picks out the key that opens the employee bathroom at the store and sticks it out toward the boy. "But she hasn't had a chance to make me a copy for the front door lock yet, on account of she's been home with the flu . . ."

"No problem," the boy says, flipping the hair out of his eyes and opening the door. He holds it for Drew to come in behind him, then stops at the door to the ground floor apartment. Drew calls, "Thanks, man," and heads up the stairs.

"Hey, tell your girlfriend not to use up all the hot water—other people need to take showers too," the boy calls back.

"I hear you," Drew laughs, and while he's walking up to the fifth floor, he feels as if what he told the boy is true: he is going to see his girlfriend who never leaves him any hot water either. This is much easier, he thinks, than worrying about what he will do once he gets a look inside her apartment. What if he's right? What if she is being abused? What will he do then?

The stairway is dark, only one dim bulb in a frosted glass fixture on each landing. On the fifth floor there are two doors, and neither is marked. Drew guesses and knocks on the one at the front of the building from which he can hear the sporadic eruption of sit-com laugh tracks. A sausage-bellied man in a white undershirt and kelly green trousers answers the door. He has a rim of thin white hair encircling a broad, shiny scalp and holds a television remote control in his beefy hand. Drew sets his jaw.

"Mister Schloss?" he asks.

"Mister, yes. Schloss, no." He points across the hall. "Schloss, yes. Mister, no." He pauses to look Drew over. "Mizz," he says in an ominous stage-whisper, nodding at Drew as though they share a great and profound understanding. Drew raises his eyebrows and nods back, uncertain what he's agreeing with.

Remote in hand, the man pivots and zaps his console. The TV flashes off, taking I Dream of Jeannie with it. Drew is beckoned to follow across the hall. The man rings the bell, announcing loudly, "Mizz Schloss, there is someone here to see you, Mizz Schloss. Mizz Schloss, you have a gentleman caller." He turns and winks at Drew, who is growing increasingly embarrassed and wishing he had just left the movies at the door and fled. In a minute the peephole flicks open, and Drew feels himself being peeped at.

"Who are you?" asks the voice behind the door. The balding man turns to Drew and gives him a look like, yeah, who the hell are you?

"I have your videos," Drew says. "Oh, and your groceries too; they were sitting in the vestibule. Something's melting, I think."

"How did you get in?" Maud demands.

"Someone was on their way in . . . they let me in," he fumbles.

"See," proclaims the neighbor, pointing at Maud through the pin-hole in the door. "I told you we need a better security system." He storms back to his own apartment as though this is what he'd come across the hall to say in the first place.

"I've asked for deliveries to be left at the door," she says. Drew can only interpret her tone as racked with pure hatred.

"I'm sorry. I . . . I didn't realize . . . but, um, I've got them, I mean, I've already carried them up here, could I just . . ."

Drew stops. The heavy door is being pulled open. Then Maud is facing him, her hair clipped up off her face, both her eyes blackened and bloodshot, surgical tape stretched across her nose. When she reaches for the bag in Drew's arms, he can see behind her a wedge of the tiny apartment: a light purple quilt littered with magazines, an alarm clock, a bouquet of dyed carnations in a florist's reusable vase, a poster of Joseph on the far wall, spreading his amazing technicolor dreamcoat in a fan behind him like a satin peacock.

"Thank you, " she says with not a shred of heart and heaves the door closed with a scrape and a thud. Drew flinches. Then he goes back across the hall to ring the neighbor's bell again. He answers, looking blank, as though he's never laid eyes on Drew before.

"Does she live there alone?" Drew asks.

"Who?" the man asks.

"Miss Schloss. Mizz Schloss, your neighbor."

The man flings open the door to his own apartment and steps aside to reveal a small room with a single bed against one wall opposite a mini fridge and stove. A door to the left opens on a bathroom the size of a broom closet. Every spare inch of the apartment is taken up by stacks of bundled newspaper.

"You gonna put two people in one of these?" he snorts and hurries back inside, shutting the door behind him.

Drew walks back to the store holding the stack of Maud's returned videos on top of his head with both hands, imagining his phone call to the police precinct. "Hello, I'd like to report a nose job." He tries to laugh at himself. He kicks at a soda can. It clatters into the gutter.

When Maud returns her movies, the swelling and bruising in her face have gone down some, but she is wearing large dark sunglasses anyway, and long pants and an army jacket although it's mid-May and nearly seventy degrees out. She's in hiding, Drew thinks. He'd be embarrassed too if he'd had a nose job. She's probably a vain, self-consumed bitch, he thinks. He hates her for making him feel so foolish. He cannot look at Maud as he checks in her returns. When he sees she's up for a freebie he grabs a box off the rack behind him and slams it down in front of her, saying, "You get a free movie with every fifteen rentals. How about this?"

It's *Roxanne*. The picture shows Steve Martin with a nose that extends from one edge of the box to the other. Maud doesn't say anything. Her knuckles whiten on the edge of the counter. Drew looks up at her big owl-eye glasses, determined to return some of her venom. Damn, he thinks, that's one hell of a nose job: they didn't even straighten it up. Maud's chest is heaving and there's a little rasping sound every time she exhales. Then she turns and slams out of the store, nearly plowing over a couple in tennis whites on their way in, holding hands. It's a blur of motion, and then the door fans slowly closed behind her, like the camera fade-out in a Mafia movie after everyone's been blown away.

He's standing there moments later, stunned, with *Roxanne* still in his hand when the door flies open and she storms back in. She comes toward Drew, panting now with uneven breaths, tearing off her sunglasses. Her eyes are bloodshot and flashing.

"You know," she yells, "you are an asshole." Customers turn around nervously, then pretend to be deeply engrossed in their movie-box blurbs. "What the fuck gives you any right in the world to act like such a smug fucking asshole?" A fluorescent light flickers. Maud is wheezing.

Everyone is staring at Drew, waiting for his response. Maud starts digging through her bag, looking frantically for something. Drew wishes he knew what. Mitch hovers a few feet from Maud like a wrestling referee. He looks like he's afraid she'll bite. When

Mitch sees her shake an asthma inhaler and put it to her mouth, he jerks around, grabs a chair from behind the counter, and pushes Maud into it. He studies her face while she breathes, then puts a hand on her shoulder and says, "Is there someone we can call for you? Someplace where you'll be safe?" Maud looks at him like he's crazy, and then her hand flies to her face.

"I am recovering from surgery to correct a deviated septum," she tries to clarify. Maud looks around, and everyone is staring back at her sympathetically as if to say, yes, we know, denial is natural. That steely look reenters her face. She stands up quickly, pulls her bag back on her shoulder, smooths her hair. "Thank you for the chair," she says, curtly polite. She glares at Drew. She seems beyond words. She strides out of the store.

Drew is rooted to the floor. He cannot move. He hopes maybe he is dead. Maybe she was carrying a .45. Maybe he has been gunned down and is now bleeding to death all over Steve Martin's profile and the linoleum floor. Oh god, he thinks, this is my life passing before my eyes, and what I am is an asshole. She is an angel, and I am an asshole.

"Man, Drew," Mitch whines. "You can't do shit like that . . ." His head goes back and forth in disbelief as if he can will away the whole scene.

Drew is already coming around the counter.

"Hey, no . . ." Mitch is going to get stern. The ground of authority is slipping from beneath him. "Drew, don't you . . ."

Drew grabs Mitch's arm, tugging his shirtsleeve as he backs toward the entrance. "I have to go . . . I have to apologize . . . I have to catch her . . ."

"You can't just . . ." Mitch's face tightens indignantly, as if he's about to assert himself for real this time. But it's too late. Drew is already out the door. This is more excitement than the Movie Place has seen in months.

He buzzes long and hard. There's a rustle of static. She is answering. She is pressing the TALK button. She is talking.

TALK: "Who is it?"

The Mushroom Girl

More static. Drew's heart is racing. She's going to push LIS-TEN. He has to think of something to say. She has to listen to him.

LISTEN: "It's Drew," he says. "I'm the . . ." How to identify himself? How to keep her on the line? He can't make his brain work fast enough. "I'm the asshole from the video store," he says.

The line goes dead. Drew starts buzzing again. He keeps buzzing. He doesn't know what else to do. He is the most pathetic person he could ever conceive of being. Buzz. Buzz. Buuuuuuuuzzzzzzzzz.

"What?" she demands. She waits a second, then presses LIS-TEN and lets him answer.

"I wanted to apologize to you . . ." She lets go.

TALK: She pauses. "Thank you," she says. "Now please go away."

She does not press LISTEN. He leans on the buzzer again. She gives in. He is confused.

LISTEN: "Hello? Hello?"

TALK: "Hello."

LISTEN: "Hello. Don't hang up," he says quickly. "Please, I just wanted to try to explain. I'm sorry. I just, I don't know why I acted like that. It's just that I've seen you around and I just didn't know how to deal with it exactly, and I didn't. Well. I mean: I didn't deal with it well."

TALK: "Could you speak a little more coherently please? It might be easier for me to understand what you're saying if you use full sentences."

Full sentences? He can barely remember how to speak English. First, he cannot make his mouth move. Then, it just sort of pops open on its own and starts spouting things and he doesn't have the power to make it stop.

LISTEN: "Did you ever . . . did you ever see that episode of *The Brady Bunch* where Marsha makes a date with a kind of nerdy guy, but then this cute guy asks her out for the same night and she forgets about the date with the nerdy guy, except then Greg and Peter are playing football in the back yard and she goes out to tell them it's time for dinner or something and she gets hit in the nose with the football, and she goes: 'Oh my nose!' and they show it in slow motion like forty times. I mean actually it's not really, totally relevant exactly, but I just . . ."

TALK: "Are you the cute guy or the nerdy guy?"

LISTEN: "What?"

TALK: "In this analogy. Are you supposed to be the cute guy or the nerdy guy?"

LISTEN: "Well, neither, I mean, maybe both. But . . ." He trails off.

TALK: "But . . .?"

LISTEN: "Maybe you'd like to come down here and punch me in the nose?" What he wouldn't give to be unconscious!

TALK: "That might be gratifying."

LISTEN: "Because, I don't really know why, but I really would like you no matter what you looked like, and I'd really like it if you'd let me take you out to dinner, to say I'm sorry . . ."

TALK: "Look, I have to go, OK?" She clicks off. He starts in with the buzzer.

TALK: "Will you stop that please."

LISTEN: "Sorry, I'm sorry. I thought you were going to hang up again."

TALK: "I was. Look, I accept your apology, OK? You don't have to take me out to dinner. Your conscience is clear. So if you'd refrain from ringing my buzzer, I'd appreciate it."

LISTEN: "Wait, I won't ring if you promise not to hang up before I'm done . . ."

TALK: "I'm supposed to wait for you to finish unburdening yourself before I can go?"

LISTEN: "No, no, wait, I just mean, warn me before you're going to not listen again . . ."

TALK: "OK. This is your last chance. I'll listen once more, then you have to leave, OK?"

LISTEN: "I get one more? Or is this it?"

TALK: "The next one is the last one. Now. Talk."

LISTEN: "Please listen all the way through, OK? You don't have to answer that, just keep listening." He takes a deep breath. "I saw you a few weeks ago, eating mushrooms on the stoop across from the store, and I watched you, and you were eating them so delicately, and you looked so lonely, and I just wanted to know you. So then you came into the store, and everything I did just made you angry, and I wasn't trying to make you angry, I just didn't know how to talk to you and it made me really nervous, and sometimes when I get nervous, I just start talking kind of a lot . . ."

TALK: "Kind of a lot?!"

LISTEN: "Wait, are you still listening? So this is my last one now. OK. Yeah, I know, a lot a lot. But it's, I mean, I know this city, and in New York, it's like . . . I just, I look at you and you don't look like you're a very happy person and maybe I'm not either, but maybe, I think maybe we could be . . ." He pauses, and she doesn't let go of the button. "Look," he continues. "I just thought that maybe we could hang out some. We could see if maybe there was something. If we were happy. I just wanted to tell you that, and maybe you'll let me take you out to dinner sometime, or not dinner, but something, anything. Or if you think, as you probably do by now, that I am a completely incoherent, unstable fool, which granted I probably am . . ."

There is a click, TALK, like she's going to say something. Only she doesn't. There is just a muffled laugh, and then another click. She is listening again. He takes another breath. "I think you think I'm crazy, and I'm not. I'm not crazy. It's just that I see a chance for something I think could make me happy in a world that is a generally not very happy place, and I can't just give up and walk away from that without doing everything I know how to do to make it happen. I'm not crazy. I'm just not giving up. I don't want to go the rest of my life thinking that maybe we could have made each other happy. So, OK. So, I guess that's all I wanted to say. I hope you'll give me a chance. I guess I'm going to go now. I'm Drew. Good-bye. I'm going, OK? OK, bye." He leaves the vestibule before he has to hear her break the connection.

———

Drew is long gone by the time Maud lets go of the LISTEN button. Shadows have begun to take over her apartment. She can't even legitimately call it an apartment. It's a room. A nearly empty room. In a couple of years she'll be like Sol across the hall and she'll stop taking out the trash; it'll be all she has to keep her company. There are no beers in Maud's fridge, no emergency onion dip. No vodka, no limes, not even flat tonic water. No one ever stops by. She never has anyone over. There's not a spare tooth-brush, an extra washcloth, no strange deodorants left behind by out-of-town guests. The evidence points to exactly what Maud's life is: empty.

Who is he anyhow? A guy who doesn't know her, doesn't know anything about her. But how can she just turn away from some-one who's picked her out of a crowd, who's seen something in her that's left him crazy and stupid, following her around, acting like a fool? Part of her wants to believe him, though. To believe in what he sees. Believe that there is something glowing under her skin, behind her eyes, something that only someone who loved her could see.

It's all bullshit, she knows. Starry-eyed fantasy. The blatant facts are that he does not know her, and—romantic notions of fate aside—cannot feel for her what he says he feels. Although he's right: she is lonely. It's also true that she's not very happy. And she knows she shouldn't be letting herself get drawn in by the romance of him: the big, fated words and the cosmic scenes he's painting her into, yet it's hard not to be drawn. Even if the wizard turns out to be a chubby man behind a curtain, when you're standing on the road, waking from the long, silent, poppy-sleep of the alone, you can't help but move toward those emerald towers, twinkling on the horizon. You can't help it: you want to know what kind of life might await you in that magic kingdom.

A breeze has picked up outside. A wind, actually. A wind which feels like it has more force than wind is supposed to. Or maybe Drew is just less resistant than he should be. His hair whips at his face. He moves away from Maud's building. He is moving to-ward the park. Brick and granite townhouses wheel past him. Curled black wrought iron flashes past like swinging Tarzan vines. Windowpanes blind like spotlights. The sidewalk sparkles, specks of hot mica, silver, like stars beneath his feet. Like he's walking in the sky.

She laughed. After he called himself a fool, an incoherent, un-stable, blithering fool, he heard her laugh. She might have been laughing at him: yes, you are a fool. But it didn't feel like that.

Maybe he's being delusional. Wishful. Ridiculous. He doesn't think she was laughing at him. It was a toss-of-the-head laugh. An eyes-closed laugh. A laugh that said, "I know!" He thinks maybe she has understood him.

People leap off buildings. They jump off subway platforms, off bridges, into the Hudson River. But they don't leap under the delusion that anyone's going to be there to catch them. In this city, nobody'd even clean up the mess on the sidewalk. Drew thinks he knows what Maud must feel like. It's as if she's walking along the street. Suddenly, from high above, someone is calling to her. Such an embarrassing lack of suicidal decorum: this guy standing on a window ledge shouting, "Hey you! You down there! You with the mushrooms . . . The blond! Yes, you with the beautifully crooked nose. You! I'm going to jump, and I want *you* to catch me. No one else. Just you. You're the . . . one, two, three, ready or not here I come . . ." And she could just keep walking, look away, pretend she hasn't heard, *I'm sorry, I didn't realize you were speaking to me.* Continue along on her way through the city of strangers.

Or she can stand there on the sidewalk and open her arms.

At
the
No. 1
Phoenix
Garden

At the No.1 Phoenix Garden my mother seats my father by a patient family friend, then positions herself across the table, a sea of shrimp boats separating husband from wife. My mother sits next to the orchestrator of this dinner party, the handsome professor of Chinese whose monologue on Tiananmen Square my mother will later call "fascinating" but during which she is distracted, her fingers feeling for the graying hair at her temples, straightening her place setting, looking across to my father hunched in his chair, the third button of his powder-blue oxford come undone to expose a tuft of whitening chest hair. His fingers, victims of premature Parkinsonian decay, can no longer maneuver button through buttonhole. He struggles with his chopsticks, trying to free the pair from the red crepe-paper ring that binds them. My mother mouths to him, over brilliantly spiced dishes and through complex conversations he cannot follow, "Do you need a fork?" at the same time motioning one from a passing waiter before my father can even begin to process her question, abandon his futile task, and muster a reply. He watches her move past him, forging on, as she does, to offer hot tea to the professor's empty cup: durable white ceramic etched with a blue pastoral scene. Two young lovers in a boat, like a gondola, steered by the young man's swift and commanding stroke. My mother glances across to her husband, the whole of his sick-stubborn being concentrated in the slow, precarious path of his fork from plate to mouth. She is remembering their once-upon-a-time expeditions, trips to Europe—Venice, canoeing the lake at Annecy, my father guiding a rental car through the twisting roads of alpine passes, uncorking bottles of French country wine, extracting escargots from their butter-slippery shells, the masterful things of which those hands were once capable. Beside my mother, the distinguished professor balances a steaming dumpling in the air between his chopsticks. Black-coffee irises wide, my mother leans toward him, her lips parted, ready.

Apple Pie

━━━━━

   At camp, when you are nine, there is a floppy-breasted Birdie-section counselor named Mary-Allison who gives you piggy-back rides to the dining hall. But when you come back the next summer you've gotten too big to carry and too awkward to be cute. Mary-Allison finds littler Birdies to carry on her shoulders across the big field. Sometimes you still get to walk alongside them and hold Mary-Allison's hand. Also: she braids your hair once before a social at the boys' camp, loans you her lifeguard whistle on camper-counselor switch day, and lets you sit in her lap while she paints a daisy on your cheek at the county fair.
   On Visiting Day you can't find her *forever*, and you ask Bobbie,

the nurse, who says Mary-Allison is running swim down at the waterfront so you drag your mom and dad down the piney hill and stand behind the do-not-cross line by the buddy-board and shout to Mary-Allison at the other end of the dock: "Mally! Mally! These are my parents!"

Mary-Allison turns for a second, startled. When she sees you, she calls to your parents, "It's nice to meet you!" waving with one hand and pulling down the bottom elastic on her orange bathing suit with the other before she turns back to the swimmers and rings the buddy bell.

"BUDDIES!" the lifeguarding counselors shout from the docks as bathing-capped girls try to grab hands with their swim partners. You want to run out onto the dock and hold Mary-Allison's hand, but you can't because it's a buddy check and besides, nobody would understand. You watch as the other girls tread water, holding their clasped fists in the air, gasping, waiting to be counted.

"She seems very nice," your mother says diplomatically as you trudge back up the needled slope. On the waterfront you can hear Mary-Allison calling for the buddy counts:

"Cindy?"

"Twenty-two deep, fourteen shallow, four on the raft!"

"Sooze?"

"Four, twenty-two, fourteen!"

You have to pinch your eyes shut not to cry. When you stumble into his leg, your dad says, "Hey kiddo, *faites attention!*" and gives your shoulders a love-squeeze right where your sunburn is.

You and Vivian are leaving. You've been scooping ice cream at Charlie's ever since you were tall enough to reach into the freezer and pull yourself back out; Vivian makes a shitload caddying at the country club. Your brother Lance has a '79 Ford Econoline van, banana yellow, and if you start saving now, when you and Viv are both seventeen and have your licenses, you'll be able to buy it off him. You live on a tiny island where, once the summer renters go home to New York City, everyone knows everything about everyone else and nothing ever changes year after year after year. Tourists call it "close-knit" and "traditional." You call it suffocating. You plan your escape for five years from now, just after the Fourth of July. Independence Day seems appropriate.

The way you imagine it, your parents will drop you off at the high school where buses will be waiting to cart you upstate to basketball camp. The Banana Van will be parked out behind the gym. You and Vivian won't ever get on the bus. Camp won't miss you; you will have withdrawn your registrations months before. You'll have a friend on the bus bound for All-Star Camp Mohawk, armed with a collection of postcards and letters addressed to your parents and to Vivian's. She'll mail one every so often and it will arrive at your island homes bearing a Lake Placid postmark, news of the game against Camp Starlight, and horror stories of poison ivy. This friend will be thrilled to be in on your diabolical plan, giddy with the importance of being the only one who knows what you're really doing: sneaking off to some boy's house or running away to New York City to become stars. Your friend will think it's the coolest thing anyone at Island High has ever tried to get away with. You won't disagree.

On the Fourth, everyone will be in town, sitting on the curbs eating salt water taffy and tossing their sticky pastel wrappers into the street like confetti as they watch the parade: three sparkling firetrucks, all buffed up for the display; Mrs. Robeson's Girl Scout troops, knee socks and pageant sashes drooping in the heat; grandfathers strutting slowly in sherbet-colored walking shorts, a perfect fez perched firmly atop each bald head.

That night you'll all go down to the beach for corn-on-the-cob and hot dogs and watermelon, and as the Catherine wheels and Roman candles shower sparks into the blackened sound, you and Vivian will watch from under the docks, tucked in the darkness, cornsilk stuck between your teeth, lips sticky from apple pie, until the last flare dies—*whizbang!*—on the horizon and parents try to out-shout each other, calling their children's names into the salty night.

You'll ride home in the back of Viv's mother's Subaru wagon, tasting of baked apples and sea air and Vivian. If you make it, that will be the last time you ever watch the fireworks from this beach, on this island, in this stifling, seagull-ridden sound.

Once in eighth grade you and Vivian are standing in line at the vending machine in the cafeteria behind Stacy Weintraub, a junior. Stacy gets the last apple pie. You stare through the glass down the long, empty aisle where silver coils disappear into the depths of the machine, turn to Viv, and say, "Bummer, no more apple."

Stacy is by the trash can and she hears you. "Hey," she says, pulling one pie-pocket from the wrapper, "do you want the other?"

Stacy Weintraub has never talked to you before. "Oh, no," you stammer. "I didn't mean you had to . . ."

She cuts you off. "Seriously, take it." She waggles the pie toward you. You try not to watch how her breast jiggles under the thin, white cotton of her T-shirt.

"Really?" you say.

"Like I need another pie!" Stacy presses the package into your hands.

"Thanks," you say. "Like *I* really need an apple pie . . ." you add, whacking yourself in the stomach.

"Oh, hush," Stacy says. "You've got nothing in the world to worry about." She takes a bite and clomps off into the cafeteria crowd, her Doc Martens—steel-toed, twelve eyelets, in oxblood—squeeching against the lunchroom floor.

Viv pulls her sack of Skittles from the mouth of the vending machine, then turns back, eyebrows raised to you. You bite into your pie.

When you are a freshman and they are seniors, Stacy Weintraub goes to the prom with Naomi Bentner. The morning after the dance, all you underclassmen go down to Charlie's Grill and wait for the seniors to show up for their postprom breakfast. They come in: the girls stockingless, dangling broken-heeled dyed-to-match pumps from manicured fingers, stiff hair pulled back in makeshift buns held in place with Class of '86 elastic garterbelts. The cuffs of the guys' tux pants dribble sand from the beach where they've been since midnight when the official prom ended. They've gotten drunk on Smirnoff, felt up their dates, and finally watched the sunrise.

Naomi and Stacy haven't rented a limo like the others. Naomi's older sister Janna, who used to date your brother Lance, is home from college and chauffeurs the girls in Lance's gigantic Banana Van: a queen-size mattress in back and a rainbow of teddy bears dancing across the rear windshield. You watch through the window of Charlie's as Janna wrenches the door handle and slides open the yellow carriage. Stacy emerges first, her silver pumps gleaming in the sun like glass slippers. She has on a shimmery stretch-velvet tank dress you've seen in the Victoria's Secret catalog. Naomi is wearing a suit. It's vintage, from one of those cool places in the City, not another rented penguin suit making its annual trip to the Island High prom. Naomi even has a cummerbund. Her bow-tie—you can see as they pass, arm in arm, and disappear into the ladies' room—is tied around Stacy's ponytail.

In the late fall of eleventh grade, Vivian's dad gets a job offer in California, three thousand miles away. There is nothing anyone can do. They leave on a gray day between Christmas and New Year's, and you say good-bye to Vivian out by the woodpile her dad chopped and stacked all summer and fall and now will never burn. Vivian has on her red parka. Her nose is red and her cheeks and ears, too.

"We can write," you say.

"Swear you will," she says.

"Swear."

"Me too."

You hug her there by the woodpile, wishing you could stay like that forever, never lift your face from the damp nylon collar of Vivian's coat. All you want—more than anything in the world—is to stay there long enough to get up the courage to do what you've wanted to do for as long as you can remember.

When their station wagon pulls out of sight, you walk home in the cold, relieved by how much it hurts. On the table in the hall there's a note from your mom: she and Dad have gone to rent a movie and are bringing back pizza, so if you're hungry . . . In your room, on your bed, your fingers are so numb you can't hold the pen to write. You watch your parent's minivan pull into the driveway, get up, and lock your bedroom door. You draft four different versions of the same letter. You flush each one down the toilet, watch the notebook confetti disappear in a porcelain whirlpool, everything spiraling down.

Weeks pass. You feel as if there is a cloudy scrim between you and the rest of the world. You are clumsy. You forget things. Your tongue is too big for your mouth.

When a letter finally comes, you can't feel it between your fingertips, as if they are frostbitten again. You slice a papercut in your thumb as you tear into the envelope, but still you don't feel anything. The words on the page are big and happy and make your mouth go to glue. *California is awesome,* she writes. *Even school is good — there are more kids in my homeroom than in all of I. High. I swear. I met a guy! Craig. I'm scared to say too much and jinx it. I'll tell you details later. I like him, I think. Really like him. I can't handle it that I get a boyfriend and you're not here! I don't know how I'll survive not talking to you every ten minutes. This is so unfair! Are you going to come visit? Come spring break, but not if it's the week of Easter because Craig'll be away and you* have *to meet him.* There is more, about her dad and his job, and her teachers, and classes, and more about Craig because in the end she just can't resist telling you all the details. No one will ever be her best friend like you are, she writes. You will be best friends forever.

You try to write back. Really. There just isn't anything to say.

—————————————

By spring you get a boyfriend too. Eli. I. High Tribune Photography editor/Yearbook staff/Environmental Club. You meet him on the Earth Day celebration planning committee which you only joined in the first place because Chloe Storfer is committee chair. Chloe Storfer looks like a cross between Michelle Pfeiffer and Melissa Etheridge and has a voice so throaty it sounds like she's seducing the cafeteria workers when she orders the lunch special with fries.

Chloe Storfer looks nothing like Vivian.

Chloe Storfer dates Peter Sanchez, who is in your algebra class. Sometimes you and he lend each other the homework. Usually you sit together, and on especially boring days you play Dots or Tic-Tac-Toe, passing the papers back and forth beneath your desks. One day while Mrs. Fiorello is putting up the "Do Now" problems on the board Peter passes you a note: *I know somebody that likes you.*

Who? you write back.

Eli Pressman.

You're such a liar, you scrawl.

Ask Chloe, he challenges.

You would never pass up an excuse to talk to Chloe.

——— ———

Chloe grins at you, her eyes twinkling like a merry matchmaker. She arranges it so you and he work the sound board together, piping R.E.M. and Carly Simon over the PA system, so you wind up spending Earth Day smushed into the sound booth with Eli Pressman. He's pretty nice and sort of cute and kind of still boylike and not all big-sweaty-manly, which makes him a lot easier to deal with. You bond over a secret devotion to Billy Joel and confess to weeping during "While the Night Is Still Young" when he sang it at the Meadowlands concert last year.

When Earth Day is over and you and Eli are outside the booth coiling wires and sorting records, Chloe skips over, flushed with the success of the celebration.

"Hey you two . . . ice cream or whatever at Charlie's . . . club fund's paying . . ."

You and Eli split a sundae: pistachio with strawberry sauce. Chloe makes gagging noises. "You guys belong together," she groans.

By Monday, you are "going out" with Eli Pressman.

Your parents think Eli is the greatest thing since sliced bread. Eli appears to think you are the greatest thing since "Uptown Girl." You go away to basketball camp the summer before twelfth grade and meet Layla, who strikes you as being the greatest thing *ever* and about whom you cannot conceive of evoking descriptions of food products or pop medleys.

"Nice shot," a voice says behind you.

You turn. "Thanks," you say.

"I'm Layla," she tells you.

"Isn't that a song?" you ask.

"You've got me on my knees ..."

"Huh?"

"My folks like Clapton," she tells you.

"Pretty hip folks." Your parents like Bach.

"They're pretty cool," she admits.

You're at a loss for words. Layla sets up a shot. She's tall—5′9″, 5′10″—with long straight blond hair and biceps that flicker like heartbeats under her skin as she shoots. It goes through. "Are they coming for Visiting Day?" you ask, feeling like a moron.

"Nah, too long a drive." She sinks another.

"You can come out with me and my folks," you spurt out, far too quickly.

She doesn't look at you funny, just cocks her head to the side. "Thanks," she smiles, but it's a smile with a question imbedded in it somewhere. "That's really nice of you to say."

You are disarmed. "Where are you from?" you manage to ask.

"New York," she tells you.

"New York where?"

"City," she says like she forgot there were other parts of New York State. "How 'bout you?"

"Long Island," you say, careful to enunciate and to pause between the *g* and the *I*. "Way out, off the eastern shore. A really little island."

"Wow," she says, trying to grasp that.

"Not really," you say. "There's not really anything 'wow' about it in the slightest."

You both laugh.

The two of you are inseparable for the rest of the summer. Layla is loud and sarcastic and fond of lapsing into a phony Brooklyn accent to tell bad jokes. You are in awe of most things about her: her basketball game (All-State champ), her wardrobe (she's from New York City after all), her breasts (low-slung and mature and utterly fascinating to 34A perhaps-you'd-like-one-with-a-bit-of-padding you), and the way she takes up space in a room. You get weird and nervous around her and live in terror of falling into a Long Island drawl. This does not stop you from wanting to spend every minute of the day with her. Somehow, miraculously, she seems to want to spend every minute of the day with you too. You make each other lanyard bracelets, on Candy Store days you get Skittles and she gets M&Ms and you share, and you save seats on your blankets for each other at Campfire Sings. You think you have never been so happy in your entire life.

Spring break, senior year, your parents invite Eli to join the family on a road trip down to Western Kentucky for your Grandma Flo's seventy-fifth birthday bash. They even let him drive their minivan, which they never let *you* drive. You sit in the passenger seat; Mom and Dad play Twenty Questions in back. "How big *is* a bread box?" Eli asks coyly, catching your mother's eye in the rear-view mirror. She laughs far too loudly. On the highway, when you pass signs for Big Bone Lick State Park, you tell Eli he has to pull off so you can buy a hat, or something, for Layla.

"That's ridiculous," your mother says. Eli looks torn between loyalties. Finally, in the exit lane, he says, "It might be good to get out and stretch, don't you think, Mrs. R.? Use the facilities, and get a bite to eat." He is stiff, waiting for her response. You are fuming at what an ass-kissing pansy he can be. A smile breaks across your mother's face. "Good thinking," she says. You know that in your mother's world, a man who caters to her daughter—no matter how absurd her daughter may be—is a good prospective son-in-law. You want to gag.

Chloe is going to the prom with Peter. You're going with Eli. One day in calc, you slip Peter a note which you wrote out last night at home but pretend to scrawl right there in class so it doesn't look premeditated.

You guys want to share a limo with me and Eli? it says.

Sure, his note answers, *that'd be good.*

Excellent, you write.

Did Chloe tell you? he asks.

You feel a little scared. You're not sure why. *Tell me what?*

We set a date, his note says. *October 16th.*

You write so hard you break your pencil point midsentence and have to switch to pen. *You're getting MARRIED?!?!*

Peter turns to you, nodding like a thirsty puppy.

After graduation you convince Lance to lend you the Banana Van, which you've never succeeded in buying from him. You and Eli and Layla are going to drive across country to see the Pacific Ocean, which you think eighteen years is too long to have gone without seeing. You haven't talked to Vivian in longer than you can remember and don't plan on calling when you get there. You just want to see California. Since the day she left you standing at the woodpile, the state itself has taken on epic proportions in your mind.

The morning you set out is so sunny it hurts. You pick up Layla in Manhattan, and she takes the driver's seat to maneuver out of the city. The Banana Mobile has a three-foot-long gear shift shooting out of the floor, more phallic than the pigs-in-a-blanket they served at your Sweet Sixteen and more unwieldy than Eli's penis, which you find to be ridiculously unwieldy and try to tangle with as infrequently as possible. Layla drives with the window rolled down, her hair whipping around her face and neck. From behind her seat you rein it all into a ponytail for her and tuck it through the back of the *Big Bone Lick* baseball cap you got her, which, she's told you, she adores and wears everywhere.

At a rest stop in Pennsylvania while Layla is in the bathroom, Eli pulls your elbow to him and whispers: "She's kind of a ditz, huh?"

You give him a look which you hope says *die* and pretend to knee him in the balls. You walk over to the vending machines and buy M&Ms. Eli's allergic to chocolate.

As Layla drives Eli keeps peering over her shoulder at the speedometer so that it looks like he's blowing in her ear, which makes you wonder if what he meant when he called her a ditz is that he thinks she's sexy.

"You're worse than my grandmother," you say to Eli, tugging at his shirt. Your grandmother is a back-seat driver prone to blatantly obvious instructions: *there's a traffic light coming up here on the corner and if it's red you'll need to stop.* Eli backs off and sulks. He picks up Layla's camera and starts taking pictures out the window. You get mad that he's wasting Layla's film without even asking her and say, "This green blur is Indiana, oh yes, and this green blur, this is Iowa. See that smudge of white? That's a cow." Eli starts to remind you just who *is* and who *is not* photo editor of the yearbook, but you do a Grandma Flo impersonation, pointing at your ears and saying, "Honey, I don't hear." Eli, who has adopted all of your mother's views of your family and thinks your grandmother is a saint, looks at you disparagingly. You turn away and stare out the window. You have vowed to stop fighting with Eli; it isn't worth it. It's only a matter of time anyway before you have to tell him. And everyone else.

The first night on the road you stay with friends of Layla's parents, professors at a little college in Ohio. They have a big, expensive house, and you each get your own room.

The second night on the road you stay in Iowa City at the Christian Community Youth Hostel even though all three of you are Jewish. To your delight there are separate dorm rooms for men and women, and you get to share with Layla while Eli has to sleep with a squawking soccer team from Des Moines. The girls' room is turquoise and green, with Sunday school drawings taped to the walls: Crayola renditions of biblical scenes titled in preschool penmanship. JOHN's *N* is backward, Ezekiel's *E* has seven prongs instead of three. The floor is covered with a gritty shag rug, swirled in shades of aquamarine and infested with fleas. You and Layla spend the night on a foam-rubber mattress, also riddled with fleas. You don't sleep much for the itching. Once, when you wake up, Layla isn't next to you. You raise your head and twist around to find her sitting by the window: the silhouette of a girl. Without turning, she speaks like she knows you're listening. We could stay, she says to the sky. Get to California and never go back. Just us. We could.

You realize you are nodding. You nod yourself to sleep.

The next day Eli drives. You and Layla sprawl in the back eating Funyun Rings and Skweez-Cheez and singing every song from every Broadway musical you've ever known. Eli threatens to pull over if you don't stop. Layla gets out her Walkman and the Red Hot Chili Peppers, clips the headphones over Eli's ears, and cranks the volume. The two of you pick up "I'm Gonna Wash That Man Right outta My Hair" right where you left off.

In Cheyenne you stay with Layla's aunt and uncle and their new baby, Fred, who sticks his fingers in Eli's ears and yells, "MAMA!" Aunt Gayle and Uncle Jim put you to sleep in their basement-turned-rec-room in sleeping bags on the floor. You sleep in between Layla and Eli and have a dream in which you are walking through a snowstorm with Layla on one side and Eli on the other. You go into a jewelry store where Eli buys a cheap mood ring and proposes to you on bended knee. Layla turns into a butterfly and flies away. You pierce your nose with the ring and walk back out into the snow alone. You wake up with a sleep-dent in your nose from lying face-down on a zipper.

You pull an all-nighter through Nevada, impatient to get to the ocean and willing to forgo the sights of Elko and Winnemucca in the name of speed. You hit San Francisco at sunrise and buy groceries from a supermarket called Lucky, because you never know: it could be. Highway 1 takes you down the coast, a stream of annoyed Porsches at your tail. The Banana Van was not designed for skinny, curvy, cliff-side roads. Eli pulls off at a scenic overlook and lets the traffic pass.

The Pacific Ocean is breathtaking. The water is the bluest thing you've ever seen and you cannot take your eyes from it, waves cresting stark white and crashing into the rocks with a force you are sure will imminently erode the cliff on which you are standing. Eli says he is exhausted and climbs into the back, heaves himself onto the mattress, and falls asleep nearly immediately, a little puddle of drool forming on the sweatshirt he's using as a pillow. You and Layla are not so much sleepy as ravenous. Layla reaches into your Lucky grocery bag and pulls out the day-old apple crumb pie you bought for a dollar ninety-nine. You've got a quart of milk in the Playmate chest your mother made you bring along "for perishables." You bought the milk at a gas-mart near Reno in the middle of the night to lighten Eli's coffee. He said he'd puke if he consumed any more nondairy creamer. You didn't really blame him.

You and Layla go up front, trying not to disturb Eli but knowing that he could sleep through an earthquake. The way you've been to him this trip, he's probably glad to leave you two alone. You think he probably won't put up with you for much longer.

Layla is curled on the passenger seat, balancing the pie between the gear shift and the open ashtray. You take the driver's seat, passing the milk between you in a Dunkin Donuts mug you find in the glove compartment. Layla eats the pie crust, making her way around the circumference, then nudging aside the apples to excavate the bottom. You pick at the crumb topping, dribbling it across the seat and through your hair on the way to your mouth. (Eli always says: Why can't you just take a whole piece of pie and eat it, like normal people? It doesn't taste as good, you tell him. You like to pick.) You hold up a sticky hand, laughing silently. Layla grins and reaches out for it. She puts your sugary fingers into her mouth and, one by one, licks them clean. There are pie-crust crumbs in Layla's hair and you straddle the gear shift and climb over into her lap to pick them out. Then you kiss her. You've always expected Layla's teeth would be somehow soft, like cooked apples. Instead, they are slick and hard, like porcelain. Eating apple pie and kissing Layla is like licking the bottom of a cereal bowl. It's like Apple Jacks.

When you join Eli on the mattress, you spoon around Layla. She snuggles backward into your arms, and you fall asleep like that, Eli's snores notwithstanding. Pie innards lie in a gelatinous heap in the box, still open on the front seat. Breakfast for Eli, you figure. When he wakes up.

You realize you haven't saved him any milk.

When
the Rain
Washes
You Clean
You'll Know

A year after my father was killed by an exploding manhole cover, Joanie Slesenger moved into apartment 2A, right above me and my mother. Soon afterward, a man who said he was Joanie's father called and asked my mother if he might speak with the landlord of the building.

"Land*lady*," my mother told him. "My husband's dead."

"So sorry, ma'am," said the man.

"As am I," my mother said.

"My daughter, Joanie," he began, "is a delicate girl. She's lovely. Harmless as bread. But sensitive. I call not to arouse concern but simply to make you aware of her circumstance."

"Which is what, Mr. Slesenger?" My mother forbade aerosol

sprays, reptiles, and rodents. Beyond that, if someone wanted to rent an apartment, she didn't ask questions.

"It's no cause for alarm. I merely thought it in everyone's best interest that I bring these issues to your attention. I wouldn't want for you to be surprised or disquieted by Joanie's behavior, should it strike you as existing outside a range which you might consider normal." He paused.

"Is your daughter a psychopath?"

"Oh no, no no no no no no no," Mr. Slesenger cried in a cadence that sounded, to me on the kitchen extension, as operatic as the trills that echoed from his daughter's apartment. Mr. Slesenger's paternity was proven. Joanie sang incessantly, along with the radio, and her floor was my ceiling, so I heard it all. She had a decent voice. Kind of loud though, too much vibrato. It was a little hard to take sometimes.

"Is she a danger to me, or my daughter, or any of my other tenants?" my mother asked.

"Oh no."

"Is she up to something illegal?"

"No no, nothing like that."

"Does she have seizures?"

"No."

"Practice voodoo? Drink sheep's blood? Sacrifice farm animals?"

"Ma'am?"

"I appreciate your concern then, Mr. Slesenger, but I think we'll all be just fine here." She hung up. Of music, my mother quite approved.

My mother was at Woodstock and claims to have sucked Janis Joplin's tit. My father was a chiropractor who capitulated finally and allowed my mother to put "Glory" on my birth certificate only after she threatened to call all his clients and tell them that the man who cracked their spines and manipulated their vertebrae smoked a fatty every single night before he went to bed. My father relented but never called me anything but Gloria. Then one night last March he went out during a thunderstorm to move our car from one side of the street to the other. Alternate Side of the Street Parking was in effect for Manhattan. From what we've been told, officials believe it was a chemical reaction caused by the winter sand and road salt that seeped, during the thaw and subsequent runoff, into the manhole. There was some sort of gas explosion then, the force of which blew the hundred-pound manhole cover thirty feet in the air. It landed on the roof of my father's brand new '82 Ford Fiesta. The crush killed him instantly.

A month after Joanie moved in, she came downstairs and knocked on our door at 7:30 in the morning wearing a blue acrylic bathrobe, her feet pushed halfway into a pair of tennis shoes, the backs flattened mercilessly beneath her heels, and asked my mother if she could have a word with me. My mother insisted it was not *because of* Mr. Slesenger's phone warning that she let Joanie into our apartment that morning and pointed her down the hall to my bedroom. Joanie had come to the door and asked to speak to me, and there was nothing in the world more to it than that. Joanie shuffled in, her robe clinging static to the pantyhose she had on underneath. My mother shouted my name and then left me to Joanie, dashing back to the kitchen to rescue her English muffin from the broiler before the smoke alarm went off.

I wasn't asleep. I had an English exam third period and had been up since six rereading the book (Ms. Friedling was partial to questions like "In Salinger's 'Just before the War with the Eskimos,' how much money does Ginny claim Selena owes her for cab fare?"), so I was quite awake when Joanie appeared in my doorway, her head cocked to one side, resting against the doorframe like I imagine my folks did when I was little and they'd come home from a yoga class or a lecture, pay the sitter, and then come in to check on me, one of them lingering in the doorway for a moment extra, gazing over their sleeping babe.

I put down my book and lifted my head from the pillow. I hadn't really talked to Joanie in the month she'd lived upstairs, just occasional hallway chitchat, but she started in as if there was nothing unusual at all about her presence in my bedroom on a weekday morning before school.

"Glory, Glory, Gloria," she said, lolling over the words like Ms. Friedling did when she read Wordsworth aloud. "Glory, Glory, Glory . . ." She was starting to singsong, her voice whispery and crackling and kind of eerie. "Gloria," she said, "there are some things that I need very much to discuss with you."

I didn't say anything. I just lay there staring at her. Joanie's hair was yellowish and looked like it had been permed once but hadn't grown out completely. She closed her eyes and took a deep, concentrated breath, like a gymnast centering herself before a routine or an actress getting into character backstage. When she opened her eyes again she said, "There are things that you will need to know in life, and most things no one can tell you. You'll have to discover those on your own. But I know some things that maybe might help you. Maybe you already know more than you should. Your father . . . you've been forced to grow up early. Knowledge is, in many ways, power. And it's not that I think power is ultimately a good thing really, but if the alternative is powerlessness, and if I can help you avoid that, that crippling, then maybe I've done you right in some way." She breathed in hard, then looked quickly around my room, like she'd suddenly realized time was an imperative. She grabbed my desk chair in one hand and set it down beside my bed, an overly dramatic gesture that reminded me of Mr. Sachs, our Guido math teacher who tried to teach geometry with moves out of *Saturday Night Fever.*

Joanie sat at my bedside. "Please remember. I'd have written you a letter, but I don't want to trivialize anything. Ballpoint can be so maudlin." She paused, as if to collect her thoughts. "When your mom is out," she asked, "when you're home alone, do you answer the telephone?"

"Yeah," I said. Joanie was sitting close, leaning in to me intently. She smelled sour but tingly—like onions and witchhazel.

"When you pick up the phone, is it ever someone asking you to donate money or telling you there's a special price on portrait sets? Like, all the wallet-size photos you'd ever want? Or a consumer survey? Someone asking questions about things? Do you know what I mean, Gloria?"

I nodded. What else was I supposed to do?

"OK, honey." She put her hand on my arm through the quilt as if to say, *OK, listen close now, OK?* "You do not ever, if you don't want to, you don't *ever* have to answer their questions. It's all right that you've said hello, but once you know it's one of them you don't have to say anything more, OK? You don't have to tell them *anything*—not why you can't pledge money to the firemen's association or the disabled veterans. You'll beat them at their own game eventually. If you can out-wait them."

"OK, but Joanie," I said, "I'm gonna have to get up soon. I've got school, and a quiz . . ." I held up Salinger, but she didn't really seem to see it. "I'm gonna need to start getting ready . . ."

Joanie smiled. She seemed somewhat charmed, like she was looking down at me with all the wisdom of her twenty-eight long years, tickled by the trivialities that masquerade as concerns in the minds of the young. "OK, sweetheart," she chuckled a little and patted my arm again. "OK, sweetheart, we'll get you there on time." Then she launched right back in.

"Gloria," she was intensely serious again. "Do you ever hear voices? Voices inside your head? Do you ever hear them calling to you?" Her eyes were wide, blue as her bathrobe and kind of buggy, as if her eyeballs were rounder than they should be or one size too big for the sockets they'd been stuck into.

I thought about voices. Everyone hears voices, I thought. Not like *I am Oz the great and powerful* voices, just regular voices. My mom telling me that if I ate Ho-hos on my way home from softball practice I'd fuck up my yin-yang balance. Or during a math test I'd try to conjure up Mr. Sachs's voice in my head intoning the Pythagorean Theorem, which I did not, no matter what I tried, seem to be capable of memorizing. Sometimes I could remember the sound of my father's voice in my head. I'd hear him singing. We'd be in the car, like when I was a baby and teething or otherwise cranky, and my parents found that the only surefire way to get me to fall asleep was to drive round and round the neighborhood crooning old campfire songs at me until I konked out, drool pooling onto the vinyl seat cushion. My dad would make up his own verses to "I Am My Own Grandpa," which he sang off-key. Those were not the kinds of voices Joanie was talking about.

"Uh uh," I said, "no voices."

"Of course not." She seemed to be berating herself for having asked in the first place. "Not yet, I should have known that. You must listen for them, though," Joanie said. "I know that they want you. They *will* call. And when they call, you have to be listening, OK?"

I nodded.

"Do you like music, sweetheart? Do you listen to the radio?"

"Sometimes," I told her. "I hear your stuff through the floor a lot." It seemed like an opportunity to say something about her radio marathons without being outright confrontational, but it didn't seem to awaken any recognition at all in Joanie. She went right on with her questions.

"Did you ever listen to Fleetwood Mac? Would your mom have any of their albums? Do you know their songs? Any of them?"

I cut her off. "Yeah, yeah, I know them." I had this awful feeling that she was going to start singing. It was annoying enough hearing it through her floor. I *really* did not want Joanie sitting in my room at eight o'clock in the morning singing Fleetwood Mac in my face.

"Good," Joanie said. "Fleetwood Mac—and Gloria, it's important you remember this, all right? Stevie Nicks—I don't know her personally, but she's the one to listen for. Listen to the heartbeat. Listen to the loneliness. Listen to the sounds the wind makes when it blows. Stevie doesn't have all the answers, and some visions we have to keep from you. At some point you'll have to go your own way. Don't look back. What's back there is painful, I know. But yesterday is gone. You can look to tomorrow. Just listen. Listen to the spirits. Promise me, Gloria. They're crying— you must listen to what they say. Promise me that."

"OK," I said.

"Good." Joanie seemed relieved to have gotten that all out and to have my word on it. She stood up quickly, then hung there at the side of my bed looking down on me. "You have to believe, Gloria. You won't know when it's time if you don't keep believing. That's how I know the time is right. The songbird knows. And when the rain washes you clean, you'll know too. Stay tuned. Keep your ears open." Joanie lifted the chair and returned it to the desk, then began edging apologetically toward the door. She gestured vaguely in the direction of upstairs. "My tea kettle," she said, as if she needed an excuse to leave me. As if I'd been keeping her from something. "It's probably been whistling for eons." She turned as if to leave, then faced me again. She looked worn, like she'd suddenly realized how much this talk was taking out of her. She put her hand to her chest and grabbed at the blue acrylic there, just over her heart, as if to illustrate the pain it caused her to say what she was about to say.

"I'm sorry I did not get to you sooner. I've not done a very good job here. If I'd made it to you before your father . . ." She seemed unable to say the word *died*, like it was just too hard to accept. "You might have been able to help him see. If you'd known." Joanie looked down, then back up at me. Her hands fell to her sides. "I feel responsible in some ways, though I know there's no way to know everything at every moment in time. Still, Gloria, I'm sorry."

Then she turned and was gone. I heard the apartment door close, and the clap-shuffle as Joanie made her way back up to 2A.

From the kitchen my mother hollered, "Poached or scrambled?"

"Neither," I called back. "I'm late." I got up, struggled into a pair of jeans. I was digging around for a decent bra when I heard Joanie's tape deck go on upstairs. The speakers were cranked so loud, I swear to god the doo-dads on my bulletin board were shaking in time to the music. She was on a serious Fleetwood Mac binge, wailing along with the lyrics, making sounds so guttural and pained you'd have pictured not Stevie Nicks but Mick Jagger, face contorted, mouth spewing.

Wearing god knows what kind of outfit, I shoved notebooks in my backpack and went into the kitchen where Mom was sipping her coffee, swaying a bit on her stool as if she was quite enjoying the musical assault from upstairs. I grabbed a banana from the fruit bowl. My mother gestured upward with her coffee cup. "Such emotion!" she said and nestled the cup back between her hands.

Upstairs one beat gave way to another, a slow snake-rattle, and I could feel the bass notes, Joanie pounding against the wall in time. *Oh Daddy, you know you make me cry. How can you love me? I don't understand why . . .*

I pulled my coat from the rack. "How'd she know about Dad?" I asked.

"Joanie?"

I nodded. "About Dad."

"I probably mentioned it. Chatting."

"You did?"

"Probably. It's not unlikely, right?"

I tapped the banana against my leg. "Why?" I asked.

She looked thoughtful, like she was trying to remember those few mailbox vestibule conversations. "I don't know," she said finally. "She talked some about her own father . . ."

"The one who called?"

"Mmm," my mom nodded, her mouth full of coffee.

"She's kind of tweaked," I said.

Mom slammed her cup down against the formica countertop. "For god's sake, Glory!" She stood up, utterly exasperated, as if ready to storm off, but only paused a moment instead and sat back down.

"I should go," I said.

"She's reaching out to you, Glory," my mother said, her eyes on me sad and intent. "Don't spurn that. Someone reaching out to you. That's something. Really." She sat with two hands cupping the coffee mug against her lap, her head nodding silently.

"It was just a little weird is all," I told her. "She wasn't making large amounts of sense."

My mother stood again. The conversation was about to be officially over. "Don't fall into the trap, my dear, of saying something doesn't make sense just because you don't understand it." Then she left the kitchen. The End.

——— ———

That afternoon just before rush hour Joanie Slesenger climbed over the guardrail of a twenty-ninth-floor terrace at 17th Street and Irving Place. It was her father who called to tell us she was dead, and his voice was detached and low.

"I'm so sorry, Mr. Slesenger," my mother said.

"It's not sorrow," he told her, "it's slower. Like resignation. Joanie's. Ours. Resignation."

My mother only nodded into the receiver, resigned.

——— ———

The night my father died, we heard the noise. Everyone did. We looked out the windows first, trying to see what the commotion was about. The rain was sheeting down; reflections from the traffic lights streaked the pavement red, yellow, white, green. We couldn't see anything from inside. My mom put a raincoat over her shoulders and glared at me for not doing the same. Outside, people in raincoats were everywhere. We ran out from the entrance of our building. All the people were across the street. They hovered, like they were circling a hurt animal, a bird fallen from its nest. Like they were afraid to get too close. When a space opened up in the group, we saw the car—our car—across the street, smashed, crushed in from the top. We heard a woman's voice rise from the inner circle, a shriek so high it was barely audible. Only it was. *There's someone inside . . .* The group recoiled, afraid. The shrieks gave way to sobs. My mother caught me in her arms. We heard the sirens scream. My mother trapped me between the wings of her raincoat, thrown over her shoulders like a cape. She wrapped herself around me, grabbed me to her, tight, her body pressed to my back, her chin clamped on the top of my head like an electric can opener. We watched from across the street: the ambulance, the crane, the men who worked in slickers to cut through the metal of the car to get to my father. The police came toward us, like they knew who we were without asking. We spoke with them. My mother held me. The rain came down. In time, the ambulance packed up and pulled away. No flashing lights. No sirens. The men in slickers continued to pry at the seams of metal, littering the street with broken glass. Sometime in the night my mother and I went back inside. She dropped the raincoat. We went to my room. We took off all that was wet and found things that were warm and that were dry. We climbed into my bed, both of us together, and we stayed there and held each other. "It was time," she said. "I didn't know that it was time already. So short. Such a short, short time." I didn't cry. I didn't cry for Joanie either. It made sense somehow. And maybe some people would call that cold and callous or strangely unfeeling. But I think Mr. Slesenger is right. That sadness is like resignation; it's a giving up. And you don't cry when you give up. You don't make a big production. You just walk away quietly, hoping no one will notice until you're already gone.

The Rather Unlikely Courtship of Edwin Anderson and Roz Rosenzweig

During the summer of 1967 Fran Kornblauser was renting a fifth-floor walk-up in a building whose buzzer system was partially and perennially incapacitated. When she threw a dinner party, which she did with characteristic frequency, her guests were able to buzz up to Fran's to announce their arrival, but Fran could not, as the system only worked in one direction, buzz back down to open the door. Thus, when the bell rang, Fran would hoist open one of the large front windows that overlooked East 11th Street, her jangling necklaces and voluminous breasts dangling over the window box, crushing the petunias planted there by the former tenant, wave hello to her prospective company stranded on the sidewalk, their necks craned upward like gawkers at a rooftop suicide, and toss a spare key out the window to the cement five flights below. "Turn it left and push hard," she'd holler. "It sticks like a motherfucker."

Roz Rosenzweig, who with her crazy ostrich legs and in an excruciatingly bright and irrevocably short Marimekko minidress looked remarkably like a strawberry lollipop, and Edwin Anderson, seersucker suit rumpled to Kennebunk perfection though he was himself not a Mainer but a Nebraskan, arrived on the stoop outside Fran Kornblauser's simultaneously and became acquainted on their knees as they scrounged in a bed of impatiens for the elusive key, which had ricocheted off a third-floor balcony and landed in the little cordoned-off flower patch. A sign hanging from the chain requested that dogs kindly be curbed elsewhere. Nonetheless, Roz was unsurprised when, instead of the key, her hand brushed what one hasty sniff proved to be a mostly but not completely hardened pile of dog shit.

"Oh fuck," she said.

"I've got it!" he exclaimed, procuring the key and holding it up so that it glinted in the light. He raised himself to standing and offered her a hand, but she declined and pushed herself to her own feet. His arm was still outstretched. "Edwin," he said, "Edwin Anderson," and he extended his hand farther toward her.

"Roz Rosenzweig," she said, "but I think we should wait and shake on that later."

"Oh," he said. "OK."

She shrugged. "Whelp . . . up to Fran's?" she suggested, and when he gestured for her to go ahead she said, "No no, after you," knowing full well all he wanted was a good view from behind for five flights. So then it was he who shrugged, and he pushed open the door.

As it turned out, it was neither her ass nor his gallantry that had prompted Edwin's offer to allow Roz ahead of him but the simple fact that he was a man who walked with a dreadful limp and knew that taking the steps behind him was bound to make for an unbearably slow and frustrating climb.

From the fourth-floor landing they could see Fran hanging out the open door, a plastic tumbler of drink in hand. "Come on, Gimpy," Fran called, not yet drunk, just naturally crass. She turned and yelled into the apartment: "One more flight and the Gimp'll have made it."

Now doubly horrified—by her shit-tainted hand and by Fran's unconscionable ridicule of this poor limping guy—she watched as Fran herded Edwin through the apartment door, and then Roz flicked a wrist and whacked Fran on the rather substantial flank of her rather formidable upper arm. Ice cubes clunked in the jostled tumbler.

"You bitch," Roz scolded, her face contorting into an overly dramatized approximation of appalled.

Fran gave Roz a reciprocal whack that nearly sent her sprawling down the stairs she'd just so arduously climbed.

"What's next?" Roz hissed. "You going to start hanging around St. Vincent's poking fun at the bedridden?"

Fran guffawed, flapped her arm toward the apartment door through which Edwin had disappeared, then gave another amused snort. "You mean the Gimp?"

"Fran!"

"Roz-Roz," Fran said, wrapping her arm around Roz and guiding her, too, into the apartment, "things are hardly as they appear, my darling."

Edwin "The Gimp" Anderson, it soon became clear, was not a cripple but a casualty of the Mad River Glen Ski Area, and there was much debate throughout the course of the evening among those party guests who were familiar to the sport (everyone, coincidentally, but Roz, who had lived her twenty-nine years on the island of Manhattan and could imagine nothing so unpleasant as a vacation in the middle of God-Knows-Where, Vermont frostbitten on the side of a mountain with six feet of deadly fiberglass strapped to the bottom of each of the only two feet she had) as to what his accident said about Edwin's downhill prowess. Roz, hands clean, sat on the floor of Fran's sparsely furnished bachelorette pad, trying not to flash her underwear to absolutely everyone in the room, sipping her vodka Collins and pondering how

she might offer herself up as an object of ridicule just to save poor
Edwin from the barrage of attention which she was sure he had
never before attracted in his short little library-squirreled life.
Though he was taking it remarkably well (some, including Barb
Carpenter, who always found it within her to come to the defense
of any marginally attractive male in distress, did, after all, believe
that Edwin's fall on a particularly icy stretch of "The Goat," a
double black diamond slope, in no way indicated that the mountain had gotten the better of him), Edwin was taking it mostly in
the face, his blush a shade of magenta not dissimilar to Roz's minidress, the purchase of which she was growing to regret more with
every passing moment, vowing that if she managed to escape
Fran's without spilling anything particularly disastrous on herself, she would return to Marimekko the next day on her lunch
hour and exchange it for the turquoise she knew she should have
gone with in the first place. Her down-the-hall neighbor, Loralee,
whom Roz had consulted for final fashion inspection that evening
before she'd headed over to Fran's, had assured Roz that only she
could pull off a dress like that so fabulously. Roz wasn't as sure.
She had always wanted to be a devil-may-care girl, proud and ir-
repressibly fuchsia. The fact was, she felt a lot more comfortable
in blue. With maybe a few more inches of material to cover up
her rather nice but very white thighs.

Edwin Anderson, a newly anointed lawyer fresh from Stanford
University who wanted to do work in civil rights, cornered Roz in
Fran's kitchen, where she'd retreated for a few moments of re-
prieve under the pretense of replenishing the bean dip. She was in
the process of adding another jigger of vodka to her Collins when
the door swung open to yield Edwin, carrying the near-empty
potato chip bowl like a monk begging for alms.

"Fran sent me for chips," he announced.

"What are you, the lackey?" Roz tossed another jigger into her
drink for good measure and pawed around the counter top for the
screw cap she'd set down somewhere. "Fran sent you to shame
me out of raiding her liquor cabinet, is what you've actually been
dispatched to do." Roz waggled the bottle toward him.

"In that case," said Edwin, "she picked the wrong spy." He set
his chip bowl on top of the fridge where he'd be sure to forget

about it completely and started opening Fran's cabinets one after another in search of a clean glass. "What're you mixing?" he asked.

"Over the sink, on the left," Roz said. "Collins. Collinses? Collinsi?"

"It could be like lice?" Edwin suggested.

"Ice? In the freezer," Roz said. "Do I look like a bartender? You've got arms."

"No, I, no, I mean, I meant the plural. Louse, lice. Mouse, mice. It could be like that. Or even like children. You know: child, children."

"Edwin," Roz said, facing him dead on. "Tonight we're making yours a triple."

Edwin Anderson had not one iota of New York savvy, yet he managed to surreptitiously extract Roz's phone number from Fran's kitchen address book and telephoned Roz the very next evening not two minutes after she'd walked in the door from work, the new Marimekko bag in hand, to ask her out on a date.

"To see the symphony," he said.

Roz was trying to wriggle out of her panty hose, the phone clamped precariously between her shoulder and her jaw. "Is that the bargain deal for people who can't afford to go and *hear* the symphony?" she asked him.

Edwin didn't laugh. "Actually," he said, "I've only got one ticket. I thought you could watch while I listened. We could switch at intermission if you'd like."

Roz, utterly unprepared for sarcasm from the mouth of a Nebraska farm boy, was speechless.

"What'd you do?" Edwin asked. "Drop the phone?"

"No," she said, grabbing hold of the receiver. She lifted her feet from the floor in front of the couch, panty hose still bunched around her ankles, and scissored her legs apart and together, thinking such an exercise might have surprising effects on her butt, which she was sure would be the first thing to go as she sagged her way into middle age.

"I could pick you up," he suggested. "Tomorrow evening, say around seven . . ."

Suddenly it felt like a challenge. "OK, sure," Roz said. He seemed harmless enough. And, honestly, when she thought about it, she could not remember once, ever, having had a man ask her to something so elegant as the symphony.

"It was perfectly adequate," Roz told Loralee, who came knocking voraciously on Roz's door, ravenous for details, when Roz came home from her evening out. Loralee was a bombshell, about as savvy as a tulip, and monogamously devoted to her incurably philandering boss, which, Roz told her regularly, quite obviously stemmed from Loralee's deep-seated fears of dating in New York City.

"Yeah, yeah," said Loralee. "So, any mushy stuff?" She sat on the carpet, her back up against Roz's front door as if to block all means of escape.

"Actually, yes," Roz said. She was flopped out on the couch, conducting Brahms in the air with her left foot. "We went for an ice cream."

"What flavor?" Loralee demanded.

"I had butter pecan."

"And the gentleman?" Loralee prodded.

"Vanilla."

"Sugar cone?"

Roz nodded.

"Uh oh."

"You said it," Roz concurred.

When Edwin called a week later to invite Roz on an architectural walking tour of Harlem, she lied, right through those mildly crooked but admirably white teeth she took such pains to brush and floss. "I'm sorry. That sounds lovely, but I'm spending the weekend up in Westchester. My aunt and uncle's place, you know."

"Sure," Edwin said, about as suspicious as a ballpoint pen. "Some other time."

"OK, well, actually, I've actually got to get off the phone, Edwin. Thanks for the thought."

"Sure," he said. "No problem."

"Well, bye," she said, taking the receiver from her ear before he had a chance to sign off, though there was no doubt that he would anyway.

Eight million people in the city of New York, what could the numerical odds possibly be of running into the one person you've told you'll be out of town? But it was Sunday afternoon, on the Fifth Avenue bus, right by the Metropolitan, that someone brushed Roz on his way toward the back door and paused there, his breath just behind her ear.

"Westchester, huh?" he said, his voice cold as chrome, and she didn't even have a chance to turn around before she spotted that telltale seersucker jacket mounting the steps of the Museum of Art.

Without thinking, Roz yanked on the signal cord, hollered "Getting off!" and plowed her way to the back door. She dashed up the museum steps and grabbed at the sleeve of Edwin's jacket. He turned, calm as only a nonnative New Yorker could be, and faced Roz on a landing halfway up the imposing bank of steps that served to weed out the faint of heart and allow only the cardiovascularly fit access to the world's great art. Now that Roz was there, panting from her sprint and still clinging to the material at Edwin's elbow, she was at a loss for words. Any excuse would be paltry and disingenuous. Thus, there was silence, and Roz, who took silence to be a sign of nothing less than death, couldn't bear it. "I just . . . I mean . . . I'm . . ." she stuttered. Edwin interrupted. "That was rude of me," he said, "not to mention juvenile. I apologize." "What?" "I said I was sorry for . . ." She cut him off this time. "You're apologizing to me? You can't apologize to me. You've been nothing but perfectly nice and I lie, and then I get caught like a kid in the cookie jar and now you think you should be . . ."

". . . Apologizing for baking the cookies in the first place?" He chuckled.

"Exactly." Roz couldn't identify her own emotions but was afraid she sounded annoyed, or self-righteous, as if she'd just said *I told you so* and was waiting for Edwin to concede to his own mistake.

Instead, he said, "Have you seen the Goya exhibit yet?"

"What?" Roz was disarmed.

"Goya," Edwin said. "That's what I came to see."

"Well, I, but . . . You want me to come with you?"

"Sure," he said, and there was nothing left to do but accept. If it was a game, she didn't know the rules. If it wasn't, if he was actually this trusting and forgiving a human being, the man was going to last about another week in New York before he fled on a train back to Nebraska, where the waves of grain were amber, the plains fruited, and the girls as simple and blond as sunflowers.

That evening they ate Indian food beneath billowing purple tapestries at a little place on 6th Street where the curry was so hot Roz had gulped her own glass of water in one breath and then moved on to Edwin's, which he pushed insistently toward her without a word. They went to Little Italy the next weekend and for drinks one evening after work in a tiny brownstone yard turned garden bistro. They strolled the Bronx Botanical Gardens and prowled Greenwich Village, Edwin's architectural guide in hand, and when they stopped for hot dogs on a bench beside a playground, he read to her descriptions of Gothic facades and flying buttresses that sounded, through his midwestern appreciation and awe, as much like poetry as any verse she'd ever heard.

It was her apartment they'd retire to at the end of an evening, since his roommate, a law student at NYU with smelly feet and an incessant marijuana habit, seemed never to venture out of doors, and though Edwin almost never stayed the night at Roz's (he worked early in the morning, and as the firm's underling lawyer, he liked to be fresh when he arrived at the office) he almost always stayed until Roz was just on the edge of sleep, when he would kiss her softly, gather his clothes, and dress in the hallway before he let himself out, pulling the door silently shut behind him.

He was not, in any way, a man Roz would have imagined for

herself. He still limped a bit from his injury, and though he wasn't short (5'8", the same as Roz), he certainly wasn't tall. He had fair and honest good looks but lacked even an ounce of the dark mystery, furtive heart, or swarthy sophistication that Roz had clambered after for most of her adult life. When Loralee pried Roz for details about the clean-cut and exceedingly polite young man she often encountered late at night in the lobby of their apartment building, he on his way out, she on her way in, panty hose tucked into her purse, all Roz could manage to say on Edwin's behalf was "I don't know, Loralee. He's not a shit," disbelieving her own words as she spoke them, as though she'd always understood shittiness to be an intrinsic male characteristic, as essential to attraction as musk.

It was one night in late October, when the die-hards were still trying to milk a few final outdoor cafe evenings before they succumbed to the winds of fall, that Roz was wide awake at eleven-thirty, having had far too much black tea at dinner due to an unexpected chili pepper in the Duck Wok's cashew chicken, and as she watched Edwin gather his clothes from the floor at the foot of her bed, she had the sudden but certain sense that Edwin actually had someplace to be.

"Hot date?" Roz asked, a brash attempt to quell her own unease.

Edwin froze, his khaki trousers clutched at his crotch like an adulterer caught in the act. "Oh," he said. "No." He tried to recover his composure, but, naked, there wasn't much to work with. "Just meeting a few folks for drinks, over by Fran's."

Roz was a bit taken aback. They'd been dating nearly four months. She knew Edwin socialized without her on occasion (of course he did), but somehow, late-night drinks with Fran's crowd—a big-drinking, smart-talking, easy-fucking crew of peripheral socialites and overgrown trust fund babies—didn't strike Roz as a perfectly innocent evening's activity.

"Which folks?" Roz asked, managing to sound about as uninterested as an inquisitor.

"Oh you know . . . Fran, Steve, Barb Carpenter . . ." he trailed off, having spotted his boxer shorts among the bedsheets, and he snapped them up and on in about the time it took for Roz to realize and identify her present emotion: she was jealous.

"Hmmph," she snorted. Barb Carpenter was a vampire vixen. Gorgeous (if one happened to find that sort appealing) and as smart and sexually conniving as she appeared vapid.

Edwin seemed to be regaining a bit more personal wherewithal with every garment he succeeded in finding and getting onto his body. "We haven't talked about making this an exclusive relationship," he pointed out.

Roz was well aware of that fact, as it was she, not Edwin, who'd insisted upon noncommitment, although it seemed like decades now since she'd dated anyone but Edwin. They were together practically every night, after all. Suddenly, Roz was defiant. "Well maybe we should!" she declared, as surprised as Edwin at the suggestion issuing from her kiss-chapped lips.

"Excuse me," said Edwin, glancing around him as if to register familiar sights. "I was looking for Roz? Roz Rosenzweig's apartment?"

"Cranky girl?" Roz asked. "Rather easy? Lousy taste in clothes?"

"That's my girl!" Edwin cried.

"Yeah? Well, I can't find her either. What'd you do with her?" Roz demanded. "What'd you do to the real Roz Rosenzweig?"

Edwin smiled, but he didn't speak. Then finally he said, "Are you serious about all that, Roz?"

"Yes," she snapped, utterly baffled by the source of her conviction. "I think you should move in here with me." It was almost a question the way it came out, like she was asking herself while she said it if that could in fact actually be what she was suggesting.

Edwin looked mildly troubled. "Maybe we could talk about this at some other time?"

"Fine," Roz snapped. "What? I'll pencil you in a week from next Thursday? Don't give me that crap."

"Maybe just when we're feeling a little less emotional . . ."

"Stop speaking to me like Queen Victoria. *We* are perfectly calm and prepared to discuss this right now. But perhaps *we* would rather go toss back a few with Barb Carpenter . . . ?"

"Is that what this is about?" he asked.

"This!" Roz yelled, then caught herself. She began again. "This is about me inviting you to move in with me and you hedging the question completely and acting like some prepubescent dimwit at a Sadie Hawkins dance. For Christ's sake, Edwin."

It was clear that Roz was going to have the conversation right then, whether Edwin wanted to or not. He looked resigned. "I just don't know about the whole idea of living together," he said.

"Oh fine," Roz shot back.

"No, no," he said. "I've got a problem with the whole living together paradigm. Living with someone is hard, but there's no commitment. It's too easy to leave if—and they're bound to—so, *when* things get rough. What's to keep us from jumping ship if the ride gets a little rocky?"

He had to be the only man she'd ever known, she thought, who could get away with a metaphor like that, and she knew then that she loved him, rotten metaphors, unflappable composure, good manners, and all. "Well," she said. "Well, so maybe we should do something trite and banal like get married."

Edwin looked like he might burst out laughing. "Is that a proposal?"

"Why not?" she said. She was warming to the idea. One could do worse than trite and banal. "What's the most awful thing that could happen? We get divorced?"

Edwin was thoughtful. "You're certainly not the kind of girl I expected to bring home to Mom . . ."

Far from insulted, Roz was extraordinarily pleased with the classification. "Well you're not exactly Cary Grant yourself," she said. Then she smiled. "Come on, Gimp, whaddaya say? You game?"

But Edwin was already slipping his trousers down over his feet and clambering back into the bed beside her.

Grover,
King
of
Nebraska

Danny didn't drive, so he was in charge of directions. Mostly he just hunched down in the back seat over the stolen Triple-A road atlas whose back cover was devoted to Danny's List: U.S. towns in which he'd concede to live if we were ever forced to stop moving and settle down.

"Admire," Danny announced.

"Where is it?" I asked, catching a glance of him in the rear-view mirror.

"Kansas," he said.

"I'm not living in Kansas."

"You'll do Nebraska but not Kansas?" Moët snapped from the passenger seat. "*That* makes a lot of sense."

"If I go back to the Midwest it'll be to Nebraska, that's all," I told her.

"Could you get over this back-to-your-roots shit already?" Moët said, her nose and lips pinched in like there was a bad smell in the car. Moët grew up in a trailer in upstate New York. Her mother got Mo's name off a champagne bottle from a drive-thru liquor store, then ditched Mo with a sister in Plattsburgh while she trotted off to a commune on the coast of Texas. Moët, understandably, does not understand about Nebraska. I think she'd like it, though. I really do.

"Santa Claus, Indiana? What Cheer, Iowa?" Danny Zaransky was a man of few words.

"Omaha," I said. "Omaha, and I don't want to hear another word about it."

Moët sent a scowl my way, then craned round in her seat toward Danny, stroking back his greasy-brown hair and cooing sweet whispers in reparation for my abuses. We had, somehow, inadvertently and against any of our intentions, begun to become a family. A warped and demented cloning of some ridiculously conventional little nuclearesque family: Papa Grover, Mama Mo, and Baby Danny Z. Those days when I tried to imagine a future for us, the only scene I could conjure was Mo in a gingham smock doing dishes down by the well, and I had started to wonder if the status quo, Ozzie and Harriet, Archie and Edith, Dick and Mary paradigm is simply inevitable no matter what path you take, no matter how far you've strayed from that proverbial interstate of convention. Even we—us! in our '76 Oldsmobile Delta 88, zipping down a highway in the middle of absolutely nowhere eastern Nevada—even we were doomed to that pathetically American fate.

We'd been making our way west since the Dead's final show of the summer tour in Chicago and had been camped, shrooming, in Zion for a few days en route to San Fran, where we had friends we could crash with until things picked back up in the fall. Danny liked to follow the green-dot roads, and I was happy to stay off the interstates, get a look at what Triple-A deemed "scenic" across this bellowing beauty of a country we call America.

"Panaca, Nevada," I said to the rear-view, jerking a thumb toward the *Now Entering* sign propped at the side of the road. *Pop-*

ulation 700, it proclaimed proudly. The town name was a peace offering from me to Danny, though it was for Mo too. Indirectly, but perhaps more necessary. Danny always forgave me my moods and flares. He always would. Moët was less intrinsic a figure in my life. Though I didn't think she would, and I didn't know where or to whom she could actually go if she ditched, I knew Moët was capable of leaving. She could slip out as quietly as she'd come, a body pressing in closer to share the warmth of my sleeping bag one night, years ago, at a show in Wisconsin when the temperature dipped nearly to frost and we made love amidst a tangle of sleeping bags and bodies before we'd even learned each other's names. Before we'd seen each other's faces in the light of day.

"Panaca sounds like mouthwash," Danny said.

"Panaca?" I said, like I was offering him a freshly grated sprinkle of some fine Italian cheese. "It's got panache . . ."

Moët groaned.

Danny grinned. "Nevada's worthless," he said.

"Well, Dan my man, you'd better get yourself ready for four hundred more miles of worthlessness."

"Yee haw," said Mo, deadpan as a door, and I knew she'd forgiven me.

Panaca, as far as we could tell, was where Route 319 dead-ended into Route 93. There was a stop sign at the three-way intersection, a boarded-up diner to the left, and a gas station straight ahead which looked about as lively as the diner but for a LOTTO light in the front window and a satellite dish in the dirt large enough to hold a skateboarding championship. As for a population of 700, either they were all underground or some eager developers had been overly optimistic. There was nothing there. Just Nevada.

"North," Danny instructed, pointing right, up 93.

I shook my head. "Gas," I replied and pulled across 93 toward the satellite dish as if it were drawing us into its force field. The Olds thunked down off the shoulder and into the dust yard with a scrape of metal we'd all grown accustomed to. The muffler dangled precariously, held up by an intricate lattice of twistie-ties which Moët claimed were the most versatile odd-end known to humankind. She kept a ready supply wound around belt loops, curled into ponytails, poked through spare earring holes, and strung into bracelets round her skinny wrists. Moët was prepared for anything. I pulled up to a pump in the shade of an overhead awning and killed the engine, but before I could get my hand to the door latch Moët stuck an elbow in my side and flicked her chin up ahead for me to look.

Parked a hundred feet ahead of us in the dirt at the side of Route 93 was a rusting red pick-up, its nose pointed east, the direction from which we'd come. Its back tires were missing; the bed was propped on stacked cinder blocks, and you could tell it had been that way for a long while. You could imagine that truck in its youth: gunning, itching, ready as fire to take off and be gone. Florida. New York. The blue-smoke mountains, three days away into the rising sun. But those cinder blocks were like cement shoes, and that truck was grounded in Panaca, Nevada. Long dead were the fly-by-night dreams of an eastern shore.

"How's that for panache?" Mo said, pleased with herself. Beside the truck stood a woman in a sea-foam prom dress trying to flash a little leg and flag down a ride. There wasn't another car for miles. And in Nevada, you could see that far.

—————   ═══════

The gas pump was a relic: the kind where you actually have to hold the trigger for the gas to flow. Mo dug a hacky sack out of the glove compartment and started kicking it around in the dusty lot while I filled the tank. Danny stepped away a few yards and took a leak, his back to the road, then joined Mo in her game. He was beautiful with a hacky sack—truly beautiful. Everything so fast and fluid it was almost like there wasn't one sack but many, with Danny at the center of them all, like the sun, in command of each intricate orbit. He was so fully himself when he was hacking, like the way he was when Jerry played, when he'd eaten a few tabs, or back when we were into ex for a while at shows, he'd climb out of the Olds stiff and jerky as the overgrown teenager he is, but something would happen as we crossed the parking lot, weaving our way through the vendors and scalpers and stoners. Inside the stadium, the amphitheater, the arena, Danny waited. And when

Jerry took the stage, when the music started, he'd squirm, twitch, like an epileptic on the cusp of a seizure, and his head would jerk, his eyes roll back in their sockets, eyelids fluttering like the near-dead. Then Danny'd start to dance. He was gorgeous. You'd fall in love with Danny dancing. I couldn't help that I wondered how it would be—how it would be to be in love with my brother Danny. I wanted so badly for there to be someone I might ask, some woman I could sit with over a few beers, late at night at someone's kitchen table and say: *Does Danny find his grace in sex?* I wanted to know if passion was a place where Danny could be free. But there was no one to ask. And you couldn't ask Danny.

Ask anyone else—ask our folks, for example—and they'd tell you Danny would never find his place in the world. That Danny needed to be somewhere with professionals to care for him, with people who knew how to deal with people like Danny. But *I* knew how to deal with Danny. Out on tour, Danny wasn't all that different from everyone else. He was always an odd kid in an interior sort of way. And it wasn't that he did so much more acid than anyone we knew, it just hit him differently. Danny wasn't unhappy living in the place he'd unearthed inside his brain. But he embodied an aberration, and that made a lot of people uncomfortable. People like our parents. Around Deadheads, though, Danny was free to inhabit the world in his own way. And when you think about it, doesn't that seem like something everyone deserves in this life?

I brought Danny with me to shows back in high school, before I left for college. I saw how he could be. I'd done two years at Brown when I went back home to Omaha for Thanksgiving and our folks said they'd had it: no more late-night naked neighborhood rampages, no more uncontrollable episodes, no more embarrassments. *We've tried,* they said. *We can't do it anymore. There's a residence, a group home sort of place — a good place. We want what's best for Danny. We're at the end of our rope.* And maybe they could have lived with that, but I could not. I said, *Danny's eighteen, and he'll decide for himself what the fuck he wants to do, and you can bet your fucking asses that it's not going to be checking into some mental ward.* I said Danny'd decide for himself, and he decided to come with me. Which then meant, of course, that I had to be going someplace Danny could come, and because nothing else made even the foggiest amount of sense, we went where the Dead went.

The old gas pump spun its numbers like a dying slot machine. My hand cramped around the trigger. Heat rode the Nevada air like an oil slick slipping across my field of vision. Moët kicked a wild one and sent Danny jogging off toward the red truck, flip-flops thwack-thwacking under his heels. He retrieved the sack without even bending down, just gave a little flick of his foot like hackers do, and the sack was airborne once again. Before he turned he raised a hand in salute to the foam-green prom queen, then started back toward Mo without even waiting for a response. There wasn't one. The queen didn't even glance his way. She stared out down the road, and though she didn't have her thumb out you'd have thought she did. There was an inner movement about her somehow, like she'd be ready to jump into any vehicle that passed her way. On the ground beside her was a nylon gym sack, the logo of some townie team stamped on its flank. I couldn't see the woman's shoes, her dress was so long, dragging the ground in back where it looked to be stretched or torn, so that it trailed out behind her in the breeze and made me think of Cinderella and those tiny, chirping bluebirds who carried her train in their beaks as they flew along behind. But this Cinderella's fairy-god-mom must've stood her up. The dress hung at her waist and sagged hor-ribly in the bust and the arms. She was emaciated, flat-chested as a cadaver, and terrible to look at: old, really, and not a prom queen at all, with drooping jowls and short, ungroomed hair the color of tarnished silver sticking out from her head in sleep-pressed cow-licks. Suddenly, she coughed: sick and thick and phlegmy. It was the first time I'd seen her move, and I averted my eyes.

I hung the nozzle back in its cradle and crossed the lot toward the LOTTO-lit shack to pay for the gas. We lived mostly off what money our folks had put away over the years for me and Danny, college fund–type money that became ours, freely, at age eigh-teen. There was also whatever money Moët made at shows sell-ing her bags—velvet sacks she pieced together, old leather belts we found at Goodwill stitched on as straps. When I had them

I sold shrooms, tabs, weed, whatever. Most of the time we got by okay.

It was dark inside the building and seemed deserted, but a bell tinkled as I came through the door and I could hear TV noise emanating from a back room beyond the counter. On the LOTTO machine next to the register hung a sign: "JACKPOT," and a handwritten "8" had been scotch-taped on in front of the "MIL-LION." The door to the back room edged slowly open and an old man came shuffling out. He was heavy, and his bedroom slippers thudded and scuffed as he made his laborious way to the register, trailing behind him a long, pale-green tube that bound him to his bedroom like a dog on an extended backyard chain. The tube snaked out from the door, threaded through a pulley that was rigged to the wall above the doorframe, then split in two, like a double-headed serpent, and coiled its heads up into the old man's nostrils. He stopped and flicked on another TV which faced out from a stand above the register. A silently raucous studio audience was overdubbed by a doodlie-doot-doo game show tune which ended abruptly, the screen flashing to a news brief before the old man could even turn round to me again.

"*This is Trudy Wells*," said a frighteningly tan woman with sideburns as sharp as a carnivore's canines shooting down her face like residual tusks, "*with a midday news brief on this, the tenth of August.*"

"Five-sixty-eight on gas," I told the man. "Unleaded."

He grunted a response and searched for the cash register buttons like a blind man, though I could see he wasn't.

"*In the news today, fans young and old across the . . .*"

"Oh, and a lottery ticket too, please." No matter how low we were on cash, we always bought them. Because you never know.

Bing-ding, said the register.

"*. . . mourn the death,*" said Trudy Wells, "*of Grateful Dead icon and musical cult figure Jerry Garcia. Mr. Garcia died yesterday in a rehabilitation center near his home in Marin County, California. Garcia was said to have entered the facility attempting to kick a lifelong addiction . . .*"

"Numbers?" the old man wheezed.

I couldn't answer. On the television screen, thousands of San Franciscans flooded through the streets of Haight-Ashbury, a sea of flowers, hair, splashes of psychedelic tie-dye—the way we always looked on camera: dirty, stringy, deluded masses weeping, laughing, sleeping, dancing. Not individuals, but that was OK somehow. The world was too individualized, I thought. We had more; we were part of a *we*.

"What. Numbers." The man coughed at me, one word at a time, for it was all he could choke out. I tried to look at him.

"Doesn't matter." I couldn't feel my head. I came apart like a pop-joint plastic doll. Disconnected, I was nothing.

"You. Want. I. Pick. 'Em." His voice came in high, thin, staccato pips.

I think I nodded. I meant to, I think.

We sat in the dirt in the shade of the gas canopy. Danny lay on the ground fanning himself with the lottery ticket, his greasy head resting in Moët's lap, her fingers combing through his hair with a fervor like it was her job, her responsibility. She could control nothing else in this world of deaths, ditches, and departures, but she could smooth the hair on the head of sweet Danny Zaransky. The hacky sack had been tucked back away, as it always eventually was—into someone's overalls pocket, or down into one of Mo's velvet bags—and Danny's grace followed it—gone—zip—as if that little leather bean bag held the secret that set my brother at ease upon this earth.

On the ground, Danny's sprawl was too languid, too comfortable for someone whose life was about to dramatically change. I sat cross-legged, staring at my limbs, limbs that I could no longer conceive of as attached to the rest of my body. Black hairs stood out too starkly against the white, midwestern skin. Too wiry. Too hairy. I knew I was wrong-looking. Too short. Mouth too big. Goofy. Eyes too wide. Hair dyed something ridiculous, blue, green, pink—I mocked nature; she hadn't done well by me on her own. I had always been too much inside my own skin, feeling and knowing its wrongness at all times. But now I could tug on my beard, touch the beads that Mo had woven into the hairs as they grew from scraggly stubble into actual hair, soft and even sort of fluttery when clean, but I could feel nothing. Like the nerve endings were dead. Like I wasn't inside. I tried to think about Jerry. Tried to imagine how it felt to be dead. Tried to imagine what this meant, but I couldn't make things link up. I felt like Danny without his magic sack, or without the music that brought him to life. The thing that had lent order to our life, however random and chaotic that order may have appeared from the outside, that thing was gone.

Out under the heat of the sun, the prom dress woman looked wilted and worn, and suddenly I could see, just then, like a revelation, that it wasn't a woman at all. It was a man. An old man. I thought, I was sure, almost absolutely sure: the prom queen was a man, standing there in the Nevada dust, sweat pouring down the sides of his face, dripping from his jowls, the prom dress wet, stained with sweat, dirty, and dragging. The man—a man!—staring off down Route 93 like he still expected at any moment a shape would appear on the horizon. Any minute now that trucker of his dreams was going to pull up, hoist his queen into the cab of that rig, and ride off into the brown Nevada wasteland. The queen looked worn, but he didn't look defeated. There was still a hope about him, a lingering certainty, deep inside, that some-day—*someday*—his prince would come.

Moët was practical. Unswervingly practical. "We should go to San Francisco," she said. "That's where we were heading. It's where we should be." And she was right, probably. There were so many of us there. If I couldn't feel myself, I could feel the others around me. Something could be postponed. There'd still be context, support in sheer numbers, arms to catch us when we fell. They'd keep us from hitting the ground too hard.

I didn't know what would happen then, after the hoopla died down, when the mourning sank in. Maybe they'd keep playing. Maybe it wouldn't really change all that much. We'd be the faithful. When the Buddha died, Buddhism didn't die with him. We'd have adjustments to make. Maybe nothing would really change.

But it would.

"Sweet, Idaho," Danny said. Mo smiled. "Ideal, Georgia. Happy Jack, Louisiana."

"Danny," I said.

"Fancy Farm, Kentucky?"

No one spoke.

"Brilliant, Alabama?"

Moët began to cry.

"Welcome, Maryland?"

"Danny," I said, "maybe we should go home."

Danny was quiet for a minute. He held the lottery ticket up to the sun like it was an envelope he could look through, like he could see what was inside. "I have a feeling," he said. "I think," said my little brother Danny Z., "I think that this time, Grove, you won. I think really. What's it now? Eight million? I think you won it, Grove. I think we won."

He looked so happy, so joyously sure. Moët sniffed, took her hand from Danny's head, and wiped her nose on her sleeve.

"You think, Dan?" I couldn't help but smile. "Well, so, eight million," I said like it was lying there on the ground before me, fanned out in glorious sweeps of tens and twenties. "So, so what'll we buy?"

Danny paused for a second, far down deep into a thought, and then turned his face to me, eyes bright as day, my brother Dan. He spoke without doubt, sure as the sun. "Nebraska," he said. "We'll buy Nebraska."

I laughed, and so did Mo, even through her tears, and it was like a breeze, almost, sweeping through the prickled desert, and Danny said, "Yeah. First we'd buy Mom and Dad's place, first. And we'd rent rooms and plant a farm and make more money and we could buy the whole block, then, and then Omaha, and then the whole thing. It would be ours. I'd be prince and Mo would be princess and Grover would be the king."

I laughed again, raised my fists to pound the hollow of my skinny chest, and sounded a fierce jungle cry: "Grover!" I hollered out into the Nevada nothingness. "King of Nebraska!"

Danny howled with delight, and Mo gave a whoop of freedom, my princess Mo, princess of the jungle. And then, seeming to notice us for the first time since we'd pulled into the dusty lot, with the hood of our Olds declaring to all in purple bold *"I've been hypnotized by the Goofaman,"* the prom queen looked at us. Prom queen, drag queen, the man at the edge of Route 93 turned and looked to us, eyes wide with hope, a gasp in his throat, a gasp of disbelief. For we'd arrived. We were here. We'd come at last to take him away.

29th Street Playground, September 1968

She laughed—she wasn't wearing the right shoes for sand and climbing—and tossed her head back, mouth wide, teeth bared as if to say *but that won't stop me.* Many years later I was responsible—*no,* she said, *the Parkinson's is responsible*—for losing her passport somewhere in Italy, and when she posed in front of a faded red curtain for a replacement at the American consulate in Florence, she wore a very different face: clenched jaw, lips closed in a tight, grim line. She no longer smiles in photographs; it's as if she remembers how a smile's supposed to go, but that doesn't make one any easier to muster.

They were sandals—Pappagallo—two thick leather straps and a back sling. It was 1968 and the photograph is black and white.

She was a shoe model then; got to keep the pairs she posed in. She'd come home nights from the showroom with a teeming shopping bag in each hand. Every color and style under the sun. She gave them to Goodwill when they got scuffed; *out with the old, in with the new,* we'd say. She tromped across the | playground—a labored stride, the sand pushing up under that arcing instep, driving down between her long toes.

It was early fall, late morning, and the playground was not crowded. Only one little boy appears in the frame, and even so, it's only the back of his head. Crew-cutted, he stands uncertainly, his feet sinking in the sand. He is looking up, the sun behind him, in his hand a toy shovel: small and plastic. Probably yellow. Or pink, or green. I can't tell. It's a black-and-white photograph.

We were not children ourselves. We'd had our loves. No one accused us of youth, naïveté. I had a Ph.D.; her father lay dying on a rented hospital bed in the living room of her childhood home in Scarsdale. The bed would not fit up the narrow flight of stairs to the bedroom her parents had shared for forty years. We'd ride the train from Grand Central to visit them some weekends. We gave her mother respite from his bedside. Some weekends we didn't want to go. Some weekends we stayed home.

Between the swing-set and the monkey bars there was a cluster of wooden pillars, all different heights, standing upright in the sand, like a fistful of pick-up sticks just before they fall. She sought out the tallest one, climbing nimbly, her long-long legs at home among the towers. *Chicken Legs,* the high school boys had called her. At her fortieth reunion, those same boys, now men—married, unmarried, widowed, divorced, disillusioned, disowned—trailed my wife across the Ramada Reception Room like they were chasing a dream. *What on earth,* they whispered, *is Haven D'Amato doing married to that man?* A man whose hands tremble like a blitzkrieg victim. Whose thoughts lurch and die before they find a way to his lips. On the tallest piling she perched, crossed her legs (a sandal wiggled; her heels are so thin!), posing for me, behind the shutter eye. She threw back her head again, and she laughed.

It was a streetcorner playground. Behind her, fire escapes climb the brick and flagstone walls as sure as ivy. We hung our laundry on a line those days—you can almost see it there: that invisible thread stretched between the buildings. There is a bedsheet and something else—something white and indistinguishable—an undershirt? There is a nightgown flapping in the wind like it should have flown away.

What Safety Is

They're not actually Deadheads, they just look the part. Darcy's 5'1" in a dress that used to be a nightgown and hangs down to her ankles; Gwynn is vein-skinny, braless in a cotton camisole and gym shorts, her crazy black curls knotted up on her head and out of the way. They know how to talk the talk. "We need a miracle . . . Looking for a miracle . . ." Darcy's better at it; it's a California thing, it seems. Gwynn, less comfortable in the voice, sticks to "Tickets? Anyone? Tickets?" Begging for miracles makes her feels like she's panhandling for the Make-a-Wish Foundation. Ticketless, the girls plunk down on a scrappy patch of grass outside the amphitheater and watch the crowds go by.

Two guys, cleanish-cut, in khakis, wander past, fingers in the air, on the same miracle quest. One of them notices Darcy sitting on the grass and does not take his gaze from her as he walks. He squints at her oddly as they slouch off into the crowd.

"What was that about?" Gwynn asks Darcy.

"What was what about?"

"That guy was seriously checking *someone* out, dearie."

"I think he was just nearsighted," Darcy says.

"You!" Gwynn moans. "You make me batty!"

Darcy leans over to Gwynn on the grass beside her and kisses her knee.

Gwynn and Darcy have lived together, best friends for four years. Matched into a dorm as freshman roommates, they moved out as soon as they could into a Berkeley co-op, where they shared a room until graduation in May. Then Gwynn got a job with a nonprofit in San Francisco and moved across the bridge to the City. Darcy, raised in the East Bay and unwavering in her devotion to it, took a room in a big old Victorian on Derby Street and a job as a smoothie blender at Whole Foods on Ashby. "I'm in a transitional phase," she maintains "I'll get a real job too, someday."

It's not a day for miracles, but the sun is nice and not too hot, and they've brought water bottles and a blanket and some left-over gado-gado, so they decide to make an afternoon of it there on the parking lot lawn, the air thick with falafel and patchouli, but with a breeze too. Some folks are hacky-sacking nearby, and Darcy joins them, tying her dress up in a knot at her waist so she can use her legs and exposing a pair of hospital-green boxers that some guy left in their room years ago after a party. They never did figure out which guy. Or which party. Darcy played soccer in high school and can handle a hacky sack pretty decently. Gwynn is a spaz and categorically refuses to engage in any sport that involves a ball, even if that ball is a bean-bag the size of an apri-cot. Gwynn has always been the difficult one. *High maintenance,* Darcy calls her.

In her nightgown amidst the hacker-guys Darcy looks like Wendy playing among the Lost Boys, stringy-green strays and overgrown adolescents. During occasional collect phone calls, the proverbial clocks ticking away, their desperate parents plead: *What about college?* tick tick tick *You're throwing your life away!* tick tick tick *Your potential! Your promise! You used to talk about law, architecture, accounting . . .* tick tick tick. The boys listen for a moment, nostalgic: they did love their parents once, they re-member, and the house was warm, the clothes clean and soft, steaming meals laid on the table every night at six . . . But now there's Jerry, Jerry who says *don't let that world get you back under its hook,* who keeps them all dancing, traveling off to a place miles beyond the moon where all that matters is the lush green of their uncharted island and the ageless glow in their wide boy eyes, and Wendy lovely Wendy . . .

And I, Gwynn thinks, I'm Nana, that old sheepdog of a nurse-maid, waiting patiently in the Darling children's nursery for her wards to return home from their flight of fancy.

The boys Darcy brings over when the hacking circle disbands are familiar-looking: the khaki guys from before.

"Gwynn," Darcy says, pointing around their little group, "Donovan, Jed." Jed is lanky, wispy, floppy-haired. Donovan's a little more solid, less pretty, but of the same post–prep school genre.

"Hi," Gwynn says, raising her head an inch, a hand shielding her eyes.

"Likewise," says Donovan. Jed gives a little salute from the other side of the blanket. He's fidgety-nervous, and Gwynn likes that: a touch of awkwardness. It's what so many of these people seem to lack. It's what pot, and California, and the Dead, and lives lived in the name of mellowness have taken from them.

"No tickets for you guys either?" Gwynn asks.

Donovan shakes his head sadly. Gwynn turns her face back to the sun.

The next time Gwynn looks up it's to say *Hey Darce, want to think about heading home?* but as she's lifting herself up and turning around, the first *Hey* only halfway off her tongue, it becomes obvious that Darcy isn't ready to go anywhere. She and Jed—cross-legged, facing each other, knees touching, the world outside the little diamond of their bodies obliterated—seem to be involved in a kiss. It's Donovan's eye Gwynn catches instead. His look is sympathetic.

"Hm," Gwynn snorts. She feels sick for a minute. Sick like: if she doesn't get away from all this right now—everything—the pot and the psychomusic and the stupid, sweet, nothing-doing hippie boys—this whole fucking state!—she's going to lose her shit completely.

But then there's Darcy.

". . . some friends of ours are having a party in San Francisco. Late-afternoon barbecue sort of thing. They're on the Panhandle . . ." Donovan is saying. "Do you guys live in the city, even?" he asks Gwynn.

"I do, she doesn't."

"Oh, well, I just . . . if you wanted to come, it should be pretty cool I think . . . good food at least . . . we could give you a lift in if you need one."

"We drove," Gwynn says.

He's sort of sweetly, cluelessly persistent. "Well, I could give you directions . . ."

"An address would be adequate, I *do* live there," Gwynn says, but she thinks it doesn't sound funny, the way she means it. She has no idea why she's even entertaining the idea of this party.

"Cool, so you'll come?" says Donovan.

Gwynn directs a thumb toward Jed and Darcy. "It's up to the little kissing smurf there. We're in her folks' car."

"Hey, Jed," Donovan calls. "Hey, unpucker for a sec?"

Darcy and Jed look up, disoriented, glazed, like they're coming out of a movie theater trying to get their bearings.

"Are you guys into checking out that barbecue thing? In the city? I'm kind of getting hungry . . ."

Jed and Darcy look to each other, then back at Donovan. *Sure,* they shrug in unison.

"That was easy," Donovan says to Gwynn.

"Cake," she mutters.

When they all start to stand up and gather things, Donovan grabs an edge of the blanket to help Gwynn fold.

"Did I say something obnoxious?" he asks. "I didn't mean to corral you into this."

"Don't worry about it," Gwynn tells him. They fold in toward each other and Gwynn takes Donovan's corners from him. He bends to pick up the opposite end.

"Please don't feel like you have to come. I mean, it would be great if you did, but I don't want you to come because you feel like you have to . . ."

Gwynn slings the blanket over her arm and gives Donovan a little thump on the back. "First of all," she says, "if Darcy has any say in it, I'm assuming that we'll be going wherever you guys are going tonight whether I want to or not. And secondly, I don't do things I don't want to do."

Donovan stiffens, looks a little surprised.

"I think I'm missing some chromosome in the guilt/obligation gene or something," she explains. "Don't mind me anyway, I'm naturally grouchy. Darcy's convinced it's my version of content-edness. I grew up in Wisconsin. She thinks it's too cold there and that human wiring goes faulty when it hits twenty-five below. Like frostbite. You never quite come back."

Donovan nods. "I'm from New Hampshire," he says.

They step out into the parking lot.

"Hey," Darcy begins as they approach the car, "should we split up so we don't get lost?" She looks to Gwynn.

Gwynn shrugs, her eyebrows lifted high in nonchalance. "You wanna take Jed and I'll ride with Donovan?" she says, as if she couldn't care less.

"Sure, OK. Gwynn, that's OK with you? You don't mind?"

"'Course not. Though I guess perhaps the person to ask is Donovan, into whose vehicle I have just insinuated myself."

"Honored by your insinuation," proclaims Donovan, the ever-valiant.

"There now," Gwynn chirps, "all better. So we'll see y'all there." She can be perky, goddamnit. She can do *easygoing* just like the rest of them. "Be good kids, you hear? No monkey business on the highway. Remember: it's only funny until someone loses a bodily fluid."

They don't see Darcy and Jed at the party. They do see the Acura, parked in front of the building, on Fell Street. The apartment is a really nice ground-floor floor-through, right on the Panhandle of Golden Gate Park, that some friends of Jed and Donovan's from school are subletting for the summer.

"Hey," some guy yells to Donovan as they enter, "Jed's come and gone. Waltzed in, stole my rolling paper, and went out again. He's out on the Panhandle grass with some hippie chick . . . Beer's in the kitchen, flaming shots in the bedroom, burgers are out back." And with a flourish of his barbecue tongs he disappears into the garden.

At first Gwynn thinks that people are square dancing in the living room. There are twenty or so of them circling the room, and one guy in the corner in a three-foot-tall Cat-in-the-Hat hat who seems to be DJing off a boom box. In the center of the room is a large pile of shoes—boat mocs, Tretorns, bluchers, Birks— and everyone appears to be limping around with one unshod foot. When the music—"*and the beer chases my blues away, oh I'll be OK, I'm not big on social graces*"—stops, the crowd dives toward the center of the circle, clamoring for shoes. Then there is more milling, the murmur of confusions, the offering of shoes to their mates' owners, and then suddenly, it seems, everyone is kissing. *Sweet Jesus*, Darcy would say, *did they not get enough of this in junior high?* Gwynn feels absurdly conspicuous, afraid they'll all assume she's some destitute groupie waif Donovan picked up at the show. That she'll fuck him in exchange for a place to crash for the night before she hitchhikes her way north for the Eugene show next week.

Gwynn turns to Donovan. She's got to get them out of this room, she's thinking. There's no way in hell she's voluntarily kissing him, but if it winds up being absolutely inescapable, there's no way she's going to do it sober. "Where was it," Gwynn asks, "that those flaming shots were happening?"

Donovan grins. "A woman after my own heart." And Gwynn wants to say, *no I'm not. I'm really not*, but Donovan has her by the arm and is guiding her away from the kissers in search of inebriation.

The back bedroom belongs to someone called Matt, who looks just like the guy who let them in, who—to Gwynn—looks just like Donovan, who looks just like Jed, who, come to think of it, looks just like Darcy's ex-boyfriend, John. Thankfully, though, unlike John (who, afraid of becoming an alcoholic like his father, did not drink and was instead a bong-hit-every-two-hours kind of guy), Matt doesn't seem to be the least bit afraid of becoming an alcoholic like his father and is lighting shots of 151, which can't, Gwynn thinks, have any legitimate purpose except to make Matt look like a big stud, which, as far as Gwynn is concerned, he is far from achieving. Donovan flounces onto Matt's bed. Matt sits backward in a desk chair, flicking a collector's edition Zippo and occasionally lifting a hacky sack between his toes and tossing it in the air. Gwynn stands in the doorway, leaning against the frame and wishing she were already drunk because she doesn't have any particular desire to *get* drunk but knows this is all going to be a lot easier once she is.

"Fire? No fire?" Matt asks her, tipping the bottle.

"I think I'll try no fire," Gwynn says, reaching out for the glass.

"No fire for a hundred, Alex. And the answer is: Bruce Springsteen."

Gwynn drinks. "Who said: you can't light a fire without a spark?" She bends to set her glass down on the milk crate that's serving as Matt's table.

Matt turns to Donovan. "She's sharp, this one, let's keep her."

Donovan and Gwynn both laugh too loudly and don't look at each other. Gwynn would really like another shot. Quickly.

"Fire? No fire?" It's Donovan's turn.

"Ooooh," Donovan deliberates. "What the fuck—light my fire, baby."

Again, Gwynn is grateful for Donovan's dorkiness.

Matt pours a hefty jiggerful, flicks his Bic, and caps the shot with a flame. He passes it across to Donovan, who reaches for it gingerly, but as soon as Matt lets go, the flaming glass burns Donovan's finger, and he jerks back his hand. A line of fire shoots across the floor, like the cord to one of Wyle E. Coyote's bombs—*fffffft*—straight to Gwynn's feet, and she's jumping backward before she even realizes what's happening, and Donovan is leaping up from the bed onto the fire-line, stomping it out under the everything-proof soles of his Doc Martens, Matt flailing to stand from his chair, Gwynn flinching, Donovan stomping until the small fire is long out and they all start to realize how silly they must look there, flailing and flinching and stomping. And then they are laughing, and the 151 bottle is in Gwynn's hand and she's taking a long, long, painful draw because who knows what's going to happen now, there's not much left in the bottle and beer's not going to do it fast enough. It burns going down, and Matt gives a low hoot of approval as Gwynn takes the bottle from her lips and passes it along. Matt tilts back his head and drinks.

"You OK?" Donovan asks her.

"*I'm* fine. Are *you* OK?" she asks back.

"Fine," he says.

He looks kind of embarrassed, which somehow makes Gwynn think, *I could kiss him if need be. I could do that. I'd be OK with that.* She gestures back out into the living room, toward the musical/shoe/kissing crowd. "Good thing we weren't out there," she says.

Donovan looks relieved. "No kidding," he says, lifting the soles of his shoes for Gwynn to see. "That would've been a lot less fun barefoot."

—————

When Gwynn and Donovan finally meet up with Jed and Darcy, it's two A.M., the barbecue is dying down, and they're all ready to pass out. Donovan and Gwynn are plowed, so it gets decided—and seems quite logical at the time—that Jed, who's only stoned, not drunk, will drive Donovan's car. They'll leave Darcy's there, pick it up tomorrow, and they'll all crash at Gwynn's since she's the only one who lives in the city.

Gwynn manages not to throw up until they get to her apartment building, whereupon she hands Darcy the door key and heaves gado-gado and 151 into the Harrison Street gutter. Darcy holds Gwynn's head, smoothing back tendrils of frizz and curl from her face while she pukes. Then Darcy unlocks the door and the four make their way up the three long, narrow flights of stairs. Gwynn's apartment is a not-very-converted warehouse space which she shares with she's not even sure how many other people, most of whom also seem to work for minimum wage at nonprofit organizations trying to save various people, places, animals, and things they've deemed less fortunate than themselves. Gwynn's room is a loftlike area, open on one side with a half-wall that overlooks the kitchen. In it are a futon, a bean-bag chair, and one layer of brick and two-by-four bookshelves encircling the room like a safety rail. The ceiling is only five feet off the floor; even Darcy has to duck when she enters.

Gwynn and Donovan collapse onto the futon, Jed disappears somewhere, and Darcy scuttles around downstairs before she appears in the loft with a toothbrush and a cup of water. She kneels down beside Gwynn.

"Bless your soul," Gwynn says, reaching shakily for the toothpaste.

"Allow me," Darcy smiles. She spreads some Colgate over the bristles. "Open up," she says.

Gwynn is on her side, propped on an elbow, her cheek in her hand. She feels woozy, swirled, but much better since she's thrown up. She drops her jaw as Darcy puts a hand behind Gwynn's head for leverage and scrubs Gwynn's teeth—firmly, but gently, like polishing silver—then holds the cup to her lips so she can rinse. Gwynn finds a coffee mug on the floor beside the mattress and spits. She lets her head fall back to the pillow, and Darcy waddle-walks on her knees around their heads to Donovan's side. "Buff and shine?" she asks. Donovan opens his mouth.

When she's done with Donovan, Darcy heads back down the loft steps.

"We can make room for you guys," Gwynn calls to her.

Darcy's head reappears in the doorframe. "That's OK," she says. "I think Jed's rigging something up outside for us. We're going to watch for shooting stars." There's a rooftop garden area on the building, accessible through a trap door. Darcy and Gwynn slept out there the night they moved Gwynn's stuff over from the East Bay. Someone had built a little lean-to, just about the only place in the warehouse that offers any privacy at all. Tied to a pole in the lean-to is a rubberized ditty bag full of condoms. "BE SAFE" reads a sign tacked to the wall, an arrow pointing to the bag. "BE SAFE."

"Sleep tight," Darcy calls, making her way down the steps again. Gwynn thinks she should respond, but she can't figure out how. There's no air in her. Like it all just sucked itself away. She hears some rustle and clink in the kitchen, the slam of the fridge, the creak of the roof-access door, and then not much else that isn't just the sound of night and Donovan on the futon next to her, shifting himself into comfort.

"How you feeling?" he asks softly.

"I'm fine," Gwynn says. "Much better."

"Thanks for letting us crash," he says.

"No problem."

And there are a few seconds of silence before Gwynn rolls over onto her stomach and into the center of the mattress, pushes herself up on her elbows, her eyes wide open, watching his open too, in shadow beneath her. She can do this. She can do this almost without thinking what she's doing. She's exhausted, sick, but she wants to do this: wants something to blot out everything else, obliterate it all—the street, the loft, the roof, the lean-to, the stars. She leans in and puts her mouth to his.

He is surprised, pulls back a few inches, studies her face in the dim moonlight for some indication of what's going on. He looks confused, tired. She kisses him again. Again, he pulls away.

"Should I assume that you're doing that because you want to?" he asks tentatively.

"That's logical," Gwynn says, her voice tight, body tensing away from his. "But if *you* don't . . ." She flops onto her back, stares up at the low-flying stick-um galaxy on the ceiling above. There's a Big and a Little Dipper that Gwynn did herself, and beside them Darcy's rendition of Orion, who's so overly studded, he's less a hunter than a sequined disco king.

"No," Donovan stammers, "I just . . . it's not that I wouldn't want to. I just didn't expect . . . I don't want you to think I expected . . ."

"Oh good grief!" Gwynn sighs.

"I didn't get the idea that *you* would want to, is all. I'm just surprised . . . It hadn't seemed . . ."

"Well maybe I don't *want* to," says Gwynn. "Maybe I just felt like *doing something*? Who knew you'd make such a production?"

"I mean," Donovan is sinking into his pillow, barely able to keep his head upright, "maybe we could hang out again . . . another time . . ."

"Maybe we should go to sleep," Gwynn says.

"Yeah," says Donovan. "I just don't want you to think . . . I mean . . . You're really cool, Gwynn. I like you. I don't want you to think I don't like you."

Gwynn's voice is losing its edge, the sleepiness dulling all emotion. "If you'll let me go to sleep I promise to think no such thing, OK?"

"OK."

"Now go to sleep." Gwynn instructs him. "You need your beauty rest."

"Gee, thanks."

"No offense intended."

"Good night," he says.

"Mmmmm," Gwynn muffles herself into her pillow. Pretty soon, fully clothed, they're out.

———

Gwynn does not hear the rain when it begins, but she smells it rising off Jed and Darcy, like wet dogs, when they creep in for shelter sometime later. They shuffle about, shedding shoes and damp wool layers, and then squeeze onto the futon with Gwynn and Donovan. It's a queen; even so, with four it's tight.

When Gwynn wakes up next it's to the steady rasp of Darcy's

breath on the pillow beside her. She is curled toward Gwynn, on her side, her face hidden under hair, the tip of one pink ear poking through, so small and discrete that it seems like it would be the most natural thing in the world for Gwynn to reach out for that ear. It looks heart-wrenchingly soft. Like tawny velvet. Like the ear of a puppy. Like newborn skin. She imagines bridging those few inches that separate her head from Darcy's. Pressing her lips, silent, to the rim of Darcy's ear. Running her tongue, there, along that inner curve of cartilage. Light, so light. Like licking an envelope. But sweet, and salty, and a bit like shampoo. Coconut, and aloe, and the tingling savory of sweat.

Then suddenly Gwynn's hand is there by Darcy's face, smoothing the hair away from that lovely, speckled, freckled skin, stroking it back over the smooth slope of Darcy's scalp. Her skull beneath Gwynn's hand is warm as an egg. Gwynn tucks flyaway strands behind the curve of Darcy's ear, pressing each sweep into place with an insistence, like assurance: *you stay, you rest, you be good now, you hear?* Darcy rolls toward her then, both hands rising to encircle Gwynn's forearm, trapping Gwynn's hand between Darcy's cheek and the pillow. Darcy presses her dry lips into the pad of Gwynn's palm and lifts them again, like a swimmer coming up for air, and they sleep like that, tucked together, the soft pressure of assurance holding them to one another, as if that's what safety is: a point of contact.

Somewhere in the night there is squishing and wriggling and a body squeezing in; Jed has gotten edged off the futon and is pushing his way back on. Jarred, Darcy's face comes free from Gwynn's palm with a wet slap of suction. Gwynn tries to shift, but she finds her arm tingling with nothingness, numb so far into the roots of her shoulder that she is powerless over it. There is more jostling, and then Gwynn can hear Darcy groan, raise her head, then a flip of hair, the shadow like windswept reeds projected huge in moonlight against the wall. She groans again and gives a snorting sort of sigh as she pushes herself up, standing, her dress falling into place around her, the fabric so sheer in the moonlight that Gwynn can see the illuminated shapes of Darcy's calves spotted in floral print from the nightgown-dress. Darcy's hair is static from sleep, rising off the back of her head like loose, live wires crackling with electricity in the moon rays, like sparks of something coming to life. Darcy shuffles out the door, downstairs to the bathroom, and is gone.

Way
Back
When
in
the
Now
before
Now

As Sari leaves her bedroom, shutting the door softly behind her, she can hear *Saturday Night Live* emanating from the master bedroom down the hall. Sari's stepfather, Isaac, has turned the volume up to mask, ineffectively, his sobs. The TV is also on in the living room, remote control at Renata's fingertips, but the channel isn't all that important to her anymore. Sari's mom pressed mute three days ago and has watched in dim silence ever since. Sari tugs on a sweatshirt over her tank top, but the zipper is broken so she can't close it. The spring night is not cold. She pulls her hair through a rubber band from around her wrist and adjusts the waistband of her cut-off sweats, folding the top down over itself to expose just an eye-slit of pale belly.

From the archway of the living room Sari watches her mother. Renata's eyes are closed, her breathing irregular and gassy. From a diagnosis in the pancreas in February, the cancer has now metastasized to her lungs. There has not been a lot of time to get used to anything—an oxymoron anyway, really: to become accustomed to change. The doctors have told Isaac that Renata has days left, maybe weeks, so she has come home from the cancer ward to die, in her own living room, on a rented hospital bed. Isaac is taking Renata's illness badly, and with scotch. He has taken an indefinite leave of absence from the investment firm where he works. Just this week, since her mom's gone so far downhill, Isaac has taken to getting up before Sari to pack her a bag lunch for school. He has offered no explanation, simply hands her the brown bag at the door as if he's been doing it for years and years. It appears to perk him up, and for fear of upsetting anything more Sari doesn't question it; she leaves the bag with Jerald, the homeless guy on the corner of 79th and Broadway who talks to her as she waits for the bus each morning. Jerald sways and keeps up a constant refrain: "Good morning, have a nice day please. Good morning, go to school please. Good morning, have a nice day please." He is gracious in accepting the lunch and, seemingly in exchange, effusively tells Sari she's the most beautiful woman in the world. It's not something a man—or a boy, even—has ever told her, and as crazy as Jerald may be, Sari likes the way his words make her feel.

Sari's heart thumps in her chest. To get to the apartment door she must cross the living room, pass directly before her mother's bed, right between Renata and the TV screen. Sari tugs again at her pony tail, leans out just slightly into the room. "Mom?" she whispers. Then louder: "Mom?"

Sari waits, but Renata gives no indication of response, just shallow, labored breathing that will go on like that and worse until it stops going on completely. "Mom?" Sari says again, stepping tentatively from the wooden hallway floor onto the living room carpet. Her eyes stay fixed on her mother as she crosses the room; she's prepared to stop at any moment and manufacture an excuse, say: *Just making sure the door's locked. You need anything?* The room's glow changes with the TV screen, shifty shadows punctuated by bursts of light, like doors opening on the sunshine, then slamming shut again. Sari tiptoes past. Renata is asleep. She looks unlike the woman who just months ago was Sari's fifty-year-old mom. This woman in the hospital bed is ancient, a wraith, a whisper. She is the echo of Renata. Yet the wizened body is somehow still Sari's mom, peering out from inside like a ghost determined to keep a watchful eye over the loved and the living.

For a moment now, the eyes flutter open, as if Renata's been aware of her daughter's presence all along but has refrained from acknowledging her until this last second when she dips into the finite and waning pool of her energy and lifts her head a little toward Sari. Sari starts—"Ma"—but Renata's eyes are closing again. Breathing is hardest for her now. Her lungs. She whispers, "Have fun." Her head nods against the pillow.

"Thanks," Sari says and would say more but Renata is gone again. Sari takes keys from the dish by the door and silently, expertly, unlatches the locks. The hallway buzzes fluorescent and the black-and-white tiling seems to ooze illusively in and out of focus. On the doormat beneath WELCOME she's left a pair of old tennis shoes which she slips on now like clogs. The door clicks shut behind her and she stretches her sweatshirt tight around her body as she pushes into the stairway. Coming from within the walls Sari can hear the clank and churl of the elevator, the swing of the gate, clinking like a handful of dropped silverware. Muffled voices tunnel up through airshafts: greetings from Vladimir, the elevator man; couples on their way in from an evening at Lincoln Center, the Metropolitan Opera, a Knicks game at Madison Square Garden. The stairwell is dimly lit, and when Sari pushes open the door on the eleventh-floor landing the overheads cut in at her jarringly. She squints her way to the Lucases' door and lets herself inside.

Dina and Harmon Lucas are in the Berkshires. Their daughter Hillary, Sari's friend since infancy, has gone tonight with friends to Loews 84th. They don't see movies, since at fifteen there is little they can get into that is worth seeing; instead they hang out under the marquee, lean against parking meters, flip their hair at the tenth-grade boys, debate crossing the street for Haägen Dazs. The

Upper West Side of Manhattan is their playground on Saturday night—all lights and life and tourist bustle, like Disney's Main Street. The sun goes down, the lights go up, and it's as if the surrounding darkness can insulate that neighborhood against anything outside its neon glow. New York City, to some a den of plagues and filth, is to them an oyster. The apartment building on 79th Street where Sari and Hillary live is packed in and padded on three sides by other apartment buildings. On the street level there are doormen and security locks and buzzers and surveillance, and the residents' sense of safety is so insidious that in twenty years of living in 11B the Lucases have never locked their apartment door.

Sari passes Hillary's room first; the door is open and she can see the bathroom light leaking across Hill's clothes-strewn floor. The next room down the hall is Jonah's room. Jonah is Hill's older brother. His door is closed. Sari gets a shudder of giddy fear at that: imagining what might be going on inside Jonah's cloistered domain. Just after her mom got sick was when Sari started coming upstairs, where her grief wasn't peripheral to Isaac's, to talk with Hill, or Dina and Harmon, or Jonah. To watch TV or drink hot milk, just to be with people still living in time. Down in 8E, day and night no longer have much meaning. It's odd, Sari has thought recently, how dying gets you ready for death: weans you off the clock before you enter that place where there's no longer time. Isaac has withdrawn himself from present time, joined his wife in her netherland. But Sari isn't allowed to do that. So while Isaac spends his days with Renata in that land of limbo, Sari's life goes on: school, softball practice, hanging out upstairs with the Lucases.

One night in March Sari let herself in, found no one in the kitchen or the living room, padded down the hall to Jonah's room. The door was partly open and Jonah was masturbating. Sari watched. It wasn't until after he'd come that he noticed her there and reached for the gray comforter which had fallen to the floor. He covered himself demurely, with a sense of propriety; he didn't grab, and he wasn't hasty or ashamed. Only when he spoke did he betray an ounce of surprise.

"Don't you knock?" he said. It wasn't really a question, and Sari didn't answer it.

"Most people would turn around and leave," he said. His head hung back slightly off the edge of the twin bed, like he was cocking his neck at her.

Sari nodded.

"I wouldn't even have known you'd been here," Jonah said. His voice was growing more impatient. "Most people wouldn't watch. That's not a normal reaction. You should have left."

Sari stood by, patient, uneasy, like she was waiting out the storm before she tried to go anywhere.

"What?!" Jonah demanded, and then his anger broke, dissolving into amusement. "What!" He grinned at her, shaking his head, his hands open, awaiting explanation.

But when Sari started toward him the quizzical look returned, only he didn't say anything else, no more questions. He just watched, waiting to see what she'd do. Sari didn't know herself right then what it was she would do. She wasn't thinking, really, just moving where her body seemed to want to go. It was a similar instinct that sent her up to the Lucases' in the first place. It was just where she ended up.

It made sense, sure. Downstairs there was her mother, who seemed to carry the yellowed stench of the hospital back home with her, trapped in the creases of her skin like oil. And Isaac, who was all but crawling inside Renata's illness himself, as if death were a suitcase and he could sneak himself along for the trip. Upstairs was Sari's childhood friend and longtime playmate, Hill. And working-mom Dina, with her portfolios and projects and something going on always, a constant state of happening. Harmon: the therapist father tugging at his beard, wearing a thin plaid shirt the color of autumn leaves or smoke and heather, his voice low and gravelly. And Jonah, in his bed, the hot sleepy boy-smell with its acrid twinge of sex now, pungent and new, but underlying it all was the soft comfort of Ivory Snow, the smell of a life that was first and foremost clean and powdery white. Sari's body moved toward that, toward Jonah's warmth, wanting it, wanting to claim some of that heat for herself, put that heat inside of her. She climbed onto the end of Jonah's bed and tucked herself under the covers beside him. Beneath the sheets the world was damp and warm, and Jonah's skin felt soft as moss. She buried her face into his side.

"Hi," she whispered.

Jonah lifted his blanketed arm like a wing and drew her to him. "Hi," he said back.

Sari has never again interrupted Jonah. Now, he waits for her. At first he'd spooned around her in his little twin bed, his thighs up against her butt, pressing into the small of Sari's back with the erection tented inside his boxer shorts. He was so catlike it almost didn't feel sexual to Sari but sensual: a sleeping cat pressing his soft belly up against the nap-warm couch cushions. And Sari liked that, the way she'd like petting that cat, or stroking a puppy's velveteen ears. She liked sensing Jonah's pleasure, the acuity of his comfort.

And then one night he took her hand from where she tucked it, as if in prayer, between her curled up knees—took her hand and drew it behind her, pressed it to his penis and held her there, his hand over hers, sandwiched between two insistences. She didn't mind, except for the angle, which was awkward the way her arm got twisted behind her. Her back was to Jonah and she was unable to watch him, to see if like a cat his eyes narrowed in contentment or if pleasure made them open wide like awe or night-blindness. She twisted around toward her arm but then could not bring herself to look at Jonah's face, buried her own instead into his chest, which smelled, as always, rich as laundry. She shifted her hand and Jonah shifted his, both of his hands now cupping hers, guiding it up and down so the skin beneath it moved, felt to Sari like the skin might slide right off in her hand. Jonah moved her hand faster and she felt like they were revving something, like a motorboat engine, waiting for the motor to gun and growl its way to a steady purr. It wasn't until the next night that Jonah placed his hand over the back of Sari's head and pushed her down under the covers. His hand was large and it fit the curve of her skull like a well-worn mitt around a softball, and it felt good, Sari thought, to have someone saying *do this, go here, yes, yes.*

There's a window open in Jonah's room tonight, and as Sari enters she hears the sounds of the street rushing in like ocean waves, the whoosh and roar of traffic, a holler, slam, siren screech fading a harried path up Broadway.

Jonah's room is sleek: wood floor, bookshelves of streamlined black aluminum, spare. On one wall: U2's Joshua Tree. The other: a map of the London Underground. It's nearly midnight, and Jonah has fallen asleep, one hand dangling off the bed, fingertips grazing the ground, caught in the stream of light emanating from beneath the bathroom door. On the floor, just within reach, is the small gray nylon stuff sack in which Jonah keeps his condoms, and the sight of it puts a little pulse in Sari, that expectant little throb in the pit of her pelvis. She likes it when Jonah's inside her. She likes how warm it is, and sometimes she likes how much it hurts.

The first time she let Jonah have sex with her, things downstairs were still somewhat normal: day was day, night was night, a kid had a curfew, and a mother left the hall light on for her teenage daughter to turn off when she got home for the evening so the mother could know she was home and stop worrying that her daughter might be lying dead in Central Park, raped and strangled with her own Maidenform.

But that night of the first sex—Sari's first anyway, she has her doubts about Jonah—that night, in the fog of it all (the odd ringing sting in her crotch; the pressure spots on her hips, neck, collarbone where bruises would surely form), she'd had to deal with all that, and so much to think about, so much swishing around in her brain: Jonah, who wasn't her boyfriend, wasn't and hadn't ever been anything but the guy who lived upstairs, Jonah, who'd suddenly become—what?—her lover? She didn't think she was old enough to qualify as a "lover." Surely lovers didn't have sex in a twin bed while his parents were away at the country house and his sister was licking a double-dip cone on the corner of 84th and Broadway. Afterward Sari sneaked back into her own apartment where her mother wasn't yet sick, not actively, and still slept in the bedroom with Isaac, so it wasn't as chancy getting in and out, but Sari came home from sex with Jonah feeling smelly and raw and had forgotten in that haze to shut off the light, just crawled into her bed to try to sleep away the things she'd done and didn't fully understand. She'd woken then when the door to her bedroom flew open, Renata there in the hallway, backlit, naked and confused, her face screwed up like she couldn't get her eyes to open all the way. "Sari?" her voice groped into the darkness. "Sari, you're home?"

Sari could smell herself beneath the covers. She could smell the musky bed-heat coming off her mother in waves like humidity. "I'm here," she said. "I'm fine. I forgot the light."

The breath fizzled out of her mother's frame and her body seemed to go slack, the fifty-year-old flesh falling loose on her bones right there in the night before Sari's eyes. "Sari," she said, clucking and pained—"Sari." Renata held herself half behind the doorframe, as though her nudity hadn't counted during the potential crisis of Sari's absence, but now, beyond the emergency, she was recognizably unclothed.

"I'm sorry. I'm sorry. I just forgot."

"OK. OK. I'll . . . OK . . ." Renata was muddled. "Yeah, OK sweetheart. I'm going to go back to bed." She shuffled in the doorway, trying to reorient herself. "Goodnight baby, we'll talk in the morning, OK?"

"OK Mom. Sleep well. G'night. See you tomorrow." Sari watched her mother's figure turn, flick the light switch, and recede down the shadowed hall. They knew Renata was sick then, but things were still mostly normal, before life became something you measured in days. Back when "See you tomorrow" was still just a thing you said, before it became a prayer.

Sari slips off her shoes, drops her sweatshirt by the door, and climbs onto Jonah's bed, whacking her knee in the process on the metal bed frame. "Ow!" she yelps, dropping into the bed more obtrusively than she'd planned. Her kneecap rings with pain like a funnybone, and she cradles the knee in her hands. The pain is sharp but throbbing also, and it strikes Sari as interesting. Her wince turns gradually back into breath. Jonah shifts beneath his dove-gray comforter.

"Hey," he says. He's been asleep awhile, Sari thinks.

"Hey," Sari says back. She's sitting now, cross-legged, by Jonah's torso, her spine resting against the wall.

"Hi," he says again. There's not much more that needs to be exchanged in words between them, and Jonah stretches a hand toward Sari, touches her thigh with his blunt fingertips, runs his hand down along her leg to the knee, and squeezes it in greeting. Where the skin is scraped it stings under his palm, but Jonah's unaware; he means nothing malicious in his touch. It feels to Sari like his hand is sticking to the wound, like summer in New York when everything sticks to everything else and the heat itself feels contagious. Sari rubs the back of her head against Jonah's bedroom wall. Jonah's hand begins again to climb her thigh. Sari is learning there are some things a boy will always wake up for.

––––––––––––

They do not hear Hillary come home. That's their own fault: Jonah on top of Sari; Sari's legs flipped up over her own head. His noises are guttural, extended, like hard pained breaths from deep in his abdomen. Sari grunts too, but staccato, caught, as if Jonah's every thrust takes her by surprise. But then suddenly he stops, half inside her, slipping slack, and every thread of energy between them shifts outward and away. Jonah slips out of Sari completely, and her legs tumble back to the bed, raggedy. Jonah's nose is aimed at the bathroom door like a pointer. Sari looks in time to see only the door to the bathroom as it closes, swiftly. The light inside goes off, then on. Then off, back on. They hear the medicine cabinet slam, pill jars and compacts rattling on the shelves inside. The toilet flushes, shower curtain grommets clatter and scrape along the rod. Plastic bottles tumble into the tub and then the shower screeches on, hammering at them like a sudden, pelting rain.

"What the fuck?!" Jonah sneers. He's peeling off the condom, pitching it to the floor. He grabs his boxers from beside the bed and pulls up the thin green cotton as he storms across the room. Wedged in the crevice between bed and wall, Sari spots her tank top and pulls it on—inside-out, right-side-to, she can't even think to care. Her shorts are in the sheets, sweatshirt and shoes by the door, underwear nowhere to be found.

Jonah hammers his fist against the bathroom door. He's not heavy, but he's big, and standing there before the closed door, poised and furious, he looks mean. "Hillary," he pounds, his voice tempered just this side of a holler. "Hillary, what the fuck are you doing?" There's no lock on the door. "Hill, I'm coming in. You better be . . . I'm fucking coming in!"

Sari wishes he'd stop, wishes he knew how stupid he looks, a stupid teenager trying to act like Marlon Brando, or Robert De Niro in *Raging Bull*. He's laughable, and Sari is ashamed, ashamed for him, but ashamed mostly that Hillary has heard them, caught them, and instead of sneaking away with their tails between their legs Jonah's striking back, mounting a defense, as if *Hillary* had offended *them* and not vice versa. Sari thinks maybe this is what it means to die of embarrassment: to have embarrassed another person so badly you want to die. She perches on the edge of Jonah's bed, unsure what to do, where to move. She scratches at the bed frame with her nails, points her toes into the floor as hard as she can, and presses them like that until she hears the joints pop and crack. Jonah shoves open the bathroom door with more force than necessary. He glances back at Sari—an odd look, like a soldier taking one last look at his homeland as he ducks his head and boards the plane to foreign wars—but then slams the door hard behind him, a fuck-you slam, as if he's as mad at Sari as he is at Hill. The bathroom noises have all ceased, and Sari hears Jonah now open the adjoining door to Hill's room. That one he doesn't shut behind him. He just starts yelling. Sari can hear it all.

"What the fuck is your problem?" he demands. Hill is slamming around her own room now; her voice is a stage whisper, too angry to maintain quiet.

"You're such a dick, Jonah. You're such a fucking dick. What the fuck do you think you're doing. Jesus! I can't believe you'd . . . you knew I'd be home . . . I don't want to *hear* whatever the fuck you do . . ."

Jonah cuts her off: "Pardon me, *Mom*. No one died and made you parole officer. No one's telling you how the fuck to spend *your* night. What time is it? One? Two? I bet you'd love for Mom to hear that, Sweetheart."

"Her mother's fucking *dying*, you asshole! You . . ." Hill sputters, speechless in her fury, and it's not clear to Sari exactly what

Hill has actually said, for she cannot help but hear the voice as directed at her—*Your mother's fucking dying, you asshole.* And Sari knows it's true. Knows what she is, what she's done—run away to fuck the guy upstairs while her mother edges her way out of the world. Sari slips out Jonah's door. She is making her way down the clammy back stairwell long before Jonah can even return to his bed, all apologies, and find her gone.

Sari puts her key in the lock. Beyond the door, not ten feet away, is the rented bed where her mother—what is left of her mother—lies. There's always a little twinge of fear coming home, late at night, with things to hide; that fear would rise in Sari's throat even if everything inside were fine—if nothing, none of this had ever happened, and Renata and Isaac had been asleep in their bedroom since the sign-off after the ten o'clock news, and if Sari was still a virgin with no scrapes on her knees, an outfit for the spring dance at the top of her list of imminent worries. If it were just a regular Saturday night, and Sari'd been out with Hill at Loews 84th, not home in bed with Hill's older brother. They'd maybe have smoked a cigarette to transgress, but most likely they'd have shared a pint of Swiss Chocolate Almond, their plastic spoons snapping like twigs in the solid, cold, sweet cream. Coming home, Sari would get off the elevator first, approach 8E, her key in hand, and she'd have that rush of nerves: *please don't let Mom be awake. Please don't let her smell the cigarettes. Please let her not ask where I've been, why I'm late, why I didn't call.* Back then, which is not even back far enough to call *then*, back in the now that used to be, when she'd wanted nothing more than to slip in silently with no one around to take notice.

Inside 8E tonight, Renata might be awake and lucid. Or awake and confused. She might greet Sari and ask *how's my girl?* She might greet someone else, someone long dead or lost, only returned through her morphine haze in the guise of the girl who used to be her daughter, when she used to be a mother. Or Renata might be asleep, the TV flashing a mute Rhoda or Mary Tyler Moore, Renata's horrible breaths rasping through the room, Sari thanking god, or someone, that her mother is not awake because all awake really means is in pain, and little else. And Sari might cross in front of the screen, past her sleeping mother, and whisper in the TV light, "Goodnight, Ma. See you tomorrow." It might happen just like that tonight, tomorrow night, the next, Sari's words like a talisman against the end of tomorrows. Or she might open the lock and step inside and find that part of the future is already gone.

Fundamentals of Communication

———————————

Communications is not my field. I teach Fundamentals of Acting I and II. I used to do the Dramatic Monologue alternating semesters with Advanced Improvisation, sometimes even staged a production spring term, but there have been cutbacks and a new dean who seems to think that art is as dispensable as coffee from the basement vending machine. Dean Ford would actually be a decent enough guy if not for his unbounded democratic enthusiasm for systems of check and balance. He's gone gung-ho about "putting the *community* back in *community college*," so suddenly he's been here six months and we're all serving on eighteen zillion different committees "for the advancement of dialogue among students, faculty, staff, administration and community." The Rhetoric/Comp. people were all in a snit for a while about the grammatical correctness of "dialogue among," but that's pretty much died down now. Pat Reiser in Economics suggested we form a committee for the Grammatical Integrity of Memos from Personnel, or GIMP, but we're all overcommitted as it is. The one committee Ford has foisted on all of us is PEAN— that's the Peer Evaluation and Advisory Network—and it's PEAN duties that have me here at 8 A.M. on a Tuesday morning sitting in on Dan Zweibic's Fundamentals of Communication.

Dan's not a bad guy, just a bad teacher. But he's so goddamn earnest it's going to break my heart to do anything short of lying through my teeth on Ford's PEAN form and proclaiming poor, dull Dan to be "dynamic," "engaging," "professional," "adept." I would too, only no one would believe me. Dan's a mouse, a sad little mouse who must have pursued a communications major in college as a goal-project in 12 Steps beyond Shyness. So here's Dan a few years later, doing the Community College thing with the best and the rest of us. 8 A.M.: preaching to the sedated.

A few compassionate, front-row souls are swigging from cans of Mountain Dew purchased at the basement vending machines in an attempt to caffeinate themselves into a modicum of functionality. And the Dew may well have twice the kick of Coke, but even that's not going to do it for Dan's students this morning. Fund. of Comm. is a required course, meets four times a week for an hour and a quarter. I have heard—through the student/faculty/staff grapevine (UNITED IN GOSSIP WE STAND!)—that four days a week Dan delivers himself of a seventy-five-minute lecture on communication. Now, as a witness, I can testify to the veracity of this oxymoron. A lecture on communication! Need my PEAN report say anything more?

The lecture hall (well, Jesus, what's the administration expect when they schedule a Comm. class in a lecture hall?) is a steeply sloped auditorium, with Dan stuck down there in front of us like a baby in a well. I've snuck in at the back, and I'm not sure he's aware I'm here. In front of me a kid in a dark trenchcoat is drawing with a full box of 64 Crayolas what appears to be a birthday card for a person called "Jeannine" whom, it would seem, he loves. A few seats down, a girl who looks like she's still in her pajamas is writing a letter, or rather the first five or six lines of a letter, over and over on sequential pages of her spiral notebook. Every few minutes she snaps up the sheet she's been working on, flips it with an angry crackle around back, and begins again. "April 15. Dear Wallace, I'm in class, which sucks, which you probably figured since I'm sitting here writing you a letter." Another row down from Friend-of-Wallace, two women pass a looseleaf binder back and forth in written conversation. From the back, one of them looks a little like Emily, my delight-of-a-daughter, who's sworn that "if it's the last thing" she does, she's moving out of state as soon as she turns eighteen this spring and that she'd "sooner die" than take classes at the same dippy college where her mother "entertains the local bimbos." Her language is clichéd, but so's the whole goddamn situation. I have no right, I'm told (guess who by?), to expect "a goddamn thing" from her. And, goddamn it, should I not have expected just that? Just precisely that.

The Emily-Girl reads her friend's latest message installment and dissolves into silent laughter, and that's more than enough to dispel her similarity to my daughter, who would not giggle, I don't think, if her life depended on it. (All clichés intended.) In the aisle of these girls' row, a young couple have eschewed the convention of desks and are sprawled on the steps. The boy, with his bobbed dark hair and tortoise-framed glasses, leans against the wall. The girl—long, fine white-blond hair skimming past a jaw that might be called horsey but is nonetheless striking—rests against her sweetie, her back propped between his open thighs, her own legs tucked beneath her. She's slipped off her shoes, a pair of tiny cork-soled clogs that sit on the carpeted step like two pet mice heeled beside their owner. The couple are among the few in the hall who are actually looking toward the front of the room, but I don't think they're listening any more than Wallace's friend or Jeannine's lover.

It's when I see Dan climbing up the aisle stairs that I realize I'm not listening either. He's describing a film of some sort, and it becomes clear that he's headed up to man the projector from the back of the hall. Dan seems to spot the stair-couple for the first time when he's about five steps below them, and there's a shudder of something like panic that crosses his eyes—this is an unanticipated obstacle!—and I can picture the adolescent that Dan really is inside seized with the adolescent fear of having to maneuver his way past a pretty girl. A pretty girl entwined with a pretty boy, the suggestion of everything that exists between them sprawled right there across the step. The girl leans toward the wall a bit to allow Dan passage, but she doesn't actually move over, just performs the gesture, the suggestion of movement. Dan seems to freeze, unable to move forward. He lifts his head, his eyes flit about, and it's then he notices me, my tell-tale PEAN clipboard out on the desk. Instantly, his hand rises in greeting, like a child's imitation of an American Indian—*How.* Dan's face cracks a goofy smile of utter relief, as though I were the familiar face in the crowd, the friend appeared suddenly to rescue him from his momentary logistical crisis. I smile back stiffly; a few heads turn to see who I am. I find myself nodding absurdly, as if I can coax Dan up the stairs the way I once rooted Emily down the slide, up the monkey bars, onto the tire swing—*I think I can, I think I can—* the Little Professor Who Could. And we're all just poised there, waiting to see what will happen.

Suddenly, the boyfriend, in a moment of divine inspiration, scoops the girl's clogs from the step, one-handed, and holds them above his head. He is the drawbridge, the starter gun, the butler gesturing *come in, come in,* and somehow, miraculously, Dan is willing to accept this young man's offer to let him pass safely: the coast is clear, full speed ahead. Dan scuttles wordlessly past, flips a light switch at the back of the hall, and resumes control of his subject: show movie, project projector, provide narration, for transcripts see textbook, *Dynamics of Human Interaction,* p. 472.

On the steps, the boy has set the girl's clogs back on the floor beside them. The girl is wearing a sleeveless shirt, and in the dim film-light I can see the boy now place his hand on the warm skin of her back just between the shoulder blades. He's wearing sandals himself, and one of the girl's hands rests atop his exposed toes. They are still, eyes trained to the screen, but all the energy is there, in these touch-points. They sit, shifting occasionally, glancing at the glowing wall clock, waiting for 9:15. I can't see them as well now, in the shadows, but I catch the occasional movement in one of their hands, the caress of a finger, press of a palm.

Flowers in the Dustbin, Poison in the Human Machine

The very first day of nursery school, when David Rogosin finds out that Addie Farber doesn't know how to read and makes fun of her, it's Kirsten Grand who comes to Addie's defense. Later, at naptime, when Mrs. Hauser turns off the classroom lights, in that midday darkness—sun slicing in at the edges of the window shades, the kids' fingers sticky with juice and Fig Newton crumbs—Kirsten and Addie are too keyed up to sleep. They've lain their sleeping mats one beside the other, far away from stupid David Rogosin, and as Mrs. Hauser settles into her chair across the room and sticks her nose into some papers, Kirsten reaches across the patch of cold, linoleum floor and takes Addie's hand. They lie like that until Mrs. Hauser turns the lights back on.

At their summer-house on the shore, the Grands spend the weekends having barbecues, swilling Scotch with Dick's business partners on the deck while they wait for the grill to fire up. This weekend, Addie is Kirsten's guest. The steaks are as thick as her torso and take a lot longer to cook than the girls' dinner: Oscar Meyer Weiners from the freezer. The adults are drunk and bored to death with each other after golf all day and corporate finance all week. Kirsten and Addie are inside watching *The Dating Game*, chewing their hot dogs quietly, the bun sticking to the roof of Addie's mouth like a wad of wet toilet paper, when they hear Dick hollering for Kirsten, *get your brainy little butt outside!* Provide the guests with a little evening entertainment. At the Grands' house Addie is treated like an extension of Kirsten: like a teddy bear she insists on toting around. All the same, Dick and Effie are glad to have Addie there; she keeps Kirsten entertained. Dick keeps forgetting Addie's name; she is "the little friend."

They set Kirsten up in a chaise lounge; Addie sits on the deck dangling her feet in the pool. It is summer. They are four. Addie watches the veiny-nosed men nodding importantly at their sick-skinny wives as Effie Grand sticks the *Arts & Leisure* section in Kirsten's lap. The adults laugh, ice clinks in refills, Dick pushes himself up with a groan to go test the fire—*sizzzzz*—a splash of his beer spattering on the coals. A twitchy, pinched wife leans across her fat husband's lap to Effie but speaking loudly, for Dick to hear, *I heard they did a study and they found out that brains come from the mother's side of the genes* . . . The man beneath her snorts, *yeah, so no wonder our kid's a moron.* And they're laughing and Kirsten doesn't know what at. She just keeps reading: *The Biennial Exhibit opens next week at the Whitney Museum of Art, on Madison Avenue and Seventy-fourth Street.* Addie hears someone say, *Dick, the kid's smarter than you. We got ourselves a new partner.*

In first grade at lunchtime Mrs. Howard does the crossword puzzle at her desk and is not to be disturbed unless someone is not breathing or has won a Nobel Prize. Tanner is supposed to be the Board of Ed's special program, the gifted program: quality education for the intellectual elite with a fifty-percent minority student mandate, a fertile ground to train young, inner-city teachers. But the school is underfunded and ill-managed. The teachers are neither young nor ready for a challenge; often they are not even students at the teachers' college. Most often what they are is tired and burnt-out, paid meagre salaries to supervise the board's "little genius" children. They live in subsidized housing an hour outside Manhattan. They schlep to and from Tanner by bus every day. It's not that they don't try. But, *Jesus*, they're tired.

Mrs. Howard's class is a zoo and it is "feeding time." Kirsten sits on top of the Turtle, a green steel hump with foot-holes for climbing. On their knees, the others surround the Turtle, carpet grit imprinting their kneecaps. Most are dogs by default: they hang their paws by their ears and pant. Some are more creative. Paige is a monkey, *eee-eee*-ing and scratching herself under the arms. Nubia is quiet, hunched over, her tongue darting in and out to catch imaginary flies. Occasionally she *ribbits*. Maisie is always Mitten the Cat. This is her early claim to fame: the leading role in every play that Kirsten writes. In the Mitten plays Addie gets to be Tracy Austin and carry a tennis racket, but at the zoo she is a dog like the rest of the unimaginative. Kirsten doesn't act in the Mitten plays; she directs. And at lunchtime she is always the zookeeper.

"Come on little animals! Who's hungry today?" Kirsten peels a strawberry fruit roll-up from its plastic and dangles the pink gummy sheet in front of their faces. "Mmmmm . . . strawberry," Kirsten coos, holding it above her own head and taking a nibble from the corner. "Boyd, do you want a fruit roll-up?" she asks. Boyd nods vigorously, shaking his butt like a tail. Animals are not allowed to speak; they must win treats through cuteness, just like the animals at the zoo, who cannot say *my mom never lets me have fruit roll-ups at home, please can I have a bite*. They must make their eyes big, faces puppylike and pathetic. They must sniffle, and whimper, and prey on the sympathy of others.

Boyd opens his mouth wide and grabs a corner with his teeth. The fruit leather tears and flops onto his chin. Hands aren't allowed, and Boyd has to slurp to get it all in his mouth. He turns back to Kirsten, panting for more.

Addie is eyeing the Starbursts resting next to Kirsten on top of the Turtle. Kirsten opens the pack and pulls out orange, waves it above the crowd for a moment, and then tosses it over their heads. A few kids scramble for it on all fours. Addie waits. She knows that now Kirsten will toss another Starburst into the thinned-out crowd which she will be able to catch more easily. Kirsten aims in Addie's direction: red. She bends and grabs it in her teeth, scraping her nose and chin against the dirty carpet. Starbursts are good because they're individually wrapped. Otherwise she'd have to eat it off the floor. The kids have learned what to ask their moms to pack in lunch bags: Hershey Kisses, Tootsie Rolls, Blow Pops. With Addie's mom, it makes no difference what she asks for because they don't buy sugar in Addie's house. Kirsten understands this and lets Addie play anyway, and the other kids go along with it OK. Some kids are not allowed to play no matter what they bring in their lunch: David Rogosin eats egg salad sandwiches and sticks his boogers in his desk and he is never allowed in the zoo. With Brittany Wilkes it just depends on Kirsten's mood. Sometimes Addie wishes Kirsten would let everybody play, but she knows that to ask Kirsten if Brittany could join or to simply invite Brittany to the game herself would be a betrayal. It would cost Addie her niche. So she follows along, barking and panting; she always gets to play. Addie is an exception.

An exception to the exceptions, really. Because Tanner is a school for the "exceptionally gifted." Admission is by test only; tuition is free. Tanner philosophy: expose these little minds to knowledge. Smart kids need not be taught; they need simply to be prompted, positioned, urged in good directions. They are gatherers of experience. So teachers, says the Board of Ed, tell your students they are exceptional. Tell them they are different. Make yourself a list of synonyms and use it religiously. Here, we'll start you off: *the cream of the crop, the crème de la crème, special, gifted, supersmart, the best.* Encourage creativity. Do a lot of art projects. Take a lot of field trips. Let them spend a lot of time in quiet study; they'll learn more from each other than you'll ever be able to teach.

On Tuesdays in second grade, Addie takes the school bus home with Kirsten and they play there at the Grands' apartment until Addie's mom comes to pick her up on the way home from work. The Grands' housekeeper seems to change nearly every time Addie goes over, always a black woman with an accent from Jamaica or Haiti who knits, watches all the soaps, and sleeps in a tiny converted laundry room off the kitchen.

The girls are finger-painting in the kitchen, kneeling up on sticky-vinyl yellow kitchen chairs, old button-down shirts of Dick's fastened around them—backward as smocks—by the housekeeper, who is in the den watching TV and folding laundry.

"I'm painting a scene," Kirsten tells Addie, dipping a finger daintily in blue, "a scene from the play."

"Which one?" Addie asks. Addie wonders if maybe Kirsten has pointier fingers than she does; she can't make her own painting look like anything.

"You don't know it," Kirsten says. "It's from a new play that's still in my head."

"A Mitten play?" Addie asks.

"Maybe," she says. "And maybe not."

"Hm," Addie says, feigning disinterest. She sips her Yoo Hoo from its glass on the table. It is deliciously sweet: something Addie doesn't get at home. It is worth enduring even some of Kirsten's moods.

The girls paint quietly until Addie begins work on a field of flowers and Kirsten peers over her shoulder to inspect. "I love the keller green, don't you?" she says, pointing to Addie's grassy planes.

"The what?"

"The keller green," she repeats. "It's so springy and glad." Kirsten gives a little hum to herself and turns back to her own work.

"What do you mean 'the keller green'?" Addie demands.

"What do you mean what do I mean?"

"Keller." Addie mimics. "You said 'keller,' instead of 'color.'"

Kirsten looks her dead on. "'Color'?" she asks benignly. "What's that?"

"What do you mean 'what's that'? Color. That's what it's called. A color. Red, orange, yellow, purple, green, blue—colors."

Kirsten pushes the hair out of her eyes, running a streak of green through her tangled blond mop, and fixes Addie with her hardest, most condescending stare. The what-a-cute-and-silly-little-mistaken-girl-you-are stare, the stare Addie most hates her for. "Addie," she says slowly, "the word is *keller*."

Addie feels paralyzed, like Kirsten is changing the rules to the world, and Addie will be left behind. There is nowhere to turn for help. The housekeeper barely speaks English. "Cut it out, Kirsten," she pleads, the panic coming up in her throat. "*Keller* isn't a word." Everything seems to hang still for a moment while Addie prays for the joke to be over.

But Kirsten isn't cracking. "Addie," Kirsten begins after a moment, "it's OK if you don't know that word. Don't worry." Kirsten reaches an arm around Addie's shoulders. "You shouldn't get so upset over a little thing like that."

Addie's body is rigid.

"Hey," Kirsten says, her tone rising, "want to go watch TV with Yolanda?"

Addie cannot nod, but she follows.

It is just past five o'clock when the doorbell rings. Yolanda pushes herself up from the couch to answer it, but Addie, who has been poised on the lip of the sofa, ready to pounce, beats her to it. She struggles with the deadbolt for a second, doesn't even remember to ask *who is it*, and flings open the door. Her mom appears at last, standing there in the Grands' foyer like a magician's assistant who has been lost too long behind the magic curtain. Addie can feel the outside cold rushing off her mother's body in waves. Her mom seems startled.

"Hi, baby . . ." she begins, but Addie can't hold it in any longer.

"Mom, right the word is *color* not *keller*? Kirsten said it's *keller* but it's not. Right it's *color*? Tell her, Mommy, tell her it's *color*. Tell her how to say it right."

Addie's mom—her eyes blinking, the glimmer of a smile flickering beneath the surface of her expression—looks to Yolanda to try and share this moment with another adult. "Hi," she says, tugging off a glove in order to shake Yolanda's hand. "I'm Anthea Farber, Addie's mom."

Yolanda, either unaware or intentionally ignorant of the hand extended toward her, gives a little nod, "Missus," and disappears into the depths of the Grand apartment.

Addie's mom looks somewhat daunted. She turns back to Addie. "What, babe? What are you saying?" Only then Kirsten appears in the archway of the hall.

"Hi Kirsten," says Addie's mom. "How are you?"

"Hi Mrs. Farber. Fine." Kirsten leans against the doorframe chewing a hangnail.

"Mom," Addie whines. She feels like she's going to burst, like there's air pressure zooming in from all around her, and she's boiling hot underneath her clothes. There is no more cold New York air coming off her mother, so she is useless, no relief, like an ice-pack left out, gone gushy and warm. Addie wants to fly at her mom and press her face into the thick canvas of her coat, pull cold out of the cloth. "Mom," she wails, her voice edging toward dissolve, "we were painting and . . ."

But her mom cuts her off, a hand smoothing the hair on Addie's small head. "That's great, Adds, do I get to see? Can we bring your painting home to show Daddy?"

Addie's desperation feels toxic. Her voice comes out loud and shaky. "Mommy! No! Wait! Listen!"

Her mom senses the panic. She snaps to attention.

"We were painting, and Kirsten said the word for *color* is *keller* and it isn't but she says it is. Only tell her it isn't. It's not *keller*. It's *color*."

Addie's mom looks to Kirsten, posed there in the archway like an old-time movie star. Her voice is instantly diplomatic. "Kirsten," she says, "Addie's right, the word is *color*."

And Addie should feel relief—the relief of rightness—but she doesn't, instead suddenly realizing what Kirsten can do now: deny having ever said anything to the contrary. Only she doesn't. From the doorframe, her face wide with innocence, pouty mouth pursed with knowing, Kirsten fixes Addie's mom with a sleepy-lidded stare. "No, Mrs. Farber," she says, her cheeks twitching, mocking a smile, "the word is *keller*."

Jimmy Carter wins a second term as president in the Tanner third grade mock election. It is a landslide victory: twenty-seven votes. Paige Sorano is the only one who votes for Anderson. Addie tries to explain to Paige what her parents have explained to Addie: that a vote for Anderson is really a vote for Reagan. "Anderson isn't going to win," Addie's mom said last night at dinner, "and if a Democrat votes for Anderson that's one less Democrat for Carter. If we force a split like that in the democratic vote, we're shooting ourselves in the feet. Practically passing Reagan the presidency on a silver platter." Her mom had made eggplant Parmesan, and there was salad, and whole wheat rolls.

"I have to vote for the candidate I like best," Paige tells Addie. "That's why it's a democracy." Addie pushes her bangs out of her eyes and lets them fall back static to her forehead, exasperated by Paige's naïveté, her starry-eyed idealism, but also by the unfairness of it all. At home Addie's told that the world is a hard place where good people fight to do the best they can. This country is a democracy, and it works. Addie's parents have taught her that good people who work hard get what they deserve, but suddenly, standing there in the coat room with Paige, this no longer makes sense. In a fair country (which her mom and dad say this is), for someone to want John Anderson to be the president but not be able to vote for him seems crazy, and Addie wishes right then that everyone could be like Paige: honest and impervious to even the simplest tactic or strategical maneuver. Paige, Addie decides, is how people were meant to be.

Kirsten Grand is the only person in Mrs. Urstle's third-grade class who votes for Ronald Reagan to be the fortieth president of the United States.

When Reagan is elected for real, Addie's mother joins the PTA. The government, she says, is falling to shit, but her daughter's school will not go the same way if she has anything to say about it. She is elected treasurer and begins to spend a lot of time on the phone with Roz DiNardo, Lydia's mom, who works afternoons in the Tanner office as a volunteer. Just wants to stay busy and involved, she says.

"Roz DiNardo is a godsend to that school," Addie's mom says one evening. They are on the crosstown bus, coming home after a PTA fund-raising drive. "But that woman has a mouth the size of the Lincoln Tunnel."

Back at the apartment, Mom plops onto the couch and nuzzles into Dad, who has been doing the crossword puzzle with the TV on. "What a catty woman I become around Roz DiNardo," she half-laughs, half-moans. Then Mom eats just cottage cheese and yogurt for dinner and gets annoyed at Addie for reading *Sweet Valley High* when there's a library of brilliant literature out there. Later, as a family, they watch *NOVA*.

The class from Tanner is walking south through the streets of Manhattan to the Stowbridge School for the annual Fourth Grade Spelling Bee. Addie and Lydia DiNardo are partners. Mrs. Oko leads the way down Madison Avenue, the head of this scrappy little troop, trudging around April puddles, instructed specifically not to splash. For the first few blocks, the children are quiet, making their way through the Tanner neighborhood. This area above 96th Street is noted mainly for trash, crime, and Optimo cigar shops on every corner where malt liquor is a better seller than coffee at nine in the morning.

Below 96th the change is abrupt. The chatter level rises. Hok jumps in a puddle and splashes dirty water all over Olu's pants. Brittany does a pirouette while they wait for a light to change to WALK. The stores they pass Addie's mom would call "cutesy": card shops, bath shops, stores that sell nothing but antique dollhouse furniture. Addie is transfixed by a window display of hanging mobiles: satin hearts and rainbows, plush stuffed stars with glittery ribbons fluttering down like a comet's tail. "I might get Kirsten a mobile like that for her birthday," she tells Lydia, pointing as they pass. Kirsten is way ahead of them, partners with Maisie.

"When's her birthday?" Lydia asks.

"Soon," Addie says. "Didn't you get an invitation yet?"

Lydia shakes her head. Her eyes flit, like she's trying to pretend she doesn't care.

"Oh," Addie says. "Maybe it got lost," she adds, "in the mail."

Lydia shakes her head again, no, but still doesn't say anything. Addie feels bad, and dumb, and clumsy. She's said the wrong thing, again. She always says the wrong thing. They walk another block in silence. The sun glints off the puddles, oily and dark.

"Kirsten shouldn't even be here in the first place."

"What?"

"She's not supposed to be here, even," Lydia says again. "Kirsten."

"What do you mean? Everybody gets to go to the spelling bee." Addie doesn't understand.

"Not here today here. Here at Tanner here," Lydia says, her eyes still down.

Addie can think of no response.

"She didn't even get in," Lydia continues. "My mom found out in the office. There was a whole big thing. I heard my mom tell someone on the telephone. She said Kirsten's parents said they'd sue Tanner if they didn't let Kirsten in, because she's so smart. So they let her in."

Still, Addie cannot process this enough to speak. It doesn't make any sense. Kirsten is maybe the smartest of all of them.

"Imagine," Lydia is saying. "Imagine what it'd be like if Kirsten wasn't here?"

"How?" Addie asks.

"I think it would be better," Lydia says. "Better if Kirsten wasn't here, don't you?" She looks at Addie for the first time. Addie has to say something.

"Maybe. I don't know."

"I think it would be," Lydia says again. Then they are quiet awhile.

The invitations to Kirsten Grand's tenth birthday are Woolworth's cards, overstock, on thin, cheap paper. *Celebrate a Grand Decade*, and someone—Dick or Effie, or maybe Kirsten—has made a little insertion mark before the word to write in *Kirsten*. A Kirsten Grand Decade.

Tanner kids call the Stowbridge School the Snob-rich School. The Snob-rich building was a mansion before it was a school, the Tanner kids have heard, and through the entrance gate Addie can see a huge marble staircase with curlicue banisters sweeping upward. The Tanner School is a converted mattress factory.

To the Tanner kids, the Snob-riches seem perfect. The boys all look cute and blond, their oxford shirts untucked, loafers scuffed. The girls are pale and porcelain-skinned. They have side parts in their hair, which falls over one eye like a model's. They have pink lips and pretty knees sticking out from their plaid miniskirts. When the gate opens, two girls bent together in a secret lift their heads in unison with a swoosh of hair that sends a cloud of Johnson's baby shampoo rushing into Addie's nostrils, and she wishes she were anywhere in the world but here right now, wishes she were anyone in the world but herself: stumpy cowlicks jutting out all over her head, curling up over the edges of the plastic headband she wears to keep them down. Suddenly she is so embarrassed she wants to be dead. Truly: dead. Everything that is OK at Tanner is no longer OK, and it never will be OK. That's something they've known maybe as long as they've known anything: it is only to each other that they will ever belong.

"Squalor. S-Q-U-A-L-O-R."
"Pharmacy. P-H-A-R-M-A-C-Y."
"Indignant." "Aspirate." "Scavenger." "Orbital." "Cloaked." "Remember." "Obnoxious." "Sentimental." "Sorcerer." "Convenient."
"Hideous." It is Paige's turn. "Hideous. H-I-D-I-O-U-S."

They win anyway. They always do. Back at Tanner they will have to make a thank-you card to send to the little Snob-riches. They have to sign their names and write how nice it was to be guests in their school and how much the fourth graders will look forward to next year's bee. Mrs. Oko spreads a big piece of oak-tag on the art table in the corner of the classroom, and they spend the afternoon doing "quiet study," working on Explorer reports or doing workbook exercises at their desks and going to the card-table in pairs to write their messages and names and to draw pictures.

Cortés is Addie's explorer, and she sort-of reads a book about him while she waits for her turn to sign the card. Paige and Maisie sit in front of Addie at their desks, and Paige has open a big book on Juan Ponce de León, only she's not reading, just sitting there with the book propped up on her desk like a shutter she's hiding behind. Addie tries to go back to Montezuma and Cortés and the Aztecs, but she hears a little gasp and a whimper in front of her and looks up again to see Paige's shoulders shudder almost imper-ceptibly. She is crying, Addie realizes, suddenly nervous and em-barrassed for Paige. It's like when Hok got hit with a dodgeball in the stomach and got the wind knocked out of him, and Addie felt so bad that everyone had to see him like that: gasping and scared and out of control. She just stood there dumbly craning over him, not wanting to get too close, saying, *are you OK? Hey, are you all right?* She puts her nose back down to Hernando Cortés and lets Paige cry in peace.

Just then Maisie leans over and puts an arm around Paige's shoulders. Paige shudders again. Addie can hear Maisie whisper: "Are you OK?" and she wants to know how Maisie can make those same words sound so earnest and real.

"It's OK," Maisie tells Paige softly. "That was a hard word." Maisie pets Paige's head, smoothing her hair out of her face like Addie's mom does when she's sick. *I will never be as good a per-son as Maisie*, Addie thinks. She looks around to see if anyone else is watching Paige break down and catches Kirsten's eye two desks down. Kirsten is mouthing something, but Addie can't un-derstand what so shakes her head: *I can't hear you.* With an exasperated huff Kirsten flings open her notebook and rips a sheet of looseleaf from the three-ring binder. She tucks her head down and scrawls, then folds the paper up tiny and drops it absently to the floor. Jenny Powilla, who sits between Kirsten and Addie, pretends not to notice.

Hands hidden beneath her desk, Addie unfolds the paper. *Does she expect us to forgive her for not being able to spell her own middle name? What a crybaby!*

Addie looks at Kirsten, confused. Kirsten rolls her eyes and pushes herself up from her chair, twitching her head to the classroom door and motioning for Addie to follow her to Mrs. Oko's desk. Mrs. Oko is eating a tuna fish sandwich.

"Mrs. Oko, can me 'n' Addie go to the bathroom?"

Mrs. Oko swallows her mouthful of rye bread and celery. There is mayonnaise in the corner of her lip. "It's not very nice to say that Addie's mean, is it, Kirsten?" This is what Mrs. Oko always says.

Kirsten shifts her weight to the other foot; she speaks in a voice so syrupy, any self-respecting teacher would send her to the principal, just for being smarmy. But discipline is not something Tanner enforces with any stringency. Kirsten begins again, "I mean, may Addie and I please be excused to use the restroom."

Mrs. Oko looks like she just wants to get back to her tuna fish. "Three minutes," she says and points the girls to the door.

In the stall, with the black metal door shut behind them, Kirsten lifts her skirt, pulls down her tights, and pees while she talks. On the wall behind her, carved crudely into the paint, is a poem: *We're the flowers in your dustbin   We're the poison in your human machine   We're the future   Your future SUCK A COCK.*

"Can you believe," Kirsten says, reaching for the toilet paper, "that she messed up on such an easy word?"

"Who? Paige?" Addie asks.

"Of course Paige," she says, yanking up her tights. "Paige 'Hideous' Sorano, who can't even spell her own name." Kirsten pushes Addie out of the stall, forgetting to flush.

When they come back into the classroom, Paige and Maisie are signing the card. It looks like Paige has stopped crying and is wrapped up in whatever she's drawing, and Addie thinks: *good.*

Paige will make a beautiful drawing like she always does and then it won't matter that she's not a good speller because she's the best artist. Paige draws pictures that make Addie never want to pick up a Magic Marker ever again as long as she lives. As they pass the drawing table, Kirsten leans over to Maisie and scratches her under the chin like a little cat.

"Pretty little Mitten," Kirsten coos.

Maisie looks up, her sweet chubby face all a-smile. She closes her eyes demurely, rubs the peach fuzz of her cheek against Kirsten's hand, and purrs.

"Good kitty," Kirsten strokes the back of her head. "Good, good kitty Mitten."

Across the table Paige is bent over the card.

Kirsten and Addie go to the card-signing table together. Maisie has made a cat next to her name, and across from it, Paige has drawn a portrait of two little girls, one in jeans and a T-shirt, the other a Stowbridge girl in her uniform skirt and sweater. The two girls are holding hands. Underneath she has signed: *Your Friend, Paige Sorano.*

When Addie gets to school a little bit late the next morning, things are in an uproar. Mrs. Oko is gone, Paige is crying, and Maisie looks like a spooked horse, her eyes wide and shifty. Some kids are crowded around the art table where the Snob-rich card was yesterday. Today, the table is empty. Addie peers over, trying to catch what people are saying, when she feels a hand on her elbow.

"Vandalism," Lydia tells Addie, her voice hushed as a TV detective.

"Someone stole the card?" Addie asks, incredulous. She thinks of her flowers: pink, green, yellow, blue.

"No, not *stolen*. Vandalized. Someone *tampered* with the card."

"Why?" Addie asks, knowing this is the wrong question. There is a nugget of fear caught in her chest like she is about to be accused of a crime she has somehow inadvertently committed.

"I don't know *why*." Lydia is getting exasperated.

"I mean, *how*?" Addie asks. "What did they do?"

Lydia leans in. "Someone wrote in things on Paige's signature," she whispers.

"What?" Addie asks after a minute, but she's faking it. She doesn't have to ask. "What did they write?"

"A bubble, like in comics," Lydia says. "Someone put a bubble coming out of her drawing, out of the mouth of the Tanner girl in her picture, that said 'DUH' and then it had the word 'hideous' spelled wrong like Paige spelled it yesterday. And they also wrote it in with her name, like it was a nickname or something: *Paige 'Hideous' Sorano*. Mrs. Oko said she was giving the 'guilty party' fifteen minutes to think about their crime and apologize to Paige and to the rest of the class. Then we're having a math quiz."

Addie's eyes hurt and she feels sweaty, like she wants to throw up, like there's something inside her that shouldn't be there.

"Hey, Tracy Austin," Kirsten's voice comes up from behind them. "Did you hear what happened?"

Addie can't talk. Kirsten's eyes are dramatic. She is doing indignity, and she's doing it well.

"Isn't that awful?" she drawls. "Can you believe someone would do that, after all the work we did on that card, can you believe someone would ruin it like that? I can't believe it."

Addie can't believe it. Kirsten seems almost giddy with excitement, with the thrill of her own performance. Addie starts to panic, starts to wonder if maybe Kirsten's set it all up as a trap— if she's telling people that "Hidious" was Addie's idea, not her own. Everything starts to crumble then, and Addie sees, for the first time, what it would be like to be on the outside—to be Brittany Wilkes, or David Rogosin. To have Maisie and Lydia and everyone else pass her in the halls and only glare. To have Paige not look at her at all. To have them think that she is evil. That she has tricked them all along—all these years—tricked them into liking her. That she is a fraud, a phony. That this terrible thing is Addie's fault. She *has* facilitated it, gone along and done nothing to protect anyone against Kirsten—nothing to warn Paige or Jenny P. or Maisie or anyone, all these years—nothing to stand in Kirsten's way. She has only made Kirsten's power possible, stronger, has been a source of that strength. Addie has basked, shimmering in the light that Kirsten casts, protected and warmed. She has bathed in the sun, swum in the pool, drunk Yoo Hoo. She has been Tracy Austin. For years. No one but Addie has ever been Tracy Austin. She has claimed all the glories. Now there is responsibility to bear. She is as bad as Kirsten. All of this—all—it is all her own fault.

No one comes forward. They take a math quiz. Addie can't remember how to find the least common denominator and has to leave three questions blank out of ten. It isn't until after Mrs. Oko has collected the papers that Addie can catch Kirsten's eye and make their bathroom signal: two sign-language *P*s. Mrs. Oko excuses them without her usual grammatical rigmarole.

Addie locks the stall door behind them. Kirsten flips down the toilet lid and takes it as a seat, her lips pursed expectantly, like she's waiting to know what the secret is she's been dragged off to the girls' room to hear. She's not giving away anything. Addie doesn't know how to begin.

"Did you?" Addie asks, hoping maybe that will be enough. Addie knows Kirsten knows that she knows, and it seems impossible—unthinkable—that she would pretend to her—Addie!— in secret, just the two of them, here in the bathroom stall where yesterday Kirsten laid it all right out, plain as day.

"Did I what?" Kirsten asks, puzzled.

"Did you . . . what you told me yesterday. About Paige. Did you?"

Kirsten gives a little chortle to herself—a soft snort accompanied by a slow shake of her head, back and forth, a grin nestled in the crook of her mouth. "I guess I wasn't the only one to make the connection between Paige's mistake in the spelling bee and her . . ." Kirsten clears her throat dramatically, "her rather *interesting* looks."

"But did you . . . I mean . . . you didn't write that there? On the card?"

Kirsten's jaw drops in determined shock. "You don't think I'd do something that stupid, Addie? God." She scoots off the toilet seat cover and stands, hands at her hips.

"I don't know," Addie says.

"Jesus, Addie, I was thinking that maybe *you* had done it, but I wasn't going to just go and *accuse* the person I thought was my best friend of doing something like *that*."

No matter where Addie goes in this conversation—in any conversation—Kirsten will always be a step ahead of her.

"Jesus, Addie, *did* you do it?" She's tapping her foot on the ground impatiently. "Not like *I'd* ever ask you that. Jesus. If you did that, Addie, you're a whole lot stupider than I thought." She shakes her head again, as if to toss off the disbelief, then unlocks the door and slams out, another *Jesus* exclaimed under her breath. The metal door swings shut again behind her, and Addie is left alone in the bathroom stall.

Except: if they took all the names of all the white kids who passed the entrance exam and put them in a hat and picked them blind, and they'd picked Addie's name, and Lydia's name, and Josh Leibowitz's name, and Paul Forrester's name, and not Kirsten's name, and Kirsten's parents said that wasn't fair and that's why Kirsten is at Tanner, then wouldn't it have been just as likely for Kirsten's name to get picked in the first place and not Addie's? Maybe Addie shouldn't be here either? Maybe she is as bad as Kirsten, and her parents are as awful as Dick and Effie? Maybe her parents, just like Kirsten's parents, threatened to sue Tanner if Addie wasn't accepted into Mrs. Hauser's nursery class? If she could take it back, she thinks, she would slip through the cracks. She would not be *special. The crème de la crème, the cream of the crop, the smartest of the smart, bright, bright, bright as a bulb. If I could take it back*, she thinks, *I would be regular. If I could take it back, I would be me.* The graffiti on the bathroom wall bleeds in front of Addie's eyes. *The future   Your future   SUCK A COCK.*

Stepping off the school bus, Addie sees her mom eating a peach, huge, pinkish-orange, beautiful, unbelievable, the first of the season—spring! She holds it out to Addie, her smile huge with anticipation. But Addie just bursts into tears. She buries her face in that familiar raincoat, her mother's hands in her hair, sweet voice and breath hushing over Addie *baby, baby, sweet baby, honey what's the matter, baby, what's happened, shhhh, shhh, baby shhhhh* and Addie sobs harder into the folds because she doesn't know if, like Maisie and Paige and Lydia and Nubia and Jenny Powilla and all of them, her mother is good. Or if she is just like Dick and Effie Grand, like Kirsten, like Addie. Bad.

"Jerks!" her mom says under her breath, slamming the silverware drawer. Her mom has coaxed the entire story out of her, here, at the kitchen table.

"So you and Daddy didn't say you'd sue Tanner if they didn't let me in?"

Her mom grabs Addie, pulls her in tight. "Oh, baby no. Of course not, no." She tugs Addie from her then, wrenches her a little so she can look right into Addie's face, right into her daughter's eyes. "You are there because you are a very very very smart girl. And Kirsten is a very smart girl too, but she's also not a nice girl. Kirsten is not a good person. You know, baby, as difficult as Kirsten is—and that child has never been anything but difficult—it isn't really Kirsten's fault. Her parents—you know her parents, Adds, they're not nice people. And that's all Kirsten's around. That's all she sees, and that's the only way she knows how to behave." Mom pauses, studying her daughter's face to see if she knows who this little girl really is. This smart girl, this good girl, *her* girl. Her Addie. Then she leans over and kisses the top of Addie's head between her bangs, stands, and swings open the refrigerator door.

"Chicken or spaghetti for dinner?" she asks.

"Chicken," Addie says and swallows hard with a fear—a fear of learning more, of knowing more things, things that once she knows, no matter how much she wishes, she can never, ever, unknow. Her mom spins around to her again, and Addie knows she will say more because she always does.

"I know you're angry now, baby, and you have a perfect right to be," she says, pulling a yellow Styrofoam tray from the freezer and *thunk*-ing down the package of rock solid breasts on the counter, "but maybe once that anger wears down some you'll realize that Kirsten is someone to feel sorry for, not someone to hate or be scared of. She's going to be a sad and nasty person just like her parents, and she'll have ugliness and unhappiness in her life just like them. She's smart, but that's not going to buy her happiness. Kirsten Grand is going to be brilliant and miserable her whole life."

At school the next day, Kirsten keeps her distance. People are still twittering about the "Hideous" thing, but Tanner life is going on pretty much as usual. Kirsten has begun plotting for the next Mitten play and is buddying up to Maisie and Paige to collaborate with her on set and costume design. Paige and Maisie are, of course, relishing the attention while Kirsten showers it on them. She can do that: cast a light over you that feels so good and so warm that you'll do anything to stay there. You'll do things you thought you'd never do just to keep that light on your face.

Excluded from the clique, Addie hangs out with Lydia, who is never part of any clique but seems glad for Addie's attention. She's doing Cortés for her Explorer report too, and they decide to make a diorama together of one of the Aztec temples. This necessitates another trip to the library, so Lydia and Addie spend the hour slotted for Social Studies looking for a book with a picture to copy.

"Out by the cubbies this morning," Lydia whispers by the card catalog, "Josh Leibowitz told Hok that he thought that *Kirsten* did the thing to the card because they were at After-School and she could've snuck back upstairs."

Addie cannot look at Lydia, so she stares down into the card file, flipping, looking for something Addie knows Lydia knows she's not really looking for. Finally, Addie speaks. "What if she *did* do it?" she whispers.

Lydia starts flipping her file faster too. "You think she did it?"

"I don't know. I'm just saying what if."

They find a picture book and take it to a corner table in the back room. And there, in the library, over the Goldyn Aztec temples of Montezuma's reign, Addie can tell Lydia everything.

Lydia is amazingly rational. "It would be petty," she says, "to tattle to Mrs. Oko. But we have to tell Paige. She's going to get hurt even worse if she doesn't know."

Addie agrees vehemently. They decide to get Paige aside, away from Kirsten and Maisie, at lunchtime and talk to her. They know they are doing the right thing.

Paige's eyes well up immediately before the words are even half out of Addie's mouth. They are standing in a corner of the bathroom, just Addie and Paige, because they'd asked Mrs. Bahtstein, who was on yard duty, if they could go inside to the bathroom, Addie, Paige, and Lydia, but Mrs. Bahtstein said only two at a time, so eventually Addie offered to tell Paige since it felt like her responsibility, really, ultimately, somehow. Lydia stayed behind.

"We just thought that you had a right to know." Addie wants to put a hand on Paige's head like Maisie did and whisper soft *everything's going to be all right, Paige, we're your real friends. I'll be your friend. I'll be the best friend you've ever had in the world.*

"Kirsten told me that's what you were going to say," Paige says, "and I don't know who to believe anymore. I hate it," she says. "I hate it. I hate it. I hate all of it." Then she pushes past and runs from the bathroom, and Addie is left alone again in that scratched ugly toilet stall.

In the yard Addie finds Kirsten, with Maisie, on the top rungs of the monkey bars. Addie has run past Lydia, unable to speak, unable to know what she even wants to say, only that she has to say it to Kirsten, has to stand there at the foot of the monkey bars and shout up to her, meaner than she's ever spoken to anybody in her whole entire life: "I hate you Kirsten Grand. I hate you more than I hate anybody. You're a jerk. You're just a jerk. Your parents are jerks. And all you will ever be is a miserable, awful, mean, stupid jerk!" Addie screams at Kirsten, the sun in her eyes, Kirsten nearly silhouetted against the sky like a giant or a demon, something beyond Addie's world, not of this world, something scary and horrible come down from the sun.

Kirsten tips her head slightly toward Maisie, and in the shift of sun Addie can see her face turned horrible, that tangled mass of blond hair framing a small and contemptuous and evil smile. She looks back down to Addie, cocks her head to the side, and says in her little sing-song voice usually reserved for teachers and house-keepers and people she hates: "A jerk is a tug, a tug is a boat, a boat lies on water, water is nature, nature is beautiful, thank you for the compliment." And then, putting her hands down on the bars beside her, Kirsten drops backward, her hair falling down in Medusa snarls as she hangs by her knees, swinging back and forth under the April recess sun, laughing.

That weekend, while Addie and her mom are playing Clue at the living room table, a telegram arrives at the door. Addie knows already that it was not Colonel Mustard, or Professor Plum, or Mr. Green, or Mrs. Peacock who did it and that it wasn't in the billiard room, the kitchen, or the conservatory. She has nothing on the weapon. It could have been anything: candlestick, rope, knife, revolver . . . She has not kept a careful enough record. She wishes they could just start over from the beginning. Her mom signs for the telegram, but it's addressed to Addie.

It's short. It says: "YOU ARE DISINVITED TO KIRSTEN'S BIRTHDAY PARTY. DO NOT COME." She reads it and under-stands but also doesn't understand at the same time. It feels like things underneath her skin are crumbling into nothing, and then Addie is gone. Addie is gone, but other things are still there—the glass top of the table, wet with the sweat of an apple juice drink-box; the square of the board; rooms in the house of Mr. Body; the red pawn (Miss Scarlet! Yes, she remembers! She is Miss Scarlet!), the red pawn on its way to the library where an accusa-tion might be made; the radio tuned to WQXR, classical music wafting over like always; and Mom's hands on her head and her *shhhhhh shhhhhh baby shhhhh* ruffling into Addie's ears like the ocean from a seashell, WQXR seeming so far, so very far away, and they will never figure out who killed whom where with what because the cards just go back in the pack to draw again next time around and nothing they've learned from this game will mean anything and they'll have to start all over again, dumb, and blind, and clueless, and Addie is scared, so scared, even in the *shhhhhhhh,* even in her mommy's *shhhhhhhh baby shhhhhh- hhh* she is more scared than she ever knew she could be.

Mailing
Incorrectly

Meredith puts cumin in her spaghetti sauce. She pours a splash of Sam Adams into the pot from the open bottle in her hand, then takes a swig and dumps in a little more. The spice shelf above the stove is crammed full of colored plastic bottles that sell five for a dollar out of a bin at Thrifty Drug. Meredith reaches for a red one and shakes a small poof of brown powder into the sauce: cinnamon. It's highly unorthodox spaghetti sauce: shredded carrots, parsnips, a can of asparagus tips, a tin of tiny shrimp, tomatoes filched from a neighbor's vine. I am in charge of the pasta.

Meredith holds her beer bottle in one hand and nestles it between her breasts. I can picture Meredith calmly placing one large hand underneath her own breast and lifting it to say "suck this" to some obnoxious customer at the coffeehouse where she works. Men try to pick her up constantly, but she's got a "sweetie," as she calls him, down at UCLA Film to whom she's committed. I, on the other hand, have Christopher, Meredith's younger brother, who—thank god—is leaving Santa Cruz to spend his junior year in Florence. He got booted from the university dorms when the summer session finished last week and is staying with Meredith until he takes off. There's only two years' difference between them, and they tend to want to throttle each other more often than not. These days I'm close to losing it with him myself. When I try to justify the fact that I didn't part ways with Christopher a month ago after our first date when he dragged me down to the beach to watch him boogie-board, I tell myself that I've been sticking around because I like Meredith. Also: Santa Cruz is lonely with Ari gone.

When Christopher comes into the kitchen he's wrapped in a towel: freshly showered and still wet. He stands over the stove sniffing and dripping into Meredith's sauce, grabs a bottle of Tabasco from the shelf, and gets ready to pour.

"Get away from my stove!"

Christopher backs off, hands raised in surrender, his sleek, hairless chest concave. "Don't get hysterical," he says and flounces back toward the bathroom, his long brown ringlets dripping behind him.

I can't figure out what I'm doing with a guy like Christopher except that since Ari left town I've been trying to make myself date. That's essentially the reason Ari and I broke up: so I could see other people. We met soon after I started at Santa Cruz, when Ari was a senior and I was a pale first-year easterner who, among the tanned, beaded, braided California Beautiful People, tended to blend in with the cafeteria linoleum or the oatmeal they served in the breakfast line. That first quarter I ate alone every morning in the Kresge cafeteria. One day, a couple of weeks into classes, this guy came and stood behind the chair across the table from me. He had a full tray and looked encumbered. He said, "Every day I watch you eat breakfast. You eat half a grapefruit and squeeze the leftover juice into your spoon. You always have a bowl of Grape-Nuts and sometimes Lucky Charms after that. You drink two cups of coffee, one regular, one decaf. Who are you? May I sit down? My name is Ari."

"Zagarella," I said, motioning him into the chair.

"Zagarella," he repeated. My name in his voice unsettled me. He sounded like a botanist discovering and naming a new species of plant. Zagarella—I think the crux of it lies right there: how long they wait before I become Zag. Christopher was doing it by our second date. "You need to marry a man named Ziegfreid: you'd be Zig and Zag," he said, obviously pleased with his own wit. As if no one had ever come up with that one before. I'm not even sure exactly how long Ari waited. I remember sometime during our first winter together finding a note stuck to my campus box that said: *Zag — come to dinner at my parents' in San Fran. It's the first night of Channukah. Ari.* And I remember thinking, yes, that's fine. When Ari graduated that spring and started his master's, we moved together into a "couple's apartment" in grad student housing and lived there two years until Ari finished his thesis: "The Psychology of Small-Group Wilderness Experience." He was planning on sticking around Santa Cruz to be with me while I finished up. I love Ari, but he's also the only man I've ever really been involved with. So when he started talking about finding a place up in the hills—our own little A-frame, with a yard, maybe a garden—I started talking about finding out what it might be like for us to see other people. Finally, Ari decided that there was a whole world to see and, with every last dollar in his Wells Fargo account, bought a plane ticket to New Zealand. He's been gone two months, and I hadn't heard a thing. Until this week, when a yellow post office slip appeared in my box saying that I had a letter to retrieve at the main branch down on Pacific Avenue. Attached to the slip was a folded form note from the post master. It was apologetic. The outside read:

SORRY SORRY

SORRY SORRY

SORRY SORRY

We're so very

SORRY SORRY

SORRY SORRY

SORRY SORRY

Inside, I was addressed as their "valued customer":

> When something like this happens the Postal Service can never say sorry enough. We take responsibility for the mail that you have entrusted with us very seriously.

DID YOU KNOW?
Using a letter envelope to mail . . .
* jewelry
* loose coins
* keys/keychains
* campaign buttons
* pens/pencils
* candy
May result in . . .
* loss of valuables
* damaged mail
* delayed mail
* injury to employee
* damage to machinery

WE NEED YOUR HELP!
Use proper packaging, i.e., small padded bags.
Share this information with someone who may be
mailing incorrectly.

The next day I went into town. It was raining and Santa Cruz looked like Freeport, Maine. People in yellow slickers held their collars against the wind, and I got a craving for lobster. Only one window at the post office was open, and there was a long line of people shaking umbrellas. Across the floor a man in a hooded sweatshirt and a navy anorak pondered the stamp machine, then turned my way to check the wall clock—it was the New Age Carpenter.

He is wherever I am. It used to spook me; now it's surprising if I go somewhere and don't see him. I spotted him in a bookstore when I first came to Santa Cruz from Massachusetts and spent my time hanging out in the Sports/Recreation sections of the used bookshops looking at photos of sailing regattas and spinnaker sails, missing home. He was by the Self-Help/Spirituality shelves. I followed him to the cash register, where he bought *Treehouses: A Do-It-Yourself Guide* and Starhawk's *The Spiral Dance*, which he paid for with an inordinate amount of change. His carrel is on the same floor as mine in the library, and I pass him every time I go to the bathroom. We attend the same lectures, frequent the student employment office, and go to all the free art films on campus. I see him by the bulk bins at the New Leaf Market, tasting the granola. We have never acknowledged each other.

I handed the clerk my yellow slip, and she presented me with a large manila envelope printed with the courier pigeon insignia, my name typed officially on the front. It was very light. I thanked her. I bought some stamps: $1.28 for a set of Elvis commemoratives. I could walk over to him, I thought. I could say: *I'll trade you an Elvis for a LOVE.* Or: *Don't you hate it when your stamps gum together in the humidity. Do you have change for a dollar?*

By the time I turned around the New Age Carpenter was gone.

Ari's letter was mutilated. I don't understand how they managed to decipher the address to get it to me; it looks like it was flown across the Pacific by a seagull. I went home the day I got it and cried, something I have not done since Ari left. Then I sat down at my desk with the letter. It was almost ripped completely in two, held together by a string of envelope gum. I began to dissect it. Most of the pieces were fragments of about an inch or so by the time I got it all separated. It is spread across my desk like a jigsaw puzzle. I am trying to piece it back together. It's not going too well. So far this is what I know: *The flight to Auckland was long. They showed "Say Anything"* which either was *romantic* and made him feel *nostalgic* or the other way around. Something about a *hostel in Okarito*, his something *getting stolen, two women named Marcella and Ja-*something, and a *feast* he was *invited to attend. P.S. Here is an address I can be reached at for a while. Apple picking. Little Sydney Valley. You hurt me. I hope you are finding what you need to be finding. I hope* other indecipherable things. *The seasons are reversed. I do* something *about you, but am trying* to something. *It's raining. Do you remember when we* something *because we needed to* something *and we just couldn't understand what was going on?* . . .

It sounds like Ari: hopeful, sentimental, understanding, and blunt. I something about him too and am trying to something.

I decided that the next step was to buy some clear contact paper so once I get a page assembled I can encase and preserve it. So this afternoon, before dinner at Christopher and Meredith's, I stopped at More's. There are plenty of drug stores up on Mission closer to campus, but I am somewhat unnaturally attracted to More's and use any excuse to make a sojourn to their superstore over on Soquel. More's is one of those drug stores that also sells a random assortment of surplus food items and overstock miscellany. And I have a strange love of going there every couple of months to stock up on all my embarrassing drug store items at once. I take absurd amounts of pleasure in setting my shopping basket down at the register and watching the cashier's face as he or she tallies my purchases.

I lose all sense of time in More's. It's like meditation: pushing my cart up and down the stocked aisles, words and colors becoming swirls before my tranced-out eyes. I lose all shopping inhibitions. When I was finally ready to leave, the sun was beginning to set outside, and my cart was piled with Jolene Creme Hair Bleach, Vaginal Contraceptive Film, a box of egg 'n' onion matzohs, four cans of sauerkraut (2 for 77¢), Compound-W, a bulk box of tampons not marked for individual sale, a tin of Danish butter cookies, some Odor-Eaters, a twelve pack of Care-Free in a variety of assorted flavors, a jar of lightly pickled cocktail okra, and a tube of Gyne-Lotrimin to have on hand just in case. And a roll of clear contact paper. I wheeled my cart through housewares around a corner display of canned soups toward the check-out line and pulled in behind a man buying Depend undergarments and a six-pack of Moosehead. I picked up a copy of *Good Housekeeping* to leaf through, but then I glanced up to check the progress of the line and realized that the person working the register was the New Age Carpenter.

I could have walked right up to him and pointed to the condoms they keep behind the cashier's booth: *And a box of the Ramses, no the Extra-Sensitive, yeah, thanks.*

Instead, I steered my cart behind the battery display, parked it, and strolled inconspicuously out the side door.

Christopher slathers his portion of spaghetti with Tabasco and tells Meredith it's really good.

"You'd eat compost with that stuff on it and never know the difference," she retorts.

"Isn't that what this is?" he says.

"How much longer till you leave the country?" she says, looking at her watch.

"Too long," he grunts.

"You can say that again."

Christopher slides his chair back and carries his plate into the living room.

Meredith tuns to me. "You have siblings?" she asks.

I shake my head.

"No wonder you're so sane," she says, and then she looks at me kind of seriously. "Zagarella," she lowers her voice and leans in to me, "what are you doing dating him?"

"I don't know." It feels good to say that: I *don't* know. I'm not sure how much more I can say, though, if there's some vestigial blood-loyalty she has to this guy who happens to be her brother. "It's just kind of a weird time right now," I tell her.

Meredith nods, a forkful of spaghetti occupying her mouth.

"You guys should come by the coffeehouse later—there's live jazz tonight," Meredith says a couple of minutes later on her way out the door to work.

"I'll talk to . . ." I gesture with my thumb toward the Christopher in the living room.

"Cool," she says. She turns to go.

"Thanks for dinner . . ." I call to her.

"No problem, let's do it again sometime," she calls back. Then she turns and peers back in around the door frame. "Without him," she mouths to me.

I am smiling as the door slams.

I find Christopher in the living room smoking a bowl and watching *Seinfeld*. He is entranced, and I find myself mourning the lost childhood days of *Carol Burnett* reruns. On the commercial break, Christopher reaches his hand over and traces a finger round and round my kneecap. He explores my shin, following the bone down to my foot and back up my leg. His hand comes over, around my thigh. Truly, I am fascinated by my own desire: this physical wanting for someone I don't even like all that much. We have sex with *90210* in the background. Dylan finally tells Brenda that while she was in France for the summer he and Kelly had a fling. Donna won't sleep with David even though she loves him because she doesn't believe in premarital sex. Andrea applies to Yale. When Christopher falls asleep, I get up and take a shower.

Later, we head downtown to the coffeehouse. It's a converted warehouse off Cedar Street, with a nondescript green door and no sign. It's just called the coffeehouse, and though there are more coffeehouses in Santa Cruz than anything else, everyone knows which one you're talking about. Inside, the large room is strangely muted. Beams, pulleys, and chains along the high, vaulted ceiling are partly obscured in shadow. The whole place is kind of like a piece of postindustrial interactive artwork. Only the tables along the walls have lamps, and students fight for patches of light. In the far corner, where the floor is covered by a deep red Oriental rug, a jazz combo is playing. Meredith stands behind the long wooden bar across the room taking orders from an endless stream of customers. She pauses at the espresso machine, her back to us, and collects her long hair from her neck. Her hands move deftly, reflex-quick, and when she resumes making her latte her hair is tied in a chignon knot. Christopher and I find a table, and he sits on the edge of his chair, tapping his feet frenetically and drumming his hands on the table. His head sways with the music and he closes his eyes, making me think of Stevie Wonder. The music is good—a bass, drums, sax . . . I start and bolt up from my chair. "I'm going to get something to drink," I tell Christopher. The New Age Carpenter is playing the piano.

"Hey Zag," Meredith says when I get up to the bar. I am strangely touched that she has called me Zag and similarly surprised at my reaction. I think for the first time that maybe I don't really have a repugnance toward nicknames assumed too early but an aversion to such implied intimacy when it comes from someone I don't want to be intimate with. From Meredith, it's nice.

"How's it going?" she asks.

"The guy playing the piano." I motion toward the band. "That's him." I've told her this story. I have not told it to Christopher. I did tell it to Ari.

"Him who?"

"Him the New Age Carpenter."

"The one who haunts you?"

"Uh huh."

Meredith cranes around me to get a better look at him. "That's him?" she says. "He's in here all the time. Mornings usually, early. We had a hell of a time getting in touch with him about playing tonight though. He doesn't have a phone. I think he lives up in Elfland."

Elfland is in the redwood forest on the UCSC campus. The moderate climate of Santa Cruz being what it is, a whole mess of people live up there in the woods in makeshift lean-tos, tents, and treehouses, gnome homes tucked among the redwoods. The leaves rustle with disembodied voices. There are people hidden in the trees.

"What's his name?" I start to ask Meredith, then change my mind. "No, don't tell me. I don't want to know."

There is a lull in the music. I could look up, straight at him, and he might be looking straight at me. Do you know "All of Me"? I'd say. Of course, he'd smile.

Meredith offers me a ride home when she gets off work, which I accept gratefully. I sit in front, Christopher in back. In my room—my single dormer cell overlooking the bay—I am up until four, permutating and deciphering the particles of Ari's letter.

How's your buddy? He's not just a carpenter, Ari, he's a jazz musician too. Does that make you even more jealous? Something *what you're thinking about. Graduation cheap fares to* somewhere. *Do you even want to try, Zag?* Blurred words *are you doing. I know* something *important. Try See what happens no matter Fiji Samoa The Cook Islands good beer missing S.C. you I didn't grovel then now not what I'm about—we are/were/can/should be about Something time isn't* something. *Maybe you are* something *we're not ready yet LONG HAUL COMMITMENT* Something *so many other travelers Europeans German to a tiny beach travel together for a while she goes back to Germany.*

At seven I stop pretending to sleep and take the bus downtown. The coffeehouse is a different place in the daytime. Clinking glasses and muted conversations echo, bouncing off the high ground-glass windows. Dust particles hover and sparkle in thick slices of sunlight. The New Age Carpenter is at the bar, reading and making pencil notes in the margins of his book. I buy a cup of coffee and take it to a corner table. The air is eerily still, dense with quiet, like the moment after an earthquake before the surface world resumes. I was here for the big one in '89. I'd lived in California for all of two months and was sitting out on one of the lawns on campus when I felt the tremors. The first thing that came to my mind was: get inside a door frame. Isn't that what they tell you to do in an earthquake? I started running toward the physics hall so I could get under a door frame. Luckily, Ari was running out of the physics hall. He turned me around. We sat on the grass together until it had passed. "Wouldn't you rather die like that," Ari said, "in the face of something real, than go down in a plane crash or get hit by a stray bullet in some crack bust?"

"Could I get a refill?" the Carpenter asks the woman behind the counter. "House. With a little steamed milk." His voice is airy and warm; the phrases settle softly, like froth.

You play the piano. You study Classics. You work at More's on Wednesday afternoons. You read Starhawk. You live in a treehouse. You stayed for two showings of Wings of Desire. *Your bicycle is green and the combination lock is so rusty it's sometimes hard to open. My name is Zagarella. Who are you?*

I spend the morning peering at the New Age Carpenter through the leaves of a potted spider plant. I watch him read.

———————

Some number *Tempo Place. Torbay. Auckland. New Zealand.* Friends of the family who'd agreed to receive and forward his mail. *I want to be here, all here but* something something *is with you   I can't lose that.* There's a big chunk I just can't find that goes in here somewhere. *She is nice. I think that's* something-*ly what you wanted me to do, in a way.* OK. I can't read this *nec-essary   this pebble on the beach at O*   Okarito?   *jagged edge, curved plane*   Dear Ari, DID YOU KNOW? Using a letter enve-lope to mail . . . rocks MAY RESULT IN . . . Zagarella going in-sane because she sits in her room all day trying to reconstruct your letter.   *send you this*   Damaged Mail   *a little piece of where I am*   Loss of Valuables   *to share this*   Information with someone who may be mailing incorrectly   *here. now.* Delayed Mail. *come. think about it.* You have entrusted very seriously. Cannot say sorry enough. *Ari.* Sorry Sorry Sorry.

The phone rings. It's Meredith. "Zag, I have a huge favor to ask . . ."

"At your service."

"Can you sub for me at the coffeehouse this weekend? Rob's film is being screened at UCLA and I want to be there. If I leave after work tonight I can make it driving. All I'd need you to cover would be the Saturday morning shift and Sunday afternoon. Pay. Tips. And all the latte you can drink . . ."

"I'm a coffee novice," I warn her.

She confides in me. "Before I started working there I was a hard-core Tasters Choice drinker."

"Hey, I'm not even that bad—just your average Maxwell House in a Mr. Coffee-type."

"We'll have you drinking Tanzanian Peaberry au Laits in no time."

"Will you promise to have dinner with me when you get back so I can hear about the screening?"

"With or without Christopher?"

"Must you even ask?"

"You are on," she says. "My treat."

"Have fun," I tell her.

"I'll see you Sunday."

Ari's letter has made me feel the way I did when I was applying to college and got rejected by one of my safety schools. I had absolutely no intention of going there but cried over the letter just the same. I never did go back to More's for the contact paper. I sweep Ari's disintegrating pieces back into the post office's manila envelope, reclasp it, and stick it in my drawer.

The coffeehouse is even quieter on Saturday morning than it was on Thursday. I have put away the clean glasses, made two cups of English Breakfast tea for an elderly couple who are reading the paper at a nearby table, poured a large coffee to go (black with one Sweet 'n Low), and eaten a "chronologically challenged" (day-old) scone.

He enters unobtrusively, wearing his same old hooded sweatshirt. He takes off his backpack and sets it by a stool at the far end of the bar. He walks toward me.

My name is Zagarella. I believe in shock and flashes of fate. I understand parts but not the whole. I'm not sure what holds the world together. Will you talk to me?

"Hi," he says. "Can I have a large coffee, for here?"

"House," I say. "With a little steamed milk, right?"

3 1/2 × 5

The postcard is tasteful: a steep and snowy slope bordered by evergreens. The Grand Teton looms regally, backed against a sky that's blue enough to sell ski passes but maintains its integrity with a few scattered clouds. Three skiers in strategically coordinated outfits send clouds of powder billowing in their wakes. In the lower right-hand corner, in a pure white field of snow, my daughter has drawn herself into the scene. She's a ball-point-blue stick figure indicated by an arrow: "ME." Me is stuck in a snowbank, arms and legs jutting every which way, skis and poles strewn across the hillside, a halo of stars and tweeting birdies orbiting her oversized head. "Tweet-tweet," they say in the bubbles by their beaks. "Tweet-tweet."

"The snow is GORGEOUS!!!" She and her father have flown to Wyoming for her spring break. "I'm thinking maybe law school in Wyoming! (?)" My daughter is a junior at Harvard. Her GPA is disturbingly high. She would like, she thinks, to be a lawyer. Civil rights, perhaps. Maybe women's issues. "Dad bought me new sunglasses at the ski shop." Hallelujah! I say. My daughter is terrified of spending money, will not shop, wears her father's old clothes, breaks down at yard sales occasionally and buys a pair of shoes. Not leather; she will not wear leather. "My nose is sunburnt!" Her father's nose, her father's eyes, his mouth, feet, coloring. She has my temperament. She has had braces but never glasses. She is, I believe, a virgin. My daughter is 5'4". I think she cannot weigh more than eighty-five pounds. This is not a question I am permitted to ask. There are few questions I am permitted to ask.

They share a room, my daughter and my husband, at the Alpenhof Mountain Inn. I do not ski. But also: I could not spend a week in the company of the wraith that used to be my baby. My husband phones me one evening when he has a moment alone.

"She's been eating," he says.

"*What* is she eating? Can you talk? She's not there, is she?"

"She's in the lobby watching TV."

"She's in the ladies' room barfing is what she's doing!"

"Stop, just stop. All right. Just stop."

No one is allowed to speak of anything. We are perfecting the art of postcard love: the glossy veneer, the ever-blue sky, just enough room to say nothing at all. My daughter is a postcard: paper thin and full of empty sentiments, canned endearments, every sentence stuck with a dunce cap of an exclamation point. My daughter has become a person of many points—!!!!!, IQ points, knees, elbows, vertebrae, accusations, "*that, Mother, is not the point*"—and little else. My daughter depicts herself in ballpoint pen; the rub of a fingertip smudges her away to nothing.

819 Walnut

We lived in that house on Walnut Street as if four
walls and a roof were going out of style. It was understood that
graduating from college was like being put out with the cat and
yesterday's empty milk bottles, and we fully expected to spend
the rest of our lives pounding on the door—"Wilma! Wiiiil-
maaaaa!"—trying to get back in. Come May we'd each be on our
own, and we passed our senior year on Walnut Street as if that
were literally true: that once the tassels were flipped, caps tossed,
housekeys handed over to our absentee ogre-of-a-landlord, we'd
strap everything we owned to our backs and step out, solitary and
directionless, into a world we knew only as "real."

  Of course, none of this was the case at all. After graduation

Nina and Claire drove to San Francisco in a U-Haul stuffed with antique housedresses, pilfered dorm furniture, and Jesus candles from Drug Mart. Margaret had that internship thing in Salem, Mass., and Isabel was going home to Charlotte to recoop for a while. Becca was headed for some women's co-op in Austin. Laylee had med school; Serena had her boyfriend; and Kate had a job lined up in consulting, though none of us could imagine what Kate could possibly be qualified to consult about, or in, or for, or who on earth was going to pay for the consult of a woman who sprinkled garbanzo beans on her breakfast cereal and locked herself out of her own house on a daily basis. The point was: we had places to go. The other point was: somehow, that did not comfort us in the least.

Fall semester we'd been snug as dwarfs, domestic as the wives we swore we'd never be. The first one up in the morning made coffee; last one to bed at night locked the door. We watched 90210 as a house every Wednesday night, telephoned if we'd hooked up with someone and wouldn't be sleeping home, and brought Thera-Flu tea trays to each other's sick beds like doting and devoted nursemaids. We loved each other and said so often. It wasn't until spring that we began to unravel.

We've never agreed as to when precisely our undoing began, and since we don't agree about much of anything now and are too far flung (except for Nina and Claire, who, last we heard, were still together, still in California) to even try, we probably never will. Some said the explosion of the upstairs toilet (on a Sunday in January when the Minnesota temperature dropped to thirty below and our landlord was vacationing in West Palm Beach) prophesied what was to come. Others blamed Elvis, Serena's boyfriend and suspected minion of Satan, who stayed for six weeks that winter, spent the most expensive daytime hours on the phone long distance to numbers he'd later claim not to recognize, and left toast crumbs in the margarine. Big clots of jam, too.

We might have blamed it on the bad karma generated by eight Macintosh Classics in one house, or by the eight largely unreadable theses we were plunking out on them at all hours of the day and night. Our parents said we were probably just ready to move on to the next stages of our lives, and our therapists earnestly validated our anxiety. Any half-baked sociologist would tell you it was a miracle we hadn't clawed each other's eyes out months earlier. Look at divorce rates. There were *eight* of us. You do the math. Still, it took us by surprise. We thought we were prepared for anything. We communicated. We *processed*. We had a job wheel, and quiet hours, and house meetings every Sunday morning which we'd sworn we'd never ever ever miss, no matter how late we'd been out Saturday night at the black light/fluorescent body paint/no feeding yourself/marshmallow fluff party. No matter who we left sleeping in our beds upstairs or in their own across town. Neither sleet, nor snow, nor freak hail storm would prevent us from convening around that kitchen table to discuss and come to consensus about the small issues that arose in the daily lives of eight women cohabiting under one rather ancient and not thoroughly raintight roof.

To celebrate that February's most obnoxious of Hallmark holidays we planned to drive to a women-only club in Minneapolis. We wanted to dance, to get done up in bustiers and flash-your-twat dresses, drink like fools, dance like banshees, and not have to contend with the throngs of depraved, dateless men who'd surely be stalking the heterobars that night like polar bears in search of flesh.

Serena addressed us at a house meeting the Sunday before the 14th. "Hey, you guys," she began. "I think I have to beg out of the dyke-bar-thing. Elvis wants to go out for dinner, just the two of us, and it is Valentine's Day, so . . ."

"Elvis?!" Nina said, her astonishment scathingly melodramatic. "*Elvis* is springing for a whole dinner for two? Elvis-whose-toenail-clippings-I-just-picked-out-of-the-couch Elvis?" Nina had begun to take the whiskers in the soapdish and cigarette butts in the coffee cups as personal affronts.

"Check your cash drawers, girls," Isa chimed in.

"You know," Serena began, slow and deliberate, like she was fighting a flight off the handle, "we talked about this initially. We said we'd *talk out* men-in-the-house issues, instead of making totally unproductive snide little passive-aggressive comments. If people are having issues with Elvis, would it be too much to ask for some mildly mature dialogue on the subject?"

There was a distinctive round of silence at the table, everyone on an intake of breath, waiting to see who'd dig in first. Finally, the quiet got to her, and Serena said, "Well . . . ?" That did it.

"We hate him," said Isa, who had never been known for her tact.

Serena's composure faltered there. She'd expected a minilecture on the importance of all-women's space and respect for personal property (i.e., shampoo, toothpaste, food in the fridge labeled DO NOT EAT, which Elvis helped himself to with abandon); she was not at all prepared for her once-considerate housemates to issue forth with such brute honesty. Her eyes darted around the table for someone to throw her a line, but we were all fed up enough at that point that no one was jumping in to perform any rescues.

"Well don't hold back," she said. "No need for politeness. We're among friends here, after all." Serena sneered that last bit, a dig that even for all the defense mounted at the table actually hurt.

It was Laylee who interceded; the woman was diplomatic down to her DNA. "It's not a question of friendship," she explained. "It's an issue of what this house is supposed to be about. Suddenly there's a man essentially *living* here, and aside from the fact that he's not paying rent, his presence alters the chemistry of the house."

"He's living *in my room*," Serena said, her anger and disbelief at the entire scene mounting. "And he chips in with food. He's cooked. Don't even try to say you didn't all partake quite happily when . . ."

Isa cut her off. "A batch of pot brownies does not a significant board contribution make."

"Oh and I suppose you didn't have any . . ." Serena spat back.

"Fuck off," said Isa.

Serena glanced around the table once more, waiting for someone to restore order to the proceedings. We must not have looked promising. She set down her mug and stood with a shaky but determined effort to have the last word. "This is not a co-operative," she said. "This is a witch hunt, " and she walked away from our circle.

Elvis was gone by evening. An emergency house meeting was called for midnight, and by 3 A.M. we were all in tears and Serena was admitting the relief she actually felt in having Elvis gone and all the ways in which he'd been manipulative and uncompromising, the abdication of power she'd allowed him to engender in her, the isolation she'd felt from us all. Six months later they were married, but for that night, at least, she was one of us again.

We bagged classes the next morning, slept in, woke late, eyes swollen but hearts and minds clear. Margaret of the Small Bladder was up first, as usual, to pee, but she hadn't even done so yet when she woke Laylee to bear witness: the toilet seat was up.

It didn't stop there. We'd pull the Land o' Lakes tub from the fridge and find it filled with toast crumbs. The long distance calls to unfamiliar numbers in New York, Albuquerque, and Springfield, Mass., continued and went unclaimed. We never again achieved a credit balance with US West. Also, when we did our weekly big clean-up, whoever had SWEEP would inevitably report finding piles of ash and stubbed-out Camels in the living room. We thought at first, naturally, that it was Serena relishing a few secret nuggets of revenge, but she left for a long weekend in March to visit Elvis, wherever he was sponging up a life by then, and it all went right on: butts, crumbs, toenails, Nina's toothpaste squeezed from the top and glooped mercilessly all over the cap, as if Elvis himself had never left at all.

It was toward the end of February that Kate and Isabel went to see the theater department's production of *Macbeth* over at Roark Auditorium. Somewhere in the middle of Act Two (Duncan was dead and someone was bemoaning drunken impotence in men), Kate felt Isabel's hand, clammy and warm, grab her own on the armrest between them. It was dark in the audience and Kate couldn't see Isa's face all that well, but there was a twist of anxiety in her whisper.

"I'm bleeding," Isa hissed.

Kate reached for her backpack with her free hand. "I probably have a Tampax . . ."

Isa's grip on Kate's hand tightened; she shook her head no. "I'm going," Isa said and began to scramble toward the aisle, over fifteen sets of knees, winter coats, stowed shopping bags, and quite a few pairs of boots dripping snowmelt slowly down the auditorium rake.

Kate sat still, half-thinking that she should be a good friend and follow Isa out, except she didn't want to leave. The play was quite good, chilling really, and though Kate hated to admit it, Brian Schwartz was doing an excellent job as Macbeth even if he had totally blown Kate off last fall and was now dating some freshman hippie-slut. Kate had kind of been looking forward to sticking around afterward to say congratulations and show the King of Scotland just who was a bigger person about the whole thing in the end. And anyway, Isa could get a pad or something from the machine in the ladies' room if she really needed one.

Meanwhile, Isa made it to the end of the row, became a *pat-pat* of feet running up the carpeted aisle, a wedge of light, thud of door, and she was gone. Kate's hand, still on the armrest, was cold, and she rubbed it with her other hand. It was wet to the touch. She held her hand toward the light of the stage. The wetness, she knew, was blood.

Kate screamed. Not loud, or long, but a scream nonetheless. And then she clawed her way out of the eighteenth row, stepping over and on anything in her path, and tore from the theater. No one followed; they must have thought her insane. And perhaps, at that moment, Kate was.

On hearing the stories and piecing together events of the afternoon into some sort of cohesive narrative, our first thought had been, Why didn't Kate check for Isa in the bathroom? But the fact was that at that moment in the theater Kate was fully convinced that there was blood on her hand and that it was the blood of the murdered king.

Kate raced from the building out into the snow, her jacket and bag and favorite green scarf forgotten at her seat. The matinee light outside was gray and soft, the air like vaporized ice, just permeable enough to allow passage and so cold Kate could hear the crackle of icicle filaments splintering in her wake. She ran straight home, her hand wielded high above her head like a torch in the victory lap of some extremist winter Olympic relay.

At 819 her voice broke the study-silence like the day's final schoolbell. "ISABEL!" she screamed. "ISABEL!" The scene was straight from a low budget horror flick: Kate standing in the open doorway, shaking, her wind-burned face streaked with near-frozen tears, choked cries rattling in her throat. She splayed her hands before her and stared at them like they were the most horrible, inhuman things she'd ever seen. They were red with cold, trembling terribly, and Kate turned them over and over, searching for something lost. Then they dropped to her sides. Her terror was palpable. "ISABEL!" she cried. "ISABEL!"

Isabel had, of course, been in the restroom at Roark Auditorium trying to wrestle a Maxi-pad out of a wall-mounted machine circa 1950 and had emerged to find the performance interrupted, a campus police car—lights flashing—parked out front, and two overweight security guards filling out an incident report about some girl who'd apparently just freaked out in the middle of the play. It was kind of a mob scene, and Isa hated crowds. To try and find Kate would have been an exercise in futility, so she didn't even try, just headed for home, a bit relieved, in all honesty, for she really did loathe Shakespeare and was a whole lot happier to spend the afternoon catching up on her sleep than sitting through five acts of a play she'd already read and knew how it would turn out. Isa arrived back at 819 a few minutes behind Kate. She never did get in that nap.

Kate spent three nights at Grace Memorial in town and another week with her folks in Milwaukee before she came back to 819, convinced, as we all were, by doctors and by each other that Kate A) was under tremendous stress formulating her thesis in comparative translations of the poetry of Rainer Maria Rilke; B) was not getting enough sleep; C) had been drinking far too much coffee; and D) had developed a relatively serious anemia from three semesters of eating in a vegetarian co-op with a lot of hippies who were mostly too stoned to light a burner on the stove, let alone plan and cook balanced lacto-ovo meals for a membership of eighty-five. Also, the theater had been hot, the drama intense, and Kate had swallowed four generic decongestants with a double espresso not twenty minutes before the curtain had gone up on Shakespeare's three weird sisters.

Kate returned to us by mid-March and was back to herself in no time. The housemate who seemed most affected by the Scottish Incident, as we came to call Kate's brief sojourn into madness, was Isabel, who had always been somewhat neurotic about her sleep but now became completely obsessed with getting the proper amount of rest. She first only napped in the afternoons, then, whenever she was in the house. She wore earplugs and a sleepmask and played a tape of white noise in the background. It was maniacal, as if she believed that the loss of one vital moment of REM time would send her right over the same edge as Kate. Their friendship, we all agreed, was never the same again; they just couldn't seem to relate to each other anymore. It was a time that made Kate get all "Carpe Diem!" about things, but Isa said it all just made her tired, and she shut her door and went back to sleep.

Claire was the only virgin among us, but it was not by virtue of virtue, or by willful abstinence, or any conventional guess you might make. She was cute as a button, bright as a bulb, and the most talented glass-blower to grace the college's art department in fifty years. The dedication she lent to her craft was ferocious, and though she had vague interests and flirtations here and there, Claire was at the art studio so many hours a day it was clear where her life's priorities lay. Sex was the sort of thing Claire wasn't particularly concerned with. It would happen someday, she didn't doubt, and until then she simply had better things to think about than who might want her, and who she might want, and other major time-sucking thoughts that occupied the hearts and minds of every other person we knew.

Claire's was the only attic room in 819, situated above the main staircase, not directly bordered by any other rooms. It might have been lonely, but early on we'd all issued open invitations to climb into each other's beds (except Isa, who had that possessive thing about her sleep) if the night got cold, or long, or frightening. We were happily accustomed to waking in the dark to the creak of our doors and the whisper of sock-footed steps across the bare wood floor, so it was without surprise, one night toward the end of March, that Claire scootched over and fumbled to find an opening in her covers when Becca appeared at the edge of the futon, her own comforter caped around her shoulders. The heat in 819 didn't clank on until five or so, and Claire's room was exposed on all sides and particularly poorly insulated. She slept under a quilt, two wool camp blankets, an afghan, and an unzipped North Face bag that was supposed to be good to twenty-five below, but she was still always glad for any warm body, especially one bearing extra blankets.

It may have been the cold. Or the delirium of exhaustion. Possibly, simply the physical manifestation of sexual desire, which had been latent in Claire for far too long and had to have been headed for some sort of ultimate release. And then, it may have been something far more mysterious, as such matters often are. The exact circumstance we may never know, but what is clear is that Claire made love that night, in the attic dark, for the first time in her twenty-one years.

Becca was gone when Claire woke in the morning. Normally, this would not have surprised her—an early class, a breakfast meeting—but under the circumstances she'd expected something—a good-bye maybe. This irked her right off the bat, and she thought that if what sex did was make you want ridiculous things like morning kisses and sweet staged farewells from people whose vague and indeterminate behavior had never before evoked your notice, let alone your disdain, then sex was something she'd been quite judicious in avoiding. This thought grew ever more distressing when later that day, and in the weeks to come, Becca would treat Claire as if nothing had happened at all. Since according to Becca, it hadn't.

And so for the next month, while Becca gallivanted about in her usual life paying no more and no less and no qualitatively different attention to Claire than she ever had, inside Claire was smoldering. She never confronted Becca directly, and she told no one else until she just couldn't stand it anymore and confessed the whole thing to Nina, who'd been Becca's roommate for two years and knew her a good deal better than the rest of us did. Nina, also peeved with Becca (for things completely unrelated), was thrilled to have someone to vent with, and thus Claire and Nina, who hadn't really known each other at all when we moved into 819, became suddenly and stubbornly inseparable. And then, when the whole thing with the garbage cans started, Claire and Nina managed to convince themselves that Becca was somehow responsible.

The rest of us simply figured raccoons, an understandable explanation as to why the back porch trash cans were getting tipped over and looted at night, garbage strewn across our already scabby yard. The mess was not as bad as you might expect since we composted all organic matter and there was nothing gross or goopy or molding waiting to be carted away by the Department of Sanitation. Every day we repacked the trash and weighted the lids with bricks and stones. To no avail. The night bandits would not be deterred. Raccoons were devious, we knew, but this question remained: why would a raccoon ransack nightly a garbage can in which it found nothing to eat when not ten yards away sat a heap of coffee grinds and carrot peels that had been decomposing for seven months and got replenished with fresh toppings daily? The other weird thing: no one ever heard a noise. Eight housemates, four aluminum trash cans, thin walls, and rampant stress-induced insomnia. We ask you. What roused us in the mornings was not the scurry of raccoons but the clanks and pissed-off clunks of Nina as she righted the cans on her way out to T'ai Chi, replacing the lids with a ferocity that seemed to necessitate her subsequent hour of silent meditation.

This was also about the time that Laylee's med school application responses started appearing in the mailbox. Laylee had been the one of us you didn't worry about; success had stamped her as clearly as the freckles on her face. She had suitors up the wazoo: lithe, long-muscled boys who courted her as ardently as the medical schools from across the country who had filled our mailbox all fall with thick brochures of Laylee's full-color future. But Laylee was unwavering in her heart's devotions: to Nick (her high school sweetie) and to Harvard, where she and Nick wanted to enroll in medical school together the following fall. Laylee and Nick were of that breed who seemed to defy assumptions of human fallibility: they worked like demons, succeeded at everything they undertook, and had an ever-present glow of physical exertion and sheer pleasure which, we decided, seemed to otherwise only afflict that segment of the population who acted in TV commercials for vitamin supplements, toothpaste, and floor cleaner. But perhaps most importantly, Laylee was a sweetheart, so well liked and well respected and sheepishly humble that no one who knew her begrudged her a thing she'd earned.

It felt almost like a blow to us all—a baffling, undercutting, rattling blow—when those thin letters postmarked from Cambridge and New Haven, Ithaca and Palo Alto arrived in the mail. One after the other: *We regret to inform . . . After careful consideration . . . Due to the overwhelming . . .* Laylee walked around campus for days so freaked she looked like she had an alien seed pod about to erupt from the side of her face. The woman had never known defeat, and as likely as Harvard had seemed just weeks before, it now seemed just as likely that we'd come home one afternoon to find her in a bathtub full of blood, wrists slit open with the precision of the surgeon she might have become.

On the last Friday evening in April, two weeks to the day before our theses were due, Becca was in the kitchen chopping onions for a quiche when she cut her finger. It was deep, and there was plenty of blood. We debated bringing her over to the emergency room at Grace Memorial, then decided we were being alarmist, but wound up having to wrap it in gauze and masking tape, because, as it turned out, Isa had not five minutes before used the last of the Band-aids tending to the chunk she'd hacked out of her shin while shaving in the downstairs shower.

Meanwhile, Kate had been in her room sticking sections of her thesis to the walls for a "different perspective" when she stepped on a dropped thumbtack, which went straight into her foot all the way up to the little yellow plastic nub. In all the drama, Nina nearly forgot about the two loaves of bread she'd stuck in the oven an hour before. She dashed out to the kitchen, grabbed a potholder from its hook, yanked open the oven door, and reached for the top metal rack that held the bread pans. We heard the commotion from the bathroom, where we were patching up Kate's foot—crashes of tin and ceramic, Nina hollering "Fuck! Fuck! Fuck!" the water coming on, Nina shouting over it all "Someone get me the god damn baking soda!" We came racing down the hall. Margaret made a poultice. Laylee bent down and retrieved the potholder where it had fallen. "I had the god damn fucking potholder! I fucking grabbed the rack with the fucking other hand!" Nina was sobbing, really shaken, and we confirmed later that it was the first time most of us had ever seen Nina cry (aside from Becca, who'd been her freshman roommate and had seen Nina through a lot more than any of us had ever considered).

Claire came home early from the studio, her lower lip sliced, swollen, and still growing. "Glass," she said. "Occupational hazard" and retreated to her attic.

At eleven or so Serena came back from having drinks with some friends at the College Inn. She held her mouth open, tongue sticking out rather ghoulishly, unable to speak clearly enough for us to understand what had happened. Finally she wrote it out on the telephone message pad: "Sliced tongue on ice cube in whiskey sour." We nodded, our faces winched in vicarious pain, as if we too were incapable of coherent speech.

"Maybe we should do something?" Margaret suggested, blowing her bangs off her forehead like she'd just finally had all the spookiness she was willing to take.

Kate, whose tryst with insanity was affording her a blunt sort of license to forgo the touchy-feely and head straight for the jugular, looked at Margaret as if she'd just suggested we step out for a brisk stroll to clear our heads. "Well now there's an idea, Margie!" she said.

Margie flashed Kate the phoniest little fuck-you smirk she'd probably ever mustered and then closed her eyes for a second before beginning again as if the exchange with Kate had simply never taken place. "I am in no way suggesting," Margie said, "that what's going on here isn't quite real, but I think we maybe need to question the origin of that reality."

"God love the religion major!" Serena hooted, then edged closer to Kate. "What the fuck are you talking about, Margie?" With her injured tongue she was hard to understand, but the tone and sentiment were clear.

Margie was getting supremely fed up with the utter lack of cohesive energy in the group. "I think that if we tried to come together a little, to unify our forces, we'd feel a lot more empowered to face whatever it is that's going on here. Anything that tries to break us down knows that we'll only fail if we're in discord. We're letting ourselves turn against each other. We're acting out the destruction on our own."

"Mom . . ." Kate cackled, "they're here . . ."

Serena cracked up and waited for the rest of us to do the same, but no one did. That made it worse. Made Kate's words actually scary and made Margie's call to unity even more imperative. Since Laylee—curled on the floor by the oven like she was thinking about crawling in and turning up the gas—was unable to assume her natural role of diplomat, Becca tried to intercede. "This isn't a Steven King novel," she declared but was then at a loss for anything more to contribute.

"But it could be just as interesting to look at under a Lacanian lens, don't you think?" Isa added, though her comic wit wasn't quite up to snuff.

"I'm not talking about holding a fucking seance," Margie cut in. "I'm talking about a god damn house meeting. Let's at least agree to talk some of this shit through. We're pitting against each other and I think we need to ask why. We're housemates for another month, and you might be halfway to Oz in your head, or wherever, but you're not, OK? We're all here for another four weeks, and I don't presume to speak for anyone else, but I damn well plan on graduating, and in order to do so I have to finish my thesis, which I'm simply not going to be able to do if the energy in the house stays as negative as it is right now and we don't address the animosity that has made its way into our home." It was quite a moving speech, Margie's voice starting to break at the end as the thesis-panic surmounted all other present forms of fear.

Nina, who'd been silently nursing her burned palm, spoke for the first time. "Margie has a point," she said, her eyes still bloated with tears. She collected herself. "I propose an emergency house meeting."

Serena looked like she was going to lose her shit. "No!" she cried. "Just no! Can we do nothing in this house without holding a god damn house meeting first?" She had conviction and the confidence that Kate was behind her, and maybe Isa too.

But Kate let her down, turned right to Margie and said, like it was an apology, "I second the proposal. If we abandon our principles when we hit a crisis point, what are we saying about the functionality of the co-operative in modern society?"

Serena rolled her eyes.

"Let's do it," Becca said, turning on the faucet and reaching for the kettle. "Anyone want tea?"

We looked to Serena then: if she said the word, preparations would be under way. The room was still for a moment, just the sound of water rushing into the tin-bottom teapot, like a rainstorm coming closer and closer to home.

"You fucking hippies!" Serena cried. She stormed across the kitchen, flung open a cabinet, and grabbed the first box of tea she got her hand on: Morning Thunder. Then she hunted around for a mug, found none clean, and turned to us again. "Can no one even wash a god damn dish around here anymore?" she said, and we knew she was with us. It was like the starter's gun, and we scattered.

"Five minutes," Margie called on her way up the stairs to fetch Claire from the attic. Then suddenly the kitchen was empty again, except for Laylee, who stood up slowly from her catatonic curl by the stove and started to wash the dirty dishes.

A few minutes later, six of us reassembled around the table, we could hear Claire and Margaret padding down the back stairs, and then Claire appeared in the kitchen at the foot of the staircase. She looked back, as if to say something to Margie, and it was like slow motion then: a yelp, a sudden cry, a thunderous crash, we watched Claire's expression go from placid to terrified like some sort of time-lapse sequence. That's when Margie burst into the frame, barreling feet-first down the entire flight of steps straight at Claire, who in the space of a blink simply bent down and caught Margie at the end of the flight, like a mom scooping her kid from the depositing tongue of a playground slide.

We rose from our chairs like one huge being and rushed at Claire and Margie, who were frozen there at the base of the stairs like a Madonna and Child. Margie let out a little chuckle, a glance behind her as if to say to the stairs *now what did I ever do to you?* and we could see she was at least that OK. Then we were all business: Becca pulled three bags of frozen peas from the ice box and slammed them against the table to break up the clumps. Claire and Serena helped Margie to the table, which Isa cleared of dishes and snacks, and they got her laid out there on her stomach, lifting her T-shirt so Becca could place those three ice packs on the welt that had pretty much gotten Margie from tailbone to shoulder blade. Otherwise, she seemed OK. The rest of us were glassy-eyed with fright. Margie's was the last blood to spill, and we stood there gaping at her sprawled across the kitchen table, three Jolly Green Giants smiling up at us. We were like a battered women's group with all our busted lips and bandaged wounds. And in the wake of everything, we were dumbfounded, which was absolutely idiotic, we knew, but we hadn't wanted to admit that anything might be truly wrong. We were stupid and disbelieving, like miniseries victims, shocked every time the drunken sadist asshole-of-a-husband starts slapping the leather hide of his belt expectantly into his palm.

It was Nina whose fear turned to anger first. She looked around the kitchen and her eyes lit on the door that led out to the back porch. She flipped the deadbolt and flung it open. There were the trash cans: on their sides, spilling J. Crew catalogs, campus mailings, squiggles of Saran Wrap, and little white Kleenex flowers from their mouths like cornucopias of refuse. Nina stood in the doorway for a moment like a diver, poised. And then it was like everything just came flying out of her, all those months of trash and pain and fighting and rejection and unspoken, unthinkable resentments, like it had all collected somewhere in the pit of Nina's body and when she opened her mouth it just heaved forward, surged like lava, liquid and lethal, in a scream so grotesque it should have wakened the entire little Minnesota town. Every resident within ten blocks of Walnut should have been on the phone to the police to report murders, slaughters, crimes against humanity, demons rising from the rich midwestern soil.

But they didn't. Not a light went on. Not a 911 was dialed. Outside of 819, no one heard a thing.

We don't know who moved first or how we knew to do what we did; we simply knew. There was Nina, wailing out the doorway into the deaf and peaceful night, and we scattered from our kitchen cluster like pool balls on the break, all except Margie, whom we left face-down on the kitchen table.

Claire threw open the three working kitchen windows, then

grabbed a rolling pin from the drawer, wrapped her hand in a dish towel and smashed out the glass of the fourth, which had been jammed shut since we'd arrived eight months before. Isabel ran to the living room, where she raised the windows she could and hurled textbooks through the glass of the ones too high above her head to reach. Kate was hopping from bedroom to bedroom on her one good foot, flinging windows open as if we'd gotten word of an imminent tornado. Becca dashed upstairs to do the same, while Laylee tore down the hall with more vitality than she'd exhibited in weeks. She threw open the front door, the one that opened onto Walnut, stood under the transom facing out into that world beyond our cursed and beloved porch, and with a pierced, bleeding harmony all her own, she joined Nina's horrible cry.

Serena sprang the downstairs bathroom windows, then ran toward a door at the base of the back stairway that, had it functioned, would have opened onto the neighbors' yard, but it was bolted off, its seams painted shut so many times over so many years and renovations that it was hard to even discern the outline on the wall. Not even Serena knows how she managed to break down that third and last door, but seconds later she was through, facing outside into the yard of 817, flakes of paint showering down over her as she took a breath—if it's my last, she thought, so be it—and lent her terrible scream to the voices shattering the sky.

Morning came, every door and window flung wide, a fierce April wind howling through our home. We have, of course, spent much time since in reconstruction and recall of the events of that night and the months that preceded it, but to this day, as far as we know, not one of us can remember the quiet. There were twenty-two years of our daily lives, then there was the weirdness, then the scream, and then there was nothing. Blank. Nothing. And then we awoke to daylight on a Saturday morning toward the end of April in a small Minnesota college town. We do not know what went on during the hours in between, we only know that moment when we opened our eyes and squinted into the sunlight. Serena was covered in plaster, beneath the picnic table across the yard at

817. Laylee was curled on the front porch between the armchair and the dead, potted spider plant. Becca found herself in the upstairs bathtub, which had not been used since the plumbing disaster five months before. Kate was upstairs in Becca's bed, Isa downstairs in her own. Claire and Nina were on Claire's futon in the attic, naked and salty, dried in sweat, entwined in one another's arms in an embrace complex enough to last a lifetime. And Margaret lay on her stomach in a pool of icy water, three bags of squishy peas strewn beside her on the kitchen table. She was wet, and cold, and had to pee like crazy. She got up and made her way, cramped and tentative, to the downstairs bathroom, wearing nothing but a pair of boxer shorts, soaked through and clinging to her thighs. In the bathroom Margie caught a glimpse of herself, over her shoulder, in the vanity mirror. She looked again, then craned around to see for sure. It was true: the skin on her back was unblemished. As if nothing had ever happened at all.

———

Things got quiet. Two weeks of keyboards tapping, coffee percolating, buckets and soup pots situated strategically throughout the house to catch the plink-plinking drips that fell from the ever-leaky roof, which hadn't taken kindly to the year's final thaw.

Laylee's outraged and well-connected professors started pulling strings, and, following a lot of phone calls and a lot of waiting, her future once again began to assume a shape she could understand. As for Claire and Nina, it was nothing short of a miracle that they finished their theses, so stunned were they by each other. They were ecstatic. We were ecstatic for them. And envious, a little bit, too. They were leaving with something. With someone. Their worlds on the outside would start out with a population greater than one. So yes, for that, some of us were a little jealous.

And, of course, Serena had Elvis, Becca had Austin, Kate had consulting, and Margaret had that Salem internship which none of us could ever seem to remember by name. And Isabel figured she'd just head back home for a while, chill out, get caught up on her rest. Maybe start trying to think about what on god's green and overwhelming earth she might possibly decide to do with the rest of her life.

Accidental Love

Steffen and I had a dance we performed ritually on mountaintops wearing our huge frame packs: a somewhat weighted pas de deux. It's amazing, the feeling when you take your pack off after that; you feel so light, like you could just leap over to the next peak on the ridge. We'd lie on top of our packs in the sun, eating peanut butter from squeeze tubes with our fingers, feeling the wind dry the sweat from our T-shirts. Steffen and I talked on the phone at least once every week this fall: he in the cramped telephone room of his freshman dorm at college, me at home in New York, my folks watching *Masterpiece Theater* in the next room. He often described his phone booth to me, the floor covered in tobacco spit. They weren't allowed to smoke in the dorm, so everyone chewed tobacco instead, including Steff, although he insisted that he always spat into a cup or an empty soda can. When we talked, I could not picture him there. I liked to think of him on top of a mountain in northern Wyoming with a smudge of Skippy on his lip.

The first time I saw Steffen he was sitting against a tree on an orange Therma-Rest sleeping pad. He told me he'd insisted on an extra-long. He was 6'2", 157 pounds, and very concerned about sleeping comfortably during the six weeks we were to spend backpacking through Yellowstone on Wilderness Adventures for Teens. The trip had been a high-school graduation gift to him from his mom, Lynn. Steffen said Lynn wished she were eighteen again because she really wanted to go herself. Steff told me that he had been somewhat less than thrilled with the whole thing, but it had looked better than another summer working maintenance crew at the small Maine college where Lynn taught mathematics, so he'd conceded to the trip. I had a purple Therma-Rest (ultralight, three-quarter length), one more year of high school left at the Convent of the Sacred Heart, and parents who were desperate for another ruse to get me out of New York City for another hot July. I have studied drama and weaving in Oxford, biked across Nova Scotia, and gone to Peace Camp in Poland. My father assures himself that I will appear well rounded on my college applications.

———————

This trip up to Maine is ostensibly a college visit, but really it's a chance to see Steff, who is home on Christmas break. He's out at the market, picking up lobsters for dinner, so it was Lynn who greeted me at the door about ten minutes ago when I arrived with a backpack full not of rain gear, gorp, and sterno gas but of college catalogs and interview clothes. And a basket of seashell soaps my mother shoved at me as I was leaving the house to give to Lynn as a thank-you-for-having-me present. I've never met Lynn before, but from all Steff's stories I kind of feel like I have.

"I was just going to make myself a cup of Lapsang souchong," Lynn says, shuffling toward the stove. Her fraying Oriental slippers whisk against the linoleum. "It's my latest passion," she confides. "Would you care to join me?" The stove ticks impatiently, and finally a flame ignites under the kettle.

I assume she's talking about some sort of tea and say, "That'd be great." Lynn gets two mugs from a cabinet and sets them down on the counter next to an open bag of Ruffles potato chips. I am leaning against the fridge, and Lynn says, "Grab the milk out of there, Lilith, would you? Do you take milk?"

"Sure," I answer, not certain as to which question I'm answering, and turn to open the fridge. Stuck to the door with a strawberry-shaped magnet is a picture of Steff in a too-tight suit, trying on his older brother's graduation cap and grinning, braces gleaming in the sun. When Geordie went off to college Steff still had a year left of high school, a year alone in the house in Maine with Lynn. It was hell, he said, hell. Lynn had hoped the boys would stay in town for college, but Geordie went away, and Steff followed a year later. Steff comes home for breaks. Geordie doesn't. On the fridge next to the photo is a shopping list torn out of a pad "From the desk of GEORDIE": wasa bread, 2% cottage cheese, green peppers (2), pine sol—mountainfresh, eggs, bourbon. At the bottom Steff has scratched in: frozen burritos, SNACKS!, brie cheese, and FOOD. I'd know his handwriting anywhere.

As I tug open the refrigerator door I hear a yelp from across the room. A large golden retriever lumbers up from its water dish in the corner and I step back, afraid it will come and sniff at my crotch. Lynn stops the dog, and it nuzzles her knee.

"Sally," she says in such a personal tone that I look around the room to see if there's anyone there besides us and the dog. "Sally, this is Lilith." It's as though she's introducing colleagues at a cocktail party: "Sally, Lilith. Lilith, Sally." The dog seems to nod politely in my direction, and I kneel down to her. "Hi Sally," I say. "It's good to meet you."

"It's good to meet you too, Lilith," Lynn says in such a way that I don't know if she's speaking for herself or for Sally, so I just smile. Lynn smiles back, and then we stand there smiling for a while until the kettle finally whistles and Lynn has to go pour the tea.

Lapsang souchong tastes like hot water that's had a ham-bone soaking in it for about three months. When Steffen finally returns home, my undrunk mug is dead cold and Lynn has moved on to wine, because, she says, there's no bourbon in the house. Sally perks up, and I jump out of my chair when we hear Steffen's keys outside. I dash for the door; Lynn and Sally saunter along behind. Then Steff steps in and I rush at him. He drops the plastic lobster bags at his sides, scoops me off the floor, and whirls me around.

When I land, we stare at each other for a minute. He looks skinnier than he did last summer, if that's even possible. Hair a little longer, skin a little worse. He's not wearing his glasses: round wire-rims. Those glasses had been my first attraction to Steffen. Everyone else on our trip was sporting cheesy Ray-Bans and seemed physically pained by the idea of giving up hair mousse for six weeks. It was the schoolteacher glasses that allowed me to think there might be at least one person with whom I might possibly, actually, be able to have a real conversation. I was right. We didn't really hang out with anyone else. All summer we kept getting lectured by the trip leaders, who wanted us to try and mingle more. They also decided it was necessary to give us a thorough pregnancy chat, which was, at best, mortifying. We weren't even fooling around, let alone having sex. With me and Steff it wasn't, *isn't*, like that.

Six weeks in the woods is different from six weeks in town. It's intense. It's all-consuming. I feel like I know Steff better than anyone else in the world. We don't just know the good parts either, the parts you show to new friends. I know what he's like at 4 A.M. when he has to pee and there's been a mosquito munching on his eyelids all night: he's peevish, whiny, abrupt. He knows me, panicked and irrational, sick from the altitude, vomiting Ramen noodles all the way up the Grand Teton. Six weeks in the woods is like life, encapsulated, and I feel like I've known Steff all of mine. Except that now it's December, not August, and though the summer was a lifetime, the time that's gone by since then has been pivotal: Steff's first semester of college, my second to last of high school. We've been apart now for much longer than we were together, not counting phone calls.

I miss his glasses.

Steffen screws his face up in a puzzled sort of bemusement. "You're here," he says, astonished, like I've just materialized out of thin air. He turns to Lynn, who is squatting by the stove, stroking Sally.

"Hi Sal. Hi Lynn." Steff says their names as though he's speaking to old people at a retirement home: *Hi Gladys. Hi Clifford. You're looking fine today.* Distant as day care. He hefts the two plastic bags back up to his shoulders and then plunks them down on the counter. "Ril Miene Lahbsta," he drawls in his most favorite and most dreaded imitation of a Maine fisherman. I've sat through entire epic sagas of Mainer life told this way. In order to appreciate the full effect, Steff says, you've got to be huddled in a deer-piss-stinking cabin out in the middle of nowhere, swigging from a bottle of Boone's wine: $1.29 tax included.

Suddenly Lynn is up and shoving a bottle of wine (not Boone's) and two glasses at me. "I'm taking care of dinner," she says. "You two go, go!" We are shooed from the kitchen. As we're heading toward the living room, Lynn calls out, "Steffen, take Lilith's backpack up to your room, would you? Let her get settled."

My composure falters here: Steff and I are sharing a room. It's not that I didn't think we would, or that we wouldn't wind up together no matter where we started out. Last summer, by the time we'd known each other two days, we were spending the nights spooned together in our sleeping bags like slugs. Somehow the idea of a bed confuses things.

A few weeks ago I was in a cab going across town to meet my mom for lunch at her office. They're digging up Central Park again—water main breaks and sewage problems—and even the cabbies can't keep straight which streets are open and which are closed. Driving anywhere in the city has become one of those rat mazes: you just keep trying different paths and hitting impasses until you find the one possible way of getting through. Usually it's easier to just get out and walk, but that day we were stuck in the middle of the park, in the middle of a tunnel, behind a crosstown bus, and there was no escaping. My driver's name was Seamus, and we were discussing, originally, traffic. He said it was time for him to get out of New York—"no place else like it, thank god." He had a beautiful wife and a beautiful baby, he told me, and enough money put away to get the three of them down to Virginia, where an old friend of his owned some farmland.

"My boyfriend goes to school in Virginia," I told Seamus.

I was able to rationalize it later: I was tired, I was annoyed, I didn't really feel like having a whole big conversation, it was easier to say that than to go into some huge explanation of this person—who is my best friend in the world, whom I love more than anybody else on this planet, whom I talk to every Sunday night with all the lights in my room turned off, who carried a mini tape recorder around campus with him once for a whole day so I could hear what it was like to be at college, whom I'm going to marry when I'm seventy-five and he's seventy-six and retire to a ranch in Montana where we'll plant beets, adopt a son named Huckleberry, and watch the sunset from the back porch every night until we die—who goes to school in Virginia. The fact of it was inescapable, though: I'd called Steffen my boyfriend.

In the far corner of the living room there's a Christmas tree with little blue bulbs made to look like tiny candles. Underneath, on a bed of fake, fleecy snow, Lynn and Steffen's gifts to each other are laid out expectantly. The squat pair of little packages wrapped in silvery foil are the tomato-shaped salt and pepper shakers which Steff described to me over the phone after he found them at the Portland Mall. He already knows what Lynn's giving him: a stack of books on the Vietnam War. He'd taken a course on it that semester. A couple of the books had actually been on Steff's syllabus, he said, but he hadn't read them. It would just be the two of them at Christmas: Steff and Lynn. Geordie had gone to Santa Fe, to their father's house in a Zen colony. Billy Strand retreated there twelve years ago, left his wife up in Maine to deal with a six year old, a seven year old, baby-sitters, boxer shorts, and baseball cards. I don't know a lot more than that. Steffen doesn't like to talk much about his father.

"It's been unbearable," Steff says, well into his third glass of Chablis. "The first few days were decent: I shoveled the snow, I went to the woods, I chopped down the tree. We spent hours trying to figure out which bulbs were burnt out so we could get all the little lights to twinkle the way they're supposed to. She made fruitcake. There were things to do." I swirl the wine in the glass which Steffen has poured for me even though I don't want it. I think wine tastes like moldy Hi-C.

"I hate Maine," Steff says. I know that he really does hate Maine. I also know that when he's nervous he talks about how depressed he is even if he's not. "I get depressed every time I set foot in this state. I can't sleep in this house. I haven't slept since I've been home. You can hear her vibrator clear across the house. It just hums and hums. I cannot deal. All I want to do is watch television. The only joy in my day is *Ren and Stimpy*. I don't think I can last another two weeks, but I don't know what Lynn would do if I left. It's so freaking desolate up here. She's alone in this house with nothing but Sally and her vibrator all winter long. Lil, I am not holding my crap together here."

Vibrators are what they sell at the Pink Pussycat Boutique in the West Village, not something your mother plays with when she doesn't feel like going out to rent a movie. I think this and feel like my mother, so I try to think something else but I don't know what to think because it's not something I've ever thought about before. I remember a story Steff once told me while we were waiting out a thunderstorm under an overhang on a mountain pass. He'd had a pretty serious girlfriend during his senior year named Daisy Spitz. Her father had died of leukemia; her mother taught fifth grade social studies. When Steffen and Daisy had been going out for a few months, Mrs. Spitz called up to do the appropriate thing and invite her daughter's boyfriend's mother over for a cup of coffee.

"Hello, Mrs. Strand," she said. "This is Mrs. Spitz, Daisy's mother . . ."

"Our children are sleeping together," Lynn said. "I think we can be on a first-name basis."

I bet that my mother, in Daisy's mother's position, would've said, "I believe I have the wrong number," and hung up.

"Lil wants to have twenty-seven children and live on a farm in Idaho," Steffen tells Lynn at dinner. I am struggling pitifully with my lobster crackers and am about to correct him and say, "Montana," when the leg gives and bits of orange shell go flying everywhere like shattered porcelain. Steff chuckles. Lynn takes another sip of wine and doesn't seem to notice.

"Twenty-seven, huh?" Lynn says. "You better get started."

It strikes me that reproduction is not the safest topic of conversation, being that it is often linked to sex.

"You don't realize," Lynn says thoughtfully, and it occurs to me that she's not laughing at me like most adults do but counseling my decision, "you don't realize how hard it's going to be." I look up at her: sitting sideways in her chair, legs crossed, an elbow on the table holding her glass up to the candlelight as she watches tears of red wine streak down the clear bowl. I recall a lifetime of my father's diatribes, quoted directly from the *Wine Spectator*. You're supposed to drink white with seafood. But Lynn isn't having lobster herself, just watching me and Steff demolish ours. I am used to this; my mother never actually eats at the dinner table, she just passes the dishes to my father and picks cucumbers out of the salad bowl with her nails.

"You have kids," Lynn says, leaning across the table toward me, "and your decisions aren't just about you anymore."

I look at her, nodding. I wish Steff would say something. I wish we could leave the table. I wish we were back in Wyoming, talking each other to sleep under the tarp: *If I were an item of camping gear*, I'd ask, *what would I be? My boots*, Steff would say. *Muddy and stinky? Indispensable.*

"Teaching freshman calculus is not what I dreamed of in my life." Lynn chuckles at herself, then regains her earnestness. "When you have kids you can't quit jobs just because they don't mesh with your ideals for the world. You need something stable. Something that's going to see those kids through. The college pays half of Steffen and Geordie's tuitions. Billy—their father—he doesn't have a pot to piss in. I pay the other half." She pauses to scratch a drip of candle wax from the table. Steff gets up wordlessly and disappears into the living room. He can't even stand to hear other people talk about his father. We hear the TV flick on.

"Cartoons," Lynn says, staring off at the wall, perturbedly shaking her empty wine glass. "Steffen's very own nudist Buddhist commune." What Steffen has conceded to tell me about Billy is that he is tall, fiercely handsome, and a genius and that Steff wants to be everything and nothing like him all at the same time.

"I have often wondered," she says, turning to face me, "if I drive them away or if it's some genetic flight instinct in the Strand male . . . Like father like son . . . Acorn never falls far from the tree . . ." Her gaze drifts back to the wall.

"Do you know, the last time I called Steffen and Geordie's father I got his answering machine," Lynn tells me. She is instantly focused again, sharp as a tack. "There was sitar music in the background, and then Billy's voice, as deep as Steffen's, Billy's voice over it saying: 'I leave a light on in my mind in case I decide to return.' I hung up. I mean, what are you supposed to do with that?" She looks at me as though I might know what you're supposed to do with it. I shake my head slowly, my mouth forming the word "wow" but not speaking it. Lynn reaches across the table for a piece of lobster meat left on Steffen's plate and feeds it to Sally under the table.

"Do you believe in love, Lilith?" Lynn asks me.

I need to believe in it too badly to say no. Yes makes it seem far simpler than it could ever really be. I love Steff, and I know that he loves me, but I don't know what any of that actually means. I feel trapped. I am pinned between my plate and my chair with only my lobster crackers to defend me.

"It depends," I say.

"I believe," Lynn says. "I believe in a love that preexists the lovers who fall into it." She lets that one fall on me while she refills her glass, then offers me the bottle. For about the tenth time tonight, I wave it away, politely.

"It's like car accidents," Lynn says. "Car accidents don't happen because you forget to look in your rear-view mirror or your brakes fail. You could spend a whole lifetime caught up in 'what if I hadn't missed the exit,' 'what if I'd had that second cup of coffee,' 'what if we'd stayed in St. Louis.' You just can't factor coincidence that way, you know?"

I nod. What else can I do?

"Car accidents exist in certain places and certain times; it's just whoever happens to show up."

"What if no one shows up?" I say. I can't bring my eyes up to Lynn's face as I speak so I am left staring at her chest. There is a chip of coral lobster shell stuck to the left breast of her angora sweater.

"The crash goes unconsummated," she says.

I wonder if vibrators hum like revving engines. I cannot nod.

"Like love," she continues. "Love is an entity unto itself. There are patches of it all over the place. It's not really tangible, but it's there, pools of it. Blue pockets, swirling like eddies. People don't meet because they both like Burmese food, or because someone's sister has a friend who's single and new in town, or because Billy's nose happened to crook just slightly to the left at an angle that made me want to weep." Lynn leans toward me again. "People don't fall in love with each other," she says. "They just fall into love."

She falls back into her chair, as if relieved to have gotten that out. I suddenly feel very stupid wearing my lobster bib, but I can't figure out what to do with it. Lynn reclines slightly onto the air behind her, wagging her crossed leg anxiously until her slipper falls to the floor. Sally picks it up and gives it back to her.

"Thanks, Sal," Lynn says, holding the slipper in her hand like a diploma, then turns back to me, laying the slipper down on the table next to her dessert spoon as if it were an extra piece of silverware.

"Some people are lucky enough to bump into each other in the middle of a patch of love," she says, feeling it necessary to clarify her point. "On the express line at Grand Union," she grins at me, her eyes sparkling, "on a mountaintop in Wyoming . . . My advice, Lilith, is just don't fall into one alone. It's devastating." She looks at me concertedly to see that I'm understanding this. "It wells in you," she says, "and there's no outlet. No place for it to go." She places the tips of her fingers to her breastbone and rubs. The chip of lobster shell is jostled free and wafts away like a speck of stray rice falling to the ground long after the bride and groom have driven off, tin cans clanking along the road behind them.

"It aches," Lynn says, rubbing. "It aches."

We clear the table together, but Lynn insists on doing the dishes herself. She tells me that there are clean towels on the rack and that I can use anything in the bathroom I need. She wishes me luck on my admissions interview in the morning. I say thank you. For everything.

I find Steffen in the living room, lying at the foot of the Christmas tree, his hands poking up into the branches from underneath. He is swearing to himself. On TV Edith and Archie are singing "Those Were the Days." The candles on the tree are flicking on and off like runway warning lights. Somewhere in the long string of lights wound round and round the tree there's a faulty bulb, somewhere a loose connection that needs to be fiddled into place.

"If I were a sitcom rerun, which one would I be?" I ask.

Steff hasn't seen me come in. Slowly he cranes his neck out from beneath the pine boughs. The tree goes suddenly dark; its lights are out again. Steff cocks his head flirtatiously and a grin spreads across his face. "My Twenty-Seven Sons," he says, laughs, and ducks back under the tree to resume his fiddling.

"If I were a Christmas tree ornament," he calls out from the branches, "which one would I be?"

The star, I think but can't make myself say. My eyes pan the tree: silver tinsel, turquoise glass balls, candy canes tied with hollyberry bows, lopsided felt cutouts in red and green probably made by two little boys on a rainy day in Maine.

"The lights," I say.

Suddenly the tree goes bright again, its glow blurry and warm. The room is perfectly still, flooded with the sleepy light of a hundred tiny blue candles. I hold my breath, prepared for the lights to flash off again, but they don't. Through the branches I hear Steff whisper, "I'm afraid if I move they'll cut out." I picture him holding that position until New Year's, and I laugh. The studio audience on the television does too. The TV is perched on a rolling cart, and I wheel it over to where we can watch before I crawl underneath the tree myself. I curl around Steff and bury my hands into the wool belly of his sweater, and we just lie like that for a while: spoons under the tree in this pocket of candle-blue. Even when we move, the lights stay on.

How
Beautifully
Resilient
the
Human
Being

On our first date John Ryan took me to Siracusa, expensive Italian in the East Village. He chose a central table and a nice Cabernet. The waiter hovered beside us.

"Do you know what you'd like, Jean?" John Ryan asked. We'd been set up on this date by the college friend with whom I'd been staying for a few weeks. She and John Ryan worked together on the floor at the Stock Exchange and, from what I understood, did not particularly like one another.

"Primavera," I announced.

At first John Ryan looked disappointed in my choice. He blinked and rearranged his silverware a little, but then his expression shifted. Suddenly he appeared to be charmed and smiled at me as if he'd known me forever. Then John Ryan held out his menu to be collected but never took his eyes from me. "I'm going to watch her eat," he said.

The waiter nodded and stalked off toward the kitchen.

"And you slept with this man?" Felicity balked.

I nodded guiltily. My life is liberally peppered with similar such lapses in logic; sometimes sense evades my orbit entirely. "It was a bad time," I said.

"Baby," Rory said, stroking back the hair from my face. She was beside me on the couch, Felicity was on the floor at my feet, her face raised, cheek resting on my knee as I talked. "Baby," Rory said again. "Baby."

Felicity is the loveliest person in the world, and it's hardly a wonder Rory pursued her the way she did: relentlessly, maniacally, with the desperate drive of the addict she'd always be no matter how many years of sobriety she had under her belt. Rory *needed*, and if she couldn't need heroin, she'd find a way to need something legal, like Felicity. I've never been addicted to drugs myself, although I often wonder why not. I recognize Rory in myself, myself in Rory—that need to make the world fall away. But I never got there chemically. I don't mean that to sound superior; it's just not the way I've gone.

I was a little drunk when the primavera arrived. The waiter stood over me, steaming dish in hand, arranging my silverware to make room for the plate.

John Ryan cleared the place before himself. "I'll take that here," he said.

A couple at the next table peered over, then busied back to their own meals.

"Of course," said the waiter. He edged out from behind my chair and set the pasta before John Ryan. From his apron pocket he whisked a tiny silver cheese grater. "Fresh Parmesan?" he asked John Ryan.

John Ryan turned to me, extending the offer.

I must have nodded.

"Please," John Ryan told the waiter, who turned the crank. Suddenly the grater disappeared, was replaced by a peppermill, angled above the plate like a lightning bolt. The waiter looked to me. I nodded again. He ground. John Ryan said, "Thank you," and the waiter left. John Ryan grabbed me in his stare. "Will you let me feed you, Jean?" he said.

I squirmed at first. Flitted my eyes around the room. I giggled, nervous. People were watching, I thought, and that embarrassed me but egged me on too, I think. If it's a show, I thought, then fuck, I'll put on a show! There was something so in-your-face about it. A thrill to shock these people a little over their nice expensive antipasto platters, to be base in the midst of their pomp. I reined in my attention and tried to return John Ryan's stare.

"OK," I said. I crossed my legs.

John Ryan picked up his fork. "What would you like in the first bite?"

"It doesn't matter," I said.

"No," he said, "you're going to choose."

"But it doesn't matter," I told him.

"Of course it matters." He set down the fork. "Don't you think you matter, Jean? I think you matter. It matters to me what you eat in your first bite of dinner tonight. I want to give you what you want."

And that was all. It was easier to give in than to fight, and I couldn't have fought long anyway. John Ryan was right there, and he wanted to take care of me.

I think I giggled a little. "Broccoli."

"With pasta?" he asked.

I shook my head. "Just broccoli."

Once you're inside, that's it: that's the logic, that's the way things are. You forget they can be any other way, that they've ever been any other way. There were amazing things with John Ryan too. The sex. The way he fed me at Siracusa—that's how it was always. He was only concerned with my pleasure. That's what got him off. It was all he cared about. After awhile, though, I started to get weird inside myself. My heart would start palpitating for no reason, and I'd get scared over things, little things sometimes: a counter clerk would ask me *for here or to go?* and I'd panic, I'd be totally incapable of responding. Of having any idea what my response even was. And maybe I partly knew that John Ryan had something to do with it, but things always got twisted because I'd think, What am I complaining about? He loved me more than he knew how to handle, treated me like a queen— he'd do anything, anything in the world for me. He'd always twist it back around to that and make it not make sense to turn away from him. Not that it made sense to be with John Ryan, but it didn't have to: I was already there.

Felicity said she could understand what made me stay. Felicity's from a different world: big, Waspy, Massachusetts clan. Boats and formal dancing lessons and family creeds. "Children should be seen and not heard." "Girls should wear their hair long." "Dungarees are for falling in dung, which is not something one does by choice, and thus is not something one dresses for." Felicity has three brothers and a sister, so she knows what it's like to want the light beaming down on just you. But in her world, too, the lights got tricky. You can crave the spot for so long, but when you finally get it, it's because you've done something like tell your parents that it's fine if they insist on throwing you a coming out party, only you're coming out as a dyke, not a deb, and then there you are, center stage, large as life, and you realize you threw away their script long before you learned your lines. There's a lot of screaming instead, and crying, and futile attempts at discussion and calm behind closed doors until suddenly those doors are slamming shut for good, and you're not sure exactly how—have you done it? Have they? Only it's you on the outside, you're the one on the bus, a bus headed west since there is no more east in Massachusetts, and you think you understand that sometimes the only thing in the world you can count on is a Greyhound bus, and you can't even begin to think about what that might really mean because you think you've begun to think like a country song, which doesn't ultimately make any less sense than anything else, so there you go—*All aboard!*

Felicity has pluck, is what Rory would say. Got off the bus at the end of the line. San Francisco was too big, so she hitched down the coast. Santa Cruz had a nondenominational church with a free lunch program. A used clothes exchange in a shack downtown. A women's center. Hippies. A climate nearly good enough to camp out year-round if need be. She got a job (waitressing breakfast and lunch at Zachary's on Pacific Avenue), and another (live-in manager of the women's hostel in a Victorian up the hill), and eventually a GED, which enabled her to take a class or two at the community college—Cabrillo—which is where she met Rory, who works there in the custodial department under the terms of her parole.

As for me, I arrived in Santa Cruz by taxi from the San Jose airport, had the driver take me straight to the hostel. It's a quarter the cost of a motel, and though money isn't my problem per se, it is a limited resource. It doesn't come in, only flows out, and while the trust from which it flows is generous, it's not going to last even a fraction of my own duration. I travel around a lot. I like to keep myself in motion, but I try to watch my spending when I can.

I don't talk about Santa Cruz. I have trouble keeping things from people, lovers especially, as if I'm compelled to relinquish everything to everyone. But Santa Cruz, somehow, I'm allowed to keep for myself. "Never been there," I can even say if someone asks. I get afraid of slipping up, of being found out, but there's a thrill in that too, a small-small secret that wouldn't mean anything to anyone anyway but is still just mine, only mine. I guard it the way I think some people guard deformities or diaries. I hide Santa Cruz. I have run to this town before.

That first week back I got my bearings, slogged around town half-looking for work, signed in at the temp agency, scanned the job boards at Saturn Cafe and Whole Earth, checked back in with my therapist, Elaine, who's like a mother the way she takes me back every time against her better judgment, incapable of saying no, of turning me away. It's too clear how much I need her. Or someone. She always thinks maybe this time we'll break through. Maybe this time I won't leave. And I think it too for a while—

a real faith that we can do it: find answers, change patterns, end the dysfunctional behavior. It's a challenge in a way: I surrender to everyone else, and Elaine's the only one to whom surrender would be safe, encouraged, and potentially helpful, but she's the only one to whom I can't. Or won't. I keep trying.

One evening I slumped into the hostel, passed the TV room on my way to the stairs, and waved hi to Felicity and the person on whose lap she was curled. Felicity said, "Hey sweetie. Join us."

"Thanks," I said, "but I'm exhausted."

Rory turned beneath Felicity. She said, "Scotch and Debra Winger . . ." dangling those two things before me like an offer I'd be powerless to refuse.

Felicity laughed, threw back that lovely blond head and laughed, her pointy chin raised to the ceiling, wide cheekbones stretching her whole face with glee. Then all at once she leaned in and put her mouth on Rory's ear, and with her eyes opened to me behind Rory's head, she raised one hand and waved me into the room.

They set me up in an easy chair with a Save-a-Tree mug of White Horse and a half-empty bag of slightly stale Circus Peanuts that stuck in my teeth like nougat. Felicity and Rory cuddled on the couch like teenagers through *Made in Heaven* and *Black Widow*. It had to have been past midnight when we put in *Terms of Endearment* and I joined them on the couch to be closer to the tissue box.

I fell in love with Santa Cruz all over again that night, brimming with it, swollen with love for Felicity and Rory both, with the whole world of the hostel, its ratty couches and stained-glass windows, the glorious buzz of scotch and crickets, and I thought I had fallen into exactly the place I needed to be: a Debra Winger film festival in a women's hostel on a couch between Rory and Felicity, who'd parted to make room for me and put the tissues on my lap where everyone could reach. By the end we were puffy and snuffling and damp.

During *An Officer and a Gentleman* Felicity took the tissues from me and set them on the coffee table, appropriating my lap for a pillow. She tucked her hands under her cheek and settled in like a little cat. Rory leaned down and kissed her brow, then planted a little kiss on my cheek so I wouldn't feel left out. I giggled. Then I dozed off, woke up in an army training camp to Lou Gosset Jr. screaming "Mayonnaise! Mayonnaise!" Felicity had slipped down to the floor at Rory's feet, and her chin rested on the lip of the couch cushion as she stared up into Rory's face. I had slumped onto Rory a bit in my sleep, and she'd wrapped an arm around me and let my head rest across her torso. I feigned sleep a little longer; I felt so peaceful. It was almost hard to believe that such a short time before I'd been a near-catatonic mess, dodging across the country to escape John Ryan as if my life depended on it. I couldn't remember if things had actually been that bad or if I'd overdramatized it all in my mind. Nonetheless, I thought, How beautifully resilient is the human being.

Rory shifted beneath me, and I could see Felicity's head nod agreement to something. Rory bent her head toward mine. She smoothed my hair from my ear and spoke into it softly. Her breath was light on my skin. Her eyes were still on Felicity.

"Jean," Rory whispered, "Jean honey. Hey there," she said, and it was like a mother waking her baby, that nice. "It's pretty late, and Fee and I were going to go up to her room and we were talking about it and we both wanted to ask you if you'd want to come with us?"

I sat up way too fast. Felicity registered something like alarm; Rory had her hands out toward me, as if to still me but afraid to touch. She said, "Oh god, I'm so sorry, Jean. We didn't mean to freak you out." Felicity was talking at the same time, saying, "It's OK, Please don't go. Are you mad? Please don't be mad, we just thought . . ."

"No, no no no no no no no no no no," I cried. "Oh god, no, it's not you. I just . . . I just I can't . . . god. I would. In a second. I swear. I'm just . . . I just got out of this awful . . . just such a huge awful mess . . . and I can't . . ." And that's when I told them the whole story: New York, John Ryan, the light, and everything that had finally gotten me from there to Santa Cruz. They were amazing—*are* amazing—they just listened, switched the whole tenor of everything in order to just be right there and listen. When we finally went upstairs to bed—them to Felicity's and me to my own—I felt light-headed, and purged, and safe.

But what Elaine would say, and has been saying for years now, is that to be safe isn't about where in the world you put your body, it's about making yourself safe from yourself from the inside. I knew she was right. If there was any possible way to fuck up, I always found it.

It would be disingenuous of me to say that I wasn't aware, sexually, of Felicity, from the start. Maybe it wasn't specifically that I wanted to sleep with her, but I wanted something. Desire, as I see it, is necessarily sexual.

In many ways—wonderful ways—Felicity was truly an innocent. She was drawn to her desires like Pooh Bear to the honey pot. I used to be like that. In the playground of my gradeschool there was a sliding pole I used to play on at recess, wrap my legs around it tight and edge myself down slowly as I could, feeling the cold hard metal against my pubic bone until my arms were too tired to hold me. Until someone complained to a teacher that Jean Suskin was hogging the pole and not letting other kids slide. After that, all the teachers on yard duty seemed to be aware that Jean Suskin wasn't supposed to be allowed on the sliding pole anymore. But Felicity as an adult was like that six-year-old me on the sliding pole, as if she hadn't picked up guilt, or self-doubt, early on. She wasn't a hedonist, but she didn't smother her passions. She filled her senses instinctually. But then, midgulp, she'd remember herself and pull back, take a degree of remove from the sensory world she couldn't resist. Some people thought she went hot and cold; they found her fickle and evasive. She wasn't. She was like a true skinny in a world of dieters. When she remembered where she was, she'd take her M&Ms into the closet and enjoy them in private. We'd flirt, Felicity and I, but then she'd catch herself, take a glance at the world around her, and find some other reasonable outlet. For me, it was tantalizing, excruciating, and ultimately unbearable.

After the Debra Winger night was when my imaginary cocktail parties started again. My mind conjured elegant foie gras and sherry events at which there was much lascivious eye-making across crowded rooms punctuated by pointed and angry declarations of love and frenetic couplings in coat closets, and bathrooms, and well-stocked kitchen pantries. My favorite was at a party in a house from which the furniture had all been cleared out to make room for dancing and was now stacked and precariously piled in the garage. We snuck in through the carport and made love on overturned tables, in a canvas butterfly chair, a children's cardboard playhouse from Sears, and a paddleboat which was raised up on cinder blocks for winter storage.

The only time we ever had sex for real, it was raining. It had been raining for eons—the rainy season, they call it—and Felicity and I had been hanging around the hostel offering up dismal suggestions of ways to pass the time until the sun came out again: "Cards?" "Checkers?" "TV?" "Scrabble?" "Charades?"

"We could go upstairs," Felicity said, her voice tentative.

I said OK.

So we went.

There was something clear-cut and settling about sex with Felicity. Very you-get-me-off-and-I'll-get-you-off. It put me at ease. Like: you do my hair and I'll do yours. Or: trade you backrubs. It was sort of contractual. I liked that. We were in her room; I felt strongly about keeping my room as a separate place, a not-sexual place, just mine. In her room we were lying across the bed. Her feet were flat on my stomach, her legs bent at the knee. She had tiny little feet. Perfect. Her ankles made me think of Audrey Hepburn. You could see all the little bones and tendons underneath the skin, and her toenails were painted like candy. Felicity's head dangled backward off the bed; she was following raindrops down the window pane with flittering fingers, being aloof to compensate for the lavish display of affection she'd just relinquished to me, and I was thinking *I'm in love with Felicity*. And I was thinking also *it could be like this, separate like this, just as long as we never have sex in my room, this can be OK.*

When she said, "What actually made you leave finally?" she wasn't looking at me.

"He was crazy," I said. "I mean, so was I, but it's not like it took more than three brain cells to realize I wasn't exactly *thriving*."

"No," she said, "no, but I mean what made you realize? What got you to the airplane?"

"A taxi," I said.

She lifted her head, picked up a pillow, and lobbed it at me, and as it hit I felt for a second like I was winning her back, back from her leave-taking across the bed.

"I hadn't had a sex drive for months. It made him crazy. Beyond crazy. He got obsessed with turning me on. It got worse than you'd even imagine—sleazier too, like his class and his horniness were inversely proportional."

Felicity grimaced. The whole concept of horny men seemed to make her a little queasy.

I said, "My sense of time, my sleep schedule, it was all off by then, but you don't know. You feel like you've beat this time thing, like you're past getting screwed by polarities. Day and night. Black and white. What you have is more organic, more whole. You're more real than everybody else."

And there was something in the way Felicity nodded that told me she understood. I told her about that day, that last day in New York when I was home in bed eating cereal. John Ryan wasn't there. The phone rang and I splashed cereal milk all over my sleeve and my lap. It was sugar cereal, and the milk was all sticky, so I guess I went to wash it off. In the bathroom I turned on the light, turned on the shower, and there was a window in the shower with a shade over it, and I tugged the shade and it retracted—*ffffft*—into a roll. The sun was out, and it came in through the window in a big dirty swatch, a big slab of sunlight. Like a chunk of cheese. And the ceiling light seemed like water then, and I knew that the two lights couldn't mix together, couldn't come together and be one light. It was like they repelled each other. And somehow it was as if I had to solve that. Like it was my responsibility. Except it was impossible. It made me afraid. Really afraid.

"And you just left?" Felicity said.

I nodded. I was talking too much. I was afraid she'd get bored.

"You think he'll try to find you?" she asked.

"I don't know." The only other thing I could imagine for John Ryan was that he'd find another me. Commit or kill himself, maybe. Or come looking for me, I guess. In a lot of ways, his options aren't all that different from mine.

It kept raining.

The night of the day that Felicity and I had sex, Rory came by with ribs, and we nuked some cornbread Felicity'd brought home from her waitressing job and took it all out to the TV room. I knew—Felicity had said so explicitly—that it would all be OK with Rory, and it was actually all OK with me too until we set the ribs and the cornbread down on the coffee table and dug out the remote from between the couch cushions. I thought, I don't want ribs. I didn't want to watch TV. But I couldn't tell what I might want instead. I had no idea what I wanted at all, and that struck me as the most insurmountable thing I could conceive of until all of a sudden "I" and "want" stopped making sense too. I got squirmy, thought, I can't sit down on that couch. There was nothing I could do, no option that would make it all OK. I didn't want Felicity to tell Rory. I didn't want her not to tell Rory. I didn't want to hide it. I didn't want to have done it at all. I didn't want to be wanting to do it again. And I didn't want to be there. I'd take a trillion other towns and cities. I *had* to be anywhere but there. But where do you go when you run from the place you've always run to?

I wish, somehow, that I could know the way it appeared to Rory and Felicity: how they thought of me then, if they think of me now, what they said to each other when fifteen, twenty minutes passed and I didn't return from the bathroom? Did they put a plate over my ribs to keep them warm for me, or did they start talking the minute I was gone from the room? I wonder if Felicity told Rory about the sex right then, or if maybe she didn't have a chance before Rory leaned over and kissed her on her wide pink mouth, restaked her claim on Felicity. I wish I knew what they saw, because what I miss out on is the reflection. My life is like standing in front of the mirror with your eyes closed, only I don't know if I have any eyes at all because I don't know how to open them to see if they're there or not. I walked to the Greyhound station from the hostel and got on the next bus east, because all there is is east from California, and where wasn't what mattered, only where not.

I don't truly think that John Ryan follows me, but sometimes I'll come home, wherever "home" seems to be at the time, and my door will be open when I'm sure I've left it locked, or the dishes will be done, or my plants will be watered and picked of dead leaves, and I wonder if that's what John Ryan does now. Keeps tabs on things. Keeps things in order. Slips a credit card or takes a bobby pin to my lock, looks around, and waters the plants on his way out just to tell himself that he's not such a bad guy really. He's concerned, honestly. Just wants to make sure I'm getting taken care of.

Jono, an Elegy

The first time I saw Jono he was hanging upside-down in a tree outside the Student Union and I walked past without letting my gaze fall his way. Richard and I had just broken up, but I was still very much under his judgmental influence, and, like Richard, I made it a point not to notice people who did things like hang upside-down in trees to call attention to themselves. Nadia and Charles were sprawled on the new-green grass, which seemed to have sprouted and covered the quad overnight. Charles was cross-legged, squinting up into the sun as if he were trying to read a clock somewhere on the horizon. Nad was on her back, sandals kicked off, her head resting on Charles's knee. She was feeling around blindly for something in her bookbag, unwilling to turn her face, even for a moment, from the long-awaited sunshine. We had survived our first Ohio winter.

I waved as I approached, wishing I had something on my mind to talk about other than Richard, to whom all conversation seemed to revert these days. I sat down and we passed a few minutes in diversion—*how was class?* etc.—before we were back to my finally-over fiasco of a relationship, and the pros and cons of dating other lit. majors, and whether it might be a good move to start looking outside the department, and how impossible love of any kind was anyway, which was a bit ridiculous since Charles and Nadia were already quite utterly in love with each other, though I seemed to be the only one aware of it at the time. The two of them then started offering me up a litany of potential suitors, everyone from Charles's roommate to the guy who worked the waffle line at Dining Service.

"How 'bout Jono?" Nadia said, waving a little and lifting her head slightly from Charles's knee.

"How 'bout Jono what?" said a person who appeared to leap into the air and land cross-legged in the grass beside me in a pose so languid and comfortable he might have been there all afternoon.

"He's perfect," Nadia said, pushing herself upright. "Attractive, easy-going, well-read—a major even—and look at those eyes. Is that Club Med blue or what?"

"Do you do windows?" Charles asked him.

"Nope," said Jono, "but I climb trees real well!" He beamed, nodding goofily, like he was aware of how silly he was, maybe even in control of it. My first impression of Jono was a cross between Huck Finn and a basset hound.

"Jono," Nadia said suddenly, "Do you know Bethany? My roommate." She gestured toward me, ever the hostess. "Bethany, Jono. We're in Fielding's class together," she explained for my benefit. "Jono, Bethany."

"Charmed," said Jono, and before I realized what was happening he'd lifted my hand from my lap and kissed it. I had a second of shock at his touch—the intrusion into personal space by a stranger, unexpected, invasive even. But that's not what stayed with me. What I remember from that moment made me start, made me lose my tongue, lose the ability to speak at all, let alone retort with something witty and place-putting. What I remember is the unnatural, perfect, ineffable softness, the coolness of his lips as they brushed the back of my hand and paused there before he pulled away again. The intensity of that moment for me I can ascribe to or blame on a slew of factors from Richard's rejection, to my jealousy over Charles and Nadia, to the quality of the air on that bursting-green May day on the quad in the grass, where we lolled until the sun had gone down in a fireball behind the library, and then we walked toward the dining hall, the four of us, under that wide, eternal Ohio sky. It's land that doesn't call much attention to itself except for a few minutes every day at sunset, when the sky comes down to meet the earth in waves of violet and crimson, alive and orange as fire. Each day goes out in a small and devastating flare of glory.

That weekend the temperature held steady, and while Nadia was at a study group meeting, Charles and I went to the annual bike derby. Outlawed by college officials, the derby, a long-standing student tradition, was now held in a sunken, muddy field behind an off-campus farmhouse known as Effigy. Effigy, its inhabitants, and everything they stood for were everything that Richard deplored. Richard was a sophomore, an English major too, and he was opinionated, moderately conservative, fastidiously directed, resolutely resolute in his convictions. For a time I admired that about him—the self-determinism, the backbone—until it became clear that I was meant not only to respect but to take after him. He chastised me routinely for any inclination I exhibited toward radical liberalism, which included owning an Ani DiFranco tape, recycling a soda can, and opting for the veggie alt at Dining Service while he sawed his way through some bastardized incarnation of roast beast. Richard called the bike derby "Monster trucks of the pseudo-intellectual poverty-pleading set," and, as astute an observation I may now recognize this to be, at the time the bike derby—or the idea of something as wacked-out as the bike derby—had taken a hold of me, much in the same way Jono had. They were part of a world quite different from mine, a world that both repelled and intrigued me. I looked into it from the outside, like a rubbernecker at a highway accident, and though I never actually altered my own course, I did slow down and gawk out the window as I passed quietly by.

"Watch for Jono," Nadia had told us. "He's riding. Dressed as Captain America, I think he said. Maybe Evel Knievel . . ." The bikers were warming up in the mud-flat arena as Charles and I made our way up the driveway. Everyone was in costume—tremendous, theatrical costumes, it was like Mardi Gras in a ruined cornfield—and we had trouble spotting Jono in the crowd. It was, in fact, he who spotted us: came barreling past with a huge, sloppy Muppet-wave hello and then sped away. He was dressed as a daredevil superhero of some indeterminate red-white-and-blue variety. His bike—one of the many junkyard salvages that had been patched together for one final ride—was pasted with silver stars that glinted in the sunlight like broken glass.

There were no rules to the bike derby. The object was to be the last one riding, which meant that the other object was to incapacitate, cripple, or otherwise maim the bikes of fellow riders by any available means. This meant closing one's eyes, howling like something undead, and plowing into people, hoping simply to do more damage than was done to you. From the sidelines onlookers cheered, but that wasn't all. The bike derby was a spectator sport. People brought superpower water guns; others had rigged a hose from the house and were blasting the riders like riot police. Some enterprising fans had set up a bucket-and-spring contraption on the roof of the porch and were using it to sling raw compost into the ring below. Most people sported ponchos and rain slickers to protect them from flying debris, but Charles and I were unprepared, in polo shirts and shorts, and we found a spot on a small rise some way off where we could observe without going home coated in pasta sauce and egg yolk. It was sad in a way, I thought, that this mattered to us, but it did. For some reason I didn't quite understand, I didn't want Jono to see me the way I sometimes saw myself: as a clean-cut, bordering-on-preppy prude. At the same time, it made me mad to find myself worrying about the impression I might be making on a weird little imp of a boy who liked to hang by his knees from tree branches. I had no reason to imagine that Jono was someone who thought particularly clearly about anything. In fact, he was the type who had probably fallen from so many roofs, bicycles, jungle gyms, and bunk beds in his time that thoughts probably migrated through his brain in patterns unrecognizable to me. I couldn't fathom how the mind of a Jono might work. And perhaps that's what captivated me.

Charles and I watched the cyclists flail madly in the flying mud. An emcee of sorts—nude but for a plastic five-gallon peanut butter tub he'd cut the bottom from and wore around his pelvis like a tube skirt—shouted incomprehensibly into a megaphone. One contestant howled on a trumpet as he rode until it became too plugged with mud and rotten tomatoes to make a sound. The beat of music was coming from somewhere but was otherwise inaudible above the shrieking. Bike parts flew through the air. It's a wonder no one was killed. Riders dropped like flies, their broken, mangled bicycles tossed onto a tremendous pile which would remain for years, slowly sinking down into the fallow earth.

There was a party after the derby, but Charles and I didn't stay. I had a Henry James paper to finish; Charles was due at rehearsal with his a cappella group for an upcoming Commencement Week performance. But we did stay long enough to see the final battle between the last two riders, long enough to watch the last contender go down, his bike literally folded in half. As it was carried to the mound it actually broke in two, and a huge roar swelled up from the crowd. The winner—a vaguely human-shaped glob of mud stuck with cabbage leaves and grapefruit peels—was hoisted up over the crowd, passed around like a punk in the mosh pit. It wasn't until the cheers unified into a loud and steady chant that we realized who it was. "JO-NO! JO-NO! JO-NO!" they cried, and he floated over their heads howling with delight, relaxed as a rag doll at the hands of his friends and classmates.

———

Jono was from Maine and was in the same class as me and Charles and Nadia. He spoke Latin, grew marijuana in his closet, tutored at the local elementary school, and was known to whip up batches of Danish crepes late at night. He had lost three fingertips to frostbite as a child and had one slightly discolored front tooth that crooked endearingly over its neighbor. He never had a girlfriend at school, but we found out later that he'd been the object of more than just *my* midwinter fantasies. It was difficult to imagine Jono touching down long enough to really get himself enmeshed with anyone. He was like a Tigger: he didn't walk; he bounced. He pissed some people off, too, with his lackadaisical, what's-a-schedule? unreliable ways. Jono was a candle: you wouldn't want to rely on him as your only source of light, and it probably wouldn't be too safe to leave him home alone, but his mere presence was enough to turn a darkened dorm room into a wondrous den of flickering sparks and dancing shadows.

I did kiss him once. It was February, senior year. Nadia and I shared an apartment in town above a general store that made its own fudge and ribbon candy and real donuts which we'd buy, hot, late at night as we came in from the library. Charles was studying at Oxford for the year, and he and Nad were making futile and paltry attempts to play the proverbial field before he came back and they got married and stayed together forever like everyone had always known they would. It was a Friday night, and I clomped up the fire escape steps that served as our entrance, kicking snow down to the alley below in soft plops, a hot donut in each mittened hand. I knocked at the door with my boot for Nadia to open up, and when she came to the door in a black beaded shift, her eyes lined in kohl, ears clipped with rhinestones, I stuck a donut at her.

"We're going out," she announced.

I pushed past her. "*You*, my dear, may be going out," I said, powdered sugar melting into my teeth. "I myself am quite distinctly on the way *in*."

"N-n-n-n-no," Nadia trilled, blocking my beeline for the couch. She set her donut down on the television and now plucked mine from my still-mittened paw. I stood still before her, closed my eyes, and opened my mouth to give her one chance to put that donut back where it belonged. Instead she grabbed my hand and pulled me into my bedroom.

"There's a kissing party at Effigy," she said, letting me down into a chair so she could rifle through my closet. She pulled out the velvet hot pants I'd worn for Halloween and held them up for my consideration. "You're going to revert into a virgin pretty soon if we don't start getting out of the house more often," she said and tossed me the hot pants.

"It's cold out there!" I whined.

"Come on," she cheered. "Hup to. It's black tie. We'll pack shoes, wear boots, and change when we get there."

I looked at her little silken slip-dress. "Nadia!" I cried, "it's subarctic out there. You'll freeze your nipples off!"

"It's better than letting them drop off from neglect." She motioned for me to get moving.

"I am not wearing hot pants out in the middle of winter when there's two feet of snow on the ground!" I wailed from my chair.

Nadia's face fell. She crinkled her eyes and nose up and made her voice sound even more pitiful than mine. "You really don't want to go?" she winced.

Of course I didn't want to go. But I was a college senior, still fighting hard not to be the kind of person who passed up an orgy invitation at 11:30 on a Friday night in favor of powdered donuts and *Taxi* reruns. "I'm not changing my clothes," I declared.

"Fine, fine," she said. "We'll find you a black scarf . . ." And Nadia was back to business, plans intact, spirits restored.

We trekked out to Effigy through the snow, Nadia promising we'd find someone to drive us home later, me consoling myself that at least Jono would be there, realizing at the same time that he was the only reason I'd relented to Nadia at all.

Inside, Effigy was gloriously warm that night, twinkling with white Christmas lights, a string of red chili pepper bulbs outlining the doorway. Everyone was beautiful, decked-out and elegant, and Nadia stripped off her layers—sweat pants, thermals, wool socks, a fuzzy blue neck warmer—until she was one of them, swirling off into the shimmering crowd. I hung my ski jacket over a chair and tapped the snow from my boots. The festivities were in full swing, everyone drunk, the wine boxes empty, and no beer to be found. On a makeshift bar full of empties and mixers I managed to find a partial fifth of cheap rum with which I slunk off into a corner to toast myself a bit before I braved the puckering masses. By the time I joined, they'd moved from Spin the Bottle onto some game that involved taking off one shoe and tossing it into a center pile of single shoes. We then circled the pile, like in musical chairs. When the music stopped, everyone grabbed for a shoe and went hunting for its owner to trade a kiss for its return.

It took me a couple rounds to figure out which were Jono's and quite a few more before I managed to grab the correct black wing-tip in the chaotic scramble. My head spun. I spotted him across the room trying to peddle a patent leather pump and started to hobble over, out of kilter in only one boot. Something knocked me on the arm halfway across the floor, and Nadia presented me with my other snowboot, pecked me on the lips, and spun back into the crowd. I felt like I had rum thumping through my heart instead of blood. I just wanted to kiss him so he'd remember it, for mine to be different from the hundred other kisses he got that night. For one moment, I thought, I could step out of the game and kiss Jono for real. A bonk-on-the-head kiss. Maybe then somewhere in him a tiny light bulb would go on, and he'd wake up the next morning feeling a little heavier in his skin, more grounded in his step, and he'd come to find me, finally, and change my life in some odd and inconceivable way.

I marched up, dropped my boot to the floor, and stuck the wing-tip into his hands. That goofy grin broke across his face like the whole thing just tickled him to death, and he dropped the shoe and stuck his face toward me, eyes shut, hands clasped behind his back, lips puckered up like Georgie Porgie. But that wasn't the kind of kiss I wanted. I put my lips to his, gently at first, to open them, soften him out of the stupid pucker-pose. I edged my body in, forcing his to straighten up, and I ran my hands insistently from his shoulders to his wrists until I'd pulled his hands apart and brought them to my hips. I needed to pull that kiss away from its context—away from the game, the scene, from everything that had led to that point of contact—in order to make it the kiss with Jono I wanted it to be. I kissed Jono as if he were the last man I'd ever kiss. The only man I'd ever kiss again.

When I pulled back, his eyes were quizzical, and his smirk broke wide into a grin. He looked at me like I'd just told him a joke that didn't make a whit of sense, and he laughed in bewilderment. "That was weird," he said, and he clapped me on the back and wandered back into the fray for yet another round of mix 'n' match musical shoes.

———————

I was only at Effigy one more time, months later, for a graduation party, one in a string of Commencement Week bashes. There's not really much to tell. Someone had gotten a motorcycle for graduation. Jono hadn't even had that much to drink, he'd just been Jono: ran the stop sign at the corner of College and Main, hit the passenger side of a big old-lady sedan whose driver was shaken but not hurt, and went flying over the hood, more than thirty feet, through the air. Long enough that I could not help but think he'd have had time to understand what was happening. And it's this that I still think about. In that moment, was Jono afraid? Did he realize as he flew through the air that he was going to hit the asphalt with a force that would shatter every bone in his twenty-two year old body? Did he know that he was about to die? Or maybe—and this is what I've hoped, what I've prayed, for Jono's sake—in those final seconds, was he still just the Jono he had always been? The Jono who would have sailed through that early summer night, the air warm and alive with crickets and celebration, living only in that moment, knowing nothing but the thrill of flight? This is what I tell myself: he had no reason to be afraid. He had never known the uncompromising resistance of the ground.

The
Girl
at
Chichén
Itzá

When I land in the hospital for the third and final time, my parents take a vacation to Mexico. I weigh sixty-
eight pounds and have a strip of satisfying bruises that span the
length of my spine caused by nothing more than sitting in a chair
or leaning against a wall. Resistant to aid and alarmingly adept
at relapse, I am sent to a tough-love clinic wherefrom I am permitted no contact with the outside world until I have jumped the
requisite hoops and hurdles and proven myself ready for reinte-
gration into society at large. This incarceration is hardest on my
parents, who've put me here, able only to see the sickness of my
sickness and blind to the glory and the triumph I've achieved.
Their love for me is fierce, but their thinking paradigmatically

narrow: *What have we done? Where did we go wrong?* The guilt hangs from their bodies like waterlogged smocks. Our family is a shipwreck, a ruin.

My roommate and "peer guardian" at the clinic is a girl named Sue who insists her name is Sioux. Sioux is my shadow and my guide. She's been in for a year, grown breasts, gotten back on her period, and is nearly ready to head home. I am the last phase of her inpatient treatment; she is the first of mine. Bluntly, I've been deemed unfit to care for myself, and that responsibility has been handed over to Sioux, who takes one look at me and says in her North Carolina twinge, "Honey, I looked bad when I showed up, but I don't think I ever looked as bad as you." This is certain testament to her wellness: she can admit not only that I am skinnier but that *I'm skinnier than she's ever been.* I am hugely comforted to know this.

For the next month Sioux will not be allowed to leave my side or let me out of her sight. I cry through the nights my first two weeks; days, Sioux trails me around, her eyes sunken in sleep deprivation. She is returning, through me, to the self she has lived beyond, yet she doesn't slip back in, back under. Sioux can take on my illness and retain her health. They love Sioux at the clinic. She's a success.

My parents fly to Cancún, a pristine strip of beach engulfed by high-rise hotels sent up one after another as if the only goal in building was to block the last guy's view. My parents loathe such places but are too exhausted to take a vacation they'll enjoy. We are existing on a far more elemental plane. Cancún is not for the fun of poolside daiquiris and orange sunsets; it is necessity. We're just working on survival at this juncture.

"I hate people," my mother declares, cranking down the back of her chaise lounge. A woman with a carcinogenic tan struts by in a white crocheted thong. Eyebrows rise in alarm as a furry man, his balls pouched in a purple spandex sling, jogs entreatingly after her.

"People are repugnant," my father says. He closes his eyes.

Within days my parents hate themselves as much as anyone

else at the hotel. "Can we take a vacation from our vacation?" my father wonders.

They are on the sixth-floor landing on their way to dinner. A bell dings and a red arrow blinks on, pointing to the ground. "Elevator to hell," says my mother. "All in! Going down!"

They travel three hours by schoolbus to the ruins at Chichén Itzá. The midday sun is scathing, and heat waves ripple before their eyes like delusions. My mother's linen shorts stick insistently to the back of her legs. The open bus windows blow dust from the rutted road, covering the passengers in a fine gray film that makes my father think of volcanic aftermaths and atomic fallout. My mother rests her head on his hot shoulder as if to sleep but never closes her eyes. Around them, cheery and chipper travelers twitter with friendliness—*So where're you all from? You don't say? Just down for the week? Milwaukee, you say. Consulting's my field. Marketing. Three grandchildren. Oh, just one. Beautiful as the sky* . . . My parents speak to no one. "I think," my mother says without even the pretense of a whisper, "that I abhor humankind." My father kisses the crown of her dusty hair.

On arrival my parents escape the irrepressible tour and strike out on their own. Chichén Itzá is beige and gray, sand and rock. It is as they feel: old, partially restored, partially unexcavated. My mother stops at the restroom and my father waits for her outside beneath an overhang of shade.

The ladies' room is shadowy in my mother's sunstruck eyes, and it takes her a moment to adjust, blots of turquoise and circles of orange clouding her vision. Inside the stall she rests her face in her hands.

As she makes her way to the sinks she hears water running. My mother glances up, and the face that meets hers in the mirrored bathroom wall is my face. My mother cannot help but gape, cannot take her eyes from the mirror. The girl smiles quickly, a tourist's smile, curt and officious but not unkind. It is my smile; it causes my mother to choke on her own.

The girl shuts her water faucet, turns to go. My mother stares into the mirror at her retreating figure. She wears a T-shirt and a long stretchy skirt. It is clear from her sneakers and her backpack—both big and neon-colored—that she is European. Across the backpack, written in white plastic block letters, is a nod of foreign worship for everything American: IT'S COOL! A flash of light from the door to outside, and the girl is gone.

My mother leaves the sink to follow her, stops a moment before opening the door in preparation for the shock of bright. Her eyes balk at the sky, scrambling to adjust, my mother for a moment blinded.

When her vision clears she looks to the shady wall where she has left my father, but he is gone. She pans the sprawling courtyard and spots him there across the path, following in the wake of the tourist girl like a man walking in his sleep. My mother runs to catch up to him and grabs at his shirtsleeve from behind. Without interrupting his stride he scoops an arm around her shoulders and pulls her in toward his hot body, and they walk together quickly like this, a three-legged race at a carnival game.

My parents miss everything at Chichén Itzá: the Temple of the Three Warriors, the Platform of Venus, the Great Ball Court, the Temple of the Bearded Man. They pass by the Nunnery with its famous Wall of Skulls; they skip the snail-shaped observatory and don't climb the steep stairway to the Temple of the Jaguar. Even the Kukulcán goes practically unnoticed, its pyramid rising eighty feet from the ground, four flights of ninety-one steps leading to the pinnacle platform, one step for every day of the year, a serpent's head guarding the base of each steep staircase. My parents are interested only in the girl.

My mother says, "It's not Amanda."
"I know," says my father. They keep following.

Chac, the Mayan rain god, is said to have lived in the Sacred Cenote, a well at the end of the Sacred Way. My parents follow the girl down this path to the well where children were sacrificed to Chac in prayer and for promise of rain. During the first exploratory dives into the well in the early years of this century, the skeletons of as many as fifty children were dredged up from the muddy water where their bones swam among offerings to the god: jade, copper, and even gold.

As the girl approaches the well, my parents see her raise both arms above her head, slowly, as if in prayer, shielding her eyes from the sun as she peers around the sacred site. And then she stops, relaxes, begins to wave her arms in the air: a greeting that from behind, where my parents stand fixed in their tracks, looks like the finish-line signal of a drag race or a runway sign for landing planes. Beside the cenote is an outdoor cafe, tables and umbrellas set upon the plaza, and it is toward one of these tables that the girl takes off. There are no more chairs, and the girl perches on the lap of one of her traveling companions, a young man wearing similarly loud tennis shoes and a funny hat that looks like a beanie. A waiter comes by and exchanges words and hand motions with the girl; she glances around, points to a half-empty glass on the table, and nods her head, smiling vehemently. She leans in and steals something from her friend's plate. A woman on the other side of the table lifts her own plate and nudges her neighbor to pass it along to the girl, who clears some space before her and accepts her friend's leftovers. She is talking as she reaches for condiments, laughing, shaking red sauce onto the plate. The man whose lap she's on reaches up and smooths the girl's pony tail behind her back, leans in and kisses absently the side of her neck, not needing to pay so much attention, the gesture as familiar to him as the girl. My parents scurry across the yard and take seats at another table nearby. If the waiter approaches they will order Cokes, or *agua mineral*, which they may or may not drink. The thing that quells them most right now is to watch as this girl takes a long sip from a tall striped straw.

The Estate

No one knew who owned the Estate, but we spent many long July evenings on the screen porch of the Carriage House, watching moths flicker at the citronella candles, inventing elaborate ancestries. We conjured profiles of eccentric old millionaires who lived in trailer homes in Arkansas and subsisted on canned sardines but secretly held the deed to the sprawling land trust which my parents and their friends—teachers and artists from New York City—called their summer home. Some of the Carriage House crew had been renting there for nearly twenty years. Checks were made out to Island Properties, a real estate company that managed the Estate, and no one ever knew into what account that money was eventually deposited. But rent was cheap, and we didn't ask too many questions for fear of rocking a boat we wanted to keep floating in.

As a kid I believed that the Estate was an old government spy camp: there was a crumbling stone wall at the shoreline that once must have barricaded the beach, and we found gun caps buried in the sand. If you cupped your lips right—over the rim—and blew, they made a sound, low and hollow, like a fog horn. A few renters insisted that Warhol was behind the Estate somehow, but everyone agreed that whatever its origins, the Estate was a haven. Each summer we fled the city for that spit of land on that tiny island off the eastern shore where our parents could spend their days volleying lazy tennis balls on the weed-covered courts under a canopy of trees and pass away the evenings sipping gin and tonics on the Great Lawn. From canvas deck chairs, whose nautical motifs were faded and frayed, they watched as the sun set and their children became silhouettes on the horizon. There were so many kids that the grown-ups let us look out for each other. We ran around all summer long as a shouting, salty-skinned, knotty-haired, sun-bleached gang. We climbed trees, swam in the old goldfish pond, did cannonballs off the crumbling pier, and played hide and seek in the Formal Gardens amidst ivy-covered pillars and chipped marble gargoyles. We slept in our bathing suits every year from May to September.

The Estate was vast: sprawling green lawns and meandering gravel paths linking a smattering of residential buildings. Summer renters lodged mostly in the Carriage House or the old Servants' Quarters. A couple usually took the one-room Honeymoon Cottage down by the beach. The Main House always remained locked. One summer, my younger sister Belle and I snuck in through a slit in a window screen which we helped along with a paring knife from the Carriage House kitchen. I think we expected a scene out of Dickens—a great summer buffet gone to dust and maggots on the dining room table, a spectral proprietress in an old-fashioned bathing costume rallying her ghost-guests for a dip in the sound. We were disappointed. The house was vacant, swept clean, and though it was stuffy and smelled like the sea (salt and brine, which made me think of sunken ships and buried treasure), it was nothing more than an empty house. No clues, no corpses, no squatters, no thieves. Just a house that nobody lived in.

My father was a painting professor at NYU, Mom managed a gallery on Greene Street, and neither of them liked the city. They probably would have gone "back to the land"—retreated to Vermont or Maine—were it not for the art culture and community that only New York offered. They appeased themselves with three-month summers in the country. Mom, Dad, Belle, and I stayed in the converted Carriage House. It slept around fifteen, always a crowd of artists from the city, so my parents really got the best of both worlds. There was Barb-Jean, a soprano who wore flowered muumuus and would not speak for days at a time when she was on vocal rest. What she had to say she wrote on little scraps of paper instead. When we cleaned the house to close it down at the end of the season we'd find fragments of conversation stuck between the couch cushions and tucked into kitchen drawers: *how many people? how many ears? Portuguese on her mother's side I think, Sot — 5 letters — ends in a y*. Once, on the back of a Scrabble score sheet left in the box, we recovered, in its entirety, her part of a rainy night conversation which included the address of a wig maker in Brooklyn and a recipe for blackened snapper.

Barb-Jean's husband, Patrick, had been a cellist with the New York Philharmonic for many years but had retired to sell antiques—eyeglasses and hat pins and other little affectations of attire—at a flea market on Columbus Avenue every Sunday in the fall, winter, and spring. Summers, he never left the Estate. "The world can get along without mother-of-pearl cuff-links for a few months," he would say. Years later, long after both Patrick and my father were gone, my mother told me that in those early years she'd always suspected Patrick of secretly owning the Estate himself. "He was so secretive," she said, "had that creepy business sense, like someone who's spent his life investing in land scams or oil rigs in Malaysia or something." As it turned out, the only cause Patrick had ever actually given money to was PBS, and he had a Channel 13 tote bag to prove it.

The Auerbachs—Yvonne and Steven, painters—had two sons, Aaron and Pete. As we grew up, Belle and I played many a game of Who's Too Chicken to Touch Who Where? with the Auerbach brothers in our hideout under a huge pine that was surrounded by rhododendron bushes. We egged each other on until the time came when no one was too chicken to touch anyone anywhere and that game lost its thrill. Unlike Who Owns the Estate? which no one ever seemed to tire of.

Janet was a soft-voiced blond who wrote children's stories, had done really well with a series of tiny books called *The Lily Chronicles*, named for her daughter. Each book came with a piece of little-girl dress-up jewelry: paste necklaces and plastic cameo brooches. Lily herself, we thought, had about as much substance as a cardboard tiara. The rest of us would be off in the woods and gardens, enacting our epic adventures: runaway orphans eluding capture by a team of vengeful Miss Hannigans; Indians protecting our island from colonization by the white men whose battleships floated stealthily just off shore. Lily stayed by the house, shooting at digital blips on her pocket Gameboy. She didn't understand our kind of play, and the feeling was quite mutual.

My favorite Carriage House kid was Maris, the only child of a sculptor dad and a stock market analyst mom, Elaine, who took the train out weekends from the city to join Harry and Maris at the Estate. Maris wore enormous T-shirts from her mom's office softball team (the Hewitt, Tulber and DeSalvo Number-Crunchers) and had crazy-curly black hair that she kept in a tight poof of a pigtail high on her head. She was four years my senior, played the flute, and left the Estate for two weeks every August to go to music camp in Michigan. I thought she was the coolest person I had ever met, not counting Delia. Delia was an astoundingly spry, white-haired woman who cooked prune compotes, wore a two-piece bathing suit with enormous daisies embroidered on it, and told us long, rambling stories of her childhood in Russia. I thought Delia had to be just about the neatest person *ever*.

In the evenings when it got too dark for us to keep playing freeze tag on the lawn and all the adults were still sitting around the porch at the dinner table, we came back inside for Delia's story. The table would be piled high with corncobs, blueberry pie stains soaking into the handwoven Guatemalan placemats. We curled into our parents' laps or at the feet of their chairs, licked the vanilla ice cream and pie crumbs from their spoons, and listened. Delia had lived through a war. She had watched the men she knew go off to fight and never saw most of them again. Her own grandfather, in order to avoid conscription—that was the word she used: "conscription"—into the army, drank a quart of white vinegar every single day.

"It damaged his heart," she told us in the accent that always seemed to grow more pronounced when she spoke of her childhood, as if to tell the stories she had to return, in a way, to Dnepropetrovsk (which I loved to try to say: *Dnepropetrovsk!*), the Russian town in which she was born in 1906. "The vinegar damaged his heart so badly," she said, "that he was rejected from the service, the military. So he didn't go to the war. He was home. He died at home instead because he injured his heart to the extent that they wouldn't take him to the war, but he couldn't last long. Those are the things that happened and those are the things that made impressions on me." Delia would pause, looking off like she had gone, for a moment, to another place, far from the Carriage House, far from our island Estate. Our parents hugged us in closer, sipped their coffee. My mother put her hand on my father, just to feel his body still next to her in his chair. Delia's stories were over when she'd get up suddenly from her chair and start clearing the dishes. The adults complied with her example, and in a moment everything was lost in a hubbub of clinking dishes and silverware and let-me-get-thats. I stood holding onto the edge of the table, the adults swirling and hovering all around, until someone stuck a bucket of corn husks in my hands and asked me to go compost.

Delia's stories were unbelievable to us in that they were completely true. We were children of comfort: fruit roll-ups in our lunch bags, subscriptions in our own names to *Highlights* magazine ("Fun with a purpose!" it said on the cover, which I read as "Fun with a porpoise!" until long after I had moved on to *Seventeen*). We were children who made up fanciful games: ingenious compared to Lily's Gameboy but tame as Monopoly in contrast with the life that Delia had actually lived. We spent one entire summer down at the beach playing Russian Revolution on the crumbling stone debris. Our imaginary walkie-talkie conversations consisted mostly of the word "nyet" and variations on the pronunciation of Delia's home town, for these were the only words we knew in Russian. We liked to keep our games as authentic as possible.

My father had cancer. We knew that from the start. But it wasn't the six-months-and-you're-gone kind of cancer. Barb-Jean knew someone who'd been in remission twenty years with Hodgkin's disease. My father had been diagnosed early, he'd gone through chemo, lost his hair, his bulk, his body. He had been a swimmer in his youth: 6'2", and he still had the thickest shock of black hair you've ever seen, not a strand of gray, and not a strand anywhere on his body besides his head. My father was sleek as a dolphin. He was beautiful, and he was strong. It was these characteristics which seemed to compound everyone's sense of tragedy. I felt like I was the only person who never found his strength tragic at all. I thought it was the luckiest thing in the world. If any of the others had had cancer (Steven Auerbach, say, with his professor's paunch and Mallomar habit; or Maris's dad, Harry, who'd probably lost more cells to LSD in his youth than my father lost to chemotherapy), their bodies would have given in to it as if drowning: they'd stop flailing and let the water close in. My father was a swimmer, too alive to die.

That summer after the chemo was the summer we discovered the Hideout. The adults seemed to be perpetually busy caring for Dad or for Belle, still a baby. We older kids, left to our own devices, spent the summer exploring every garden path and back stairway the Estate had to offer. One afternoon during a game of hide and seek I crawled under a rhododendron bush down by the Honeymoon Cottage. When I came through on the far side of the shrub I found myself in a little clearing at the base of a pine tree. The branches didn't begin until a few feet above my head, so the space around the trunk was a little alcove. It was deeply shaded; no plants could grow. The ground was dusted with dry pine needles, and it was soft and cool. No one could see in from the outside through the thick rhododendrons. It was the perfect hideout, and we guessed we were not the first to use it as one.

"I bet it's the owner's," Aaron said. "I bet this is where he stays, watching us." He grinned devilishly.

"Shut up," Pete snapped. He looked a little scared.

"Yeah," I said. "Anyway, it's our hideout now."

Inside the pine clearing we were Medicine Women, even Aaron and Pete, and we set out to heal my dad. We scurried around the Estate collecting flowers and leaves in old plastic yogurt containers. In the stillness of the Hideout, with mortars and pestles of rock and clam shell, we ground honeysuckle, dandelion, and wild chives and set the pulp in the sun to steep in water-filled mason jars. We brought our concoction to Dad's couch on the screen porch. I poured some into a teacup for him and he sipped it, making sure to stick out his pinkie finger. He grinned then and his eyes sparkled the way they had when he was well. "I feel better already," he said.

Dad did start to feel better that summer, mostly thanks to Delia, who knew everything there was to know about health and loved my father too much to let him stay sick. Delia believed in vitamins. She kept all her bottles in a suitcase which I found fascinating as a jewelry box. There were tiny round pills, flat and chalky; huge oval-shaped ones speckled like robins' eggs; shiny brown oil-filled capsules which gleamed like polished amber. Delia took about twenty different ones after each meal. She laid them out in a saucer by her place at the table. When the meal was over, the kid who was sitting next to Delia got to preside over her vitamin taking, placing the pills one by one into Delia's open hand for her to swallow, each with a sip of milk. We raced one another to the table just to sit by her. When Delia got Dad started on a vitamin regime, he let one of us dole his pills out to him too. Then we kids would go off to catch salamanders or collect beach glass, and when we came back inside, Dad and Delia would still be at the table, talking about health and balance and wholeness. Delia might have been old, but she had more spunk than anyone. Every morning she ate a bowl of oatmeal big enough for six, and she played tennis and volleyball with the rest of us. I'd overheard the adults talking about how Delia had once cured herself of some awful disease through vitamins and good nutrition and exercise. And will, my mother said, will to live.

We stayed at the Estate through the winter that year; just us and Delia, who didn't have any job to go back to. My mother took a leave of absence from the gallery and taught me at home instead of sending me to school. Mostly I read and did a lot of art projects. I remember Delia in the house cooking all the time—enormous salads and big pots of bulgur and barley. The vitamins had a whole cabinet to themselves by then. My father spent a lot of time by the fireplace reading herb books and art books to himself and Dr. Seuss books to Belle. My mother and father took long walks around the Estate every day. Dad put on some weight. His eyes laughed again. By spring he was strong enough to work. He said he felt vital. He painted every day for five months, and when we left after Labor Day the next summer to return to our lives in New York, he seemed, for all we could discern, to have become the man he had once been. "Remission," they told us. No one could say how long it would last. When my father was healthy, it was nearly impossible to imagine that he might ever be sick again.

We came back to the Estate every summer. In my memory, each blurs into the next: just one long, lazy, August hammock dream of barbecues and late-afternoon volleyball games, walking back to the house from the beach on the gravel paths, soaking in the sun's heat through the soles of our feet as the air around us cooled to evening. Some days Dad woke us up before dawn to go fishing off the pier, and on weekends we'd drive to yard sales at 8 A.M. to get first pick at the good stuff. On rainy days we'd color and make collages out of old magazines we found in the attic. Mom would feed us Doritos and garlic cheese and the fried bologna we adored, and Dad would cast a disparaging glance and say in both mock and actual disapproval, "Hannah, how can you let them eat that stuff?" He put away a bowl of morning oatmeal bigger than Delia's now and swam with us kids in the bay every day, no matter the weather. We played GI Joe at the water tower fort, tossed bread crumbs to the goldfish we bought to populate the pools in the Formal Gardens, sucked honeysuckle blossoms, and sunbathed on the roof. Dad helped us build kites, and we flew them on the Great Lawn. Belle grew up. So did I. Faces changed, but the spirit of the Estate remained the same.

In junior high I started going to sleepaway camp for half the summer. By high school I wanted to stay in the city and scoop

Häagen-Dazs like all my friends. Sometimes I'd take the train out to the island to spend a weekend and see the Carriage House crew. It was nice for a few days, but I liked to get back to the city, to my friends, my job. That was where my life was.

I did leave New York City in order to go to college in another: Chicago. I was accepted at a small university where I could study art and made the move midwest. I liked school, even liked Chicago, though it wasn't New York, and adapted pretty quickly and happily into college life. I spoke with my parents on the phone every few weeks. Dad was still teaching, and Mom was still at the gallery. Belle was starting high school.

My father died in April. He was at home, and we were all there with him. I left school without finishing the semester and returned to New York. Delia came too, from wherever it was she spent her winters. She'd gotten my parents through their initial crisis years before, and although this time there was nothing more she could do to help my father, it was Delia, I think, who kept Mom from going with him. My parents had met at a summer arts program when they were seventeen. For as long as my mother had functioned in the adult world, she had done so with my father. When he died, what Delia offered to Mom was continuum. Delia showed her how you keep going when you've lost someone you can't live without.

After the funeral, I went back to Chicago. I immersed myself in work, took summer classes, spent whole nights at the studio, painting, trying to do what he had done: live life right now. I spoke to my mother often; she was out at the Estate with Delia, and Belle, and everyone. It was a full house, but still, the Estate seemed enormous with Daddy gone: so much empty space. The stories after dinner were not of Russia any longer; no one spent idle hours in extravagant conjecture about the ownership of the Estate. They spoke of our father, Belle told me. They missed him. Flavors were dulled, my mother said; everything was watered down: the sweet corn, fruit pies, fresh scallops from the island fish market.

Still, life was going on. Belle and I wrote occasionally, and it sounded like she'd found some paths through the Estate she could still walk with happiness. She was spending most of her time with Aaron Auerbach, who had loved our father and—he told her, and then she told me—had always loved Belle. The familiarity of Aaron and the intimacy of that first love—sleeping on the beach, feeling another body that close—made it somehow bearable for her. She was sad, she told me hesitantly, but sad in a way that was so overwhelming it almost felt like joy. I understood, I thought. Sometimes, especially when I was painting, I got so flooded with emotion that the sensation of *sadness* was overtaken by the sensation of *sensation*. It might have been despair. It might have been bliss. I only felt the filling.

The way I figure things, Delia didn't want to make us all go through it twice. We'd only have to spend one summer in mourning like this, she must have thought, and then we'd be free. Next summer, the corn would need to be sweet again, the berries bursting with juice, day lilies as orange as the sun, the bay a glory, the Estate a haven once again from the rest of the world. Delia died the way she would have wanted: it was the middle of July, and she had a stroke in the kitchen of the Carriage House while washing the greens for supper. She always made a green salad. I remember when she and Dad would eat three heads of lettuce between the two of them.

Her grave is in the eastern corner of the Formal Gardens marked by one of Harry's sculptures, a smaller work in stone. At Delia's lawyers' request, the whole Carriage House clan—Mom, Janet, the Auerbachs, Barb-Jean and Patrick, Harry and Elaine—went to the reading of the will. She had no living relatives, and the Estate family could certainly have been her own, if families were determined by love, not merely blood. Sound in mind and body, Delia left everything—fourteen acres, the lawns and gardens, the houses, and pools, and beaches—she left it all to us. The Estate, all those years: it was hers. Her will made clear what she had wanted us to feel all along: that it was ours. She had lived there as she'd wanted to, as one of us, and she wanted to make sure that summers at the Estate would continue long after she was gone. That the Carriage House would keep on smelling like Salvation Army tweed coats, pine cleanser, and garlic rubbed into the tips of your fingers. That the screens would always have holes made by loose-limbed children so that the bugs might forever hurl their bodies at bedside reading lamps. That someone would keep track of the erosion of the pier, watch as it got shorter and shorter each season, make jokes about its disintegration into the bay. Kids and grown-ups would run around half-dressed, drape damp towels over every door and lawn chair, leave Scrabble tiles on top of the radio or on a shelf in the bathroom cabinet, soak cauldrons of chick peas on the old gas stove, and plant sprawling tomato plants in washtubs on the sun porch. The Estate would be as it had always been.

A Bungalow, Koh Tao

Peace Corps was platonic. Two of us, a tiny refugee village outside Mae Sot just over the Thai border from Burma where shells rained down nightly beyond our camp. Where would we have done it anyway? On your bedroll in the schoolroom, Banchong on one side, Joe on the other, Van's hammock above swaying side to side as he snored? Or at my place? Among the looms in the Pongyilah house, four generations tucked asleep amidst bright cotton skeins and the woven sacks that were their livelihood? *That* would've been colorful.

We barely slept as it was. Two years. We needed each other too badly to fuck it up—such an appropriate term, really. A perfect example of what it is that makes English so impossible sometimes.

To fuck up: to have an interaction which renders all further and future interaction irrevocably altered. In Mae Sot, to fuck up was a luxury.

When we were done, we were done. No third year's service extensions, no continuing. We were tired. There are things you never get used to. We knew ex-pats who'd been in Thailand since Vietnam without a solid shit. Two years. Fifteen pounds underweight and ultimately of no great use to anyone. We didn't regret anything—it wasn't like that. We were just tired.

The plan was to go back to the States to recoup and then set off again, make ourselves useful in some other part of the world. But all that was vague and obligatory. One can't very well leave the Peace Corps and take a job at Blockbuster Video. Can't leave the Peace Corps with no clearer vision of one's life than one had arriving. We had thinking to do. A lot.

But we couldn't make ourselves go. We'd thought that's what we wanted. But home was almost intangible by then. What if we got there and grew back into Americans, cushy and slow? What if we got there and couldn't make ourselves leave? We were afraid to cross that ocean. Afraid the equator would rise like a great wall and seal us out of this land forever. And I was afraid to leave you. Afraid to leave before I understood what I was leaving.

So instead of home, we took the train south to the gulf. Rented a bungalow on an island the size of Central Park five hours by ferry from the mainland, paid five bucks a day for roof, mattress, mosquito net, a tiny earring-baggie-ful of weed wedged under the door each morning. The bed had one sheet, though we hardly needed it in that kind of heat, only used it with obliging modesty to cover the parts of ourselves the other was not supposed to see. There you were in your boxers, I in my tank top, settling down for another night where your fingernails crept up my arm and I rubbed your belly until you purred like the cats back in Mae Sot sunning on the trails around camp. The difference was that, at night, those cats screeched.

When our restraint got unbearable we looked for screeches elsewhere. You went for travelers: German girls with chunky sneakers and bright backpacks. That blond from New Zealand. The Israeli, whom I honestly liked, though she didn't stick around. Resigned, I hooked up with an American who'd come down for a full moon party and never left. He had a rollicking little drug trade going on from a thatch hut on stilts with a local woman who was the mother of his child. He could never meet me for long. We snatched moments on white sand beaches, mosquitoes poised in our sweat.

Nonetheless, and quote-unquote lovers notwithstanding, nights found us back at our Haad Sai Ree bungalow, where we lay like lovers ourselves, whispering in weedy swirls inside our white cocoon. Whispering: *how will our lives happen?* Not passively. Not: *what's to become of us?* We were curious. We wanted answers. *When it's all over, what paths will our lives have taken?*

I lay across you, and you kissed my forehead. "What happens will happen," you said and rested your head back down.

And I wanted to say *que será será to you too, buddy, but it doesn't happen. Nothing happens. We lie here pushing this line as far — farther — than this line should go. We push; we reinscribe.*

I wanted to cross. It was like going underwater when I finally asked, "If I love you as much as I do, why am I fucking *him*?"

I held my breath as you reached, like a mother, to brush the hair from my face, your voice so loving, but not in a way that answered anything. Not I-love-you loving. Not *not* I-love-you loving. Instead, "I'd love you no matter who you let in your bed."

And I just kept pressing my ear to your heart as if I could hear there something to know if what you were was scared, or respectfully misguided, or just protective of this thing you knew we'd fuck up, knew better than I did what a good thing we had. Or maybe I knew and by then didn't care. I wanted you so much that the worst thing we could ever have done—whatever that was— the worst thing would've hurt less than wanting you. And still we lay there. We came no closer; we didn't move. We were stoned and sunburned and nowhere near anywhere we knew.

Grog

"I'm cleaning today," Maud proclaims. She's been threatening for weeks to scour the pit of a laundry room where she works at the College Inn, a decaying hotel and bar on campus where students go for watery, overpriced Long Island iced teas.

"Excellent," Drew says. Maud imagines this is how he sounds when he tutors at the campus Writing Center: smiling, encouraging illiterate rich kids to use semicolons correctly.

"Finally!" she snorts. She wishes he didn't always insist on seeing the pathetic as heroic.

"You want help," Drew offers, "I've got time this afternoon . . ."

"Like that's really the way you want to spend it." She means: do this and you will prove yourself spineless. He says nothing.

If she cleans, things will move efficiently. She'll be able to read while the laundry spins, maybe keep up with course readings, audit one next semester even. Have something, besides Drew, binding her to the college. Be someone other than a woman who followed her boyfriend back to school because she had nothing better to do.

———————

Maud and Drew walk together until the edge of the Inn grounds. Drew crosses the quad toward class; Maud crosses the parking lot to the laundry shack. As she opens the door she can hear laugh tracks; the television stays on twenty-four hours a day. There's an old upright fan in the corner, its grate choked with mouse-gray lint. The room is engulfed in junk: yellowing Lillian Vernon catalogs ringed with coffee stains, cellophane Cheez-n-Cracker packs full of cigarette ash, buckets crammed with cleansers and stiff sponges and balled-up paisley neckties. On the floor by the doorway lies a crisp, dead bumblebee, perfectly preserved, like a science display, wings like shimmering eucalyptus leaves. Maud is always careful to step over the bee; to disturb it, she feels, would be somehow sacrilegious.

She knows then: to disturb anything here would be sacrilegious. She cannot clean. She can't throw out the piles of dryer lint, go through the back closet and ditch the tablecloths with six-month-old pork chop stains. If she swept the floor, what would she do: bury the poor old bee in a pencil-box grave behind the shack?

Instead of scouring, Maud spends the afternoon atop a dryer, cradled by the rock and lull. Even in its chaos, the laundry room is somehow soothing. Or maybe it's the fact of the laundry, in spite of the room. In the face of seediness and grime, still: soapy becomes rinsed, wet becomes dry, wrinkled becomes folded, dirty becomes clean.

Maud does not hear Drew's knock over the drone of the dryer and the chaos of *Rescue 911*, which she is watching rapturously. She doesn't even realize he's there until a pint of Cherry Garcia and two spoons clatter onto the table. Drew is beaming down with the bemused pleasure she first loved in him—loved that he took in all of her confusion and craziness and accepted them as the things that went into making her, not problems that needed to be fixed or issues she needed to resolve. Lately, though, this unconditional acceptance is striking her as simple, bordering on insipid. But she's not actually thinking about him at all; she's thinking about the ice cream. Fuck him, she thinks, he knows she loves Cherry Garcia. That's why he brought it. Fucking bastard.

"Buenos días, fair laundress."

"Yo no hablo español."

"Do you get off soon?"

"You haven't even touched me yet."

Drew smiles. He tries again, all earnestness: "Do you want to go eat at the hospital?"

In her Ben and Jerry's paranoia Maud thinks for a moment that he means he's going to check her into the psychiatric ward for forced feedings. She's ready to tell him he can go to hell when she realizes he means the picnic area: grassy little knolls in the hospital parking lot where they've gone before to lie on wooden tables and watch clouds. Maud feels a surge of sticky guilt and reaches her arm out to Drew. His T-shirt is soft and pilled, and she pets at it absently, never once taking her eyes from the crack bust on channel 19.

They leave the dryer running and cut over to College Street, passing the house of someone in Drew's Gnosticism seminar where they'd once gone to a party. Maud had felt out of place and left Drew there to drink tepid Schlitz and talk Jesus. She'd walked home alone. So had he.

At this time of afternoon, doctors and nurses stroll through causeways, and patients are wheeled along the cement paths of Grace Memorial Hospital. It looks like a sanatorium in an eighteenth-century novel, and Maud gets a sudden flash of herself propped up in a white bed like a Victorian heroine. She knows Drew would probably visit her, but she can't picture him getting farther than the parking lot. He'd sit at a picnic table shelling pistachios from a bag. He'd feed them to the birds.

"What are people supposed to do," Maud whispers, "come out here and dig into IGA potato salad while their loved ones are having dialysis?" Pringles and pap smears. Sweet gherkins and a colonoscopy. Maud is milking a joke they've told to death.

They find a spot, and Drew sets down the pint, pulling the spoons from the back pocket of his cut-offs while Maud pries off her sneakers and positions herself cross-legged on the table. Facing her from the bench like a schoolboy at detention, Drew pries the cardboard lid from the container with a slow, resistant suck. He scoops a spoonful and holds it toward her, but she pushes his arm down. His face falls. He looks so defeated and Maud is washed with such guilt that there is nothing she can do except raise his arm back up to her mouth and take the proffered bite. The ice cream is sweet: sweet and smooth, and Maud watches Drew watching her as it slides down her throat, easy and sentimental. Not once does he lift his flat, wide stare from hers.

When Drew leaves for his evening seminar, Maud goes back to the laundry. The humidity is reaching a critical level: the sky clouding over, darkening fast. She sprints and makes it to the shack just as the heavens open up. Inside the air is thick and muggy. Maud flips on the light and plugs in the fan. She takes out her dinner: one half-pint of white rice from a take-out container. *Hunan: the East in the Midwest.* She eats and sucks at a Canfield's diet chocolate fudge soda. When it's gone, she wants more chocolate. Every night she lets herself buy one Milky Way Dark from the vending machine in the hotel lobby, eats off the chocolate coating, and smashes the rest into a dusty crevice or a crusted cat-food bowl before throwing it out. Otherwise she's liable to go into the garbage and polish it off.

It's dark, and the rain is coming down hard as Maud runs across the parking lot. Some students have ducked inside to escape the downpour and are huddled by the lobby couches. Maud walks quickly past. The candy machine stands in an alcove next to a pay phone outside the rest rooms. Maud drops in her quarters and jams hard on the button: D6. The coil inside turns slowly and releases a Milky Way Dark. Maud reaches down for it, but the coil keeps turning, and as she's pushing open the flap, another Milky Way tumbles down. She's pausing, a candy bar gripped in each hand, when the door to the men's room swings open and a man in a green apron walks out, wiping his hands.

"Now there's a sugar rush in the making," he says, grinning.

"It gave me two," Maud snaps. "I mean, they just fell out; I only paid for one. I only want one—not even a whole one, really . . . Would you like one?"

"Allergic," he says.

"What do I do with two chocolate bars?" Maud says. The man begins to move toward the lobby and as he passes claps a hand on Maud's back.

"Feast," he says. "Go wild."

Maud watches his green apron disappear into the bar.

She drops one of the candy bars into an ashtray by the phone booth and dashes back to the laundry shed. Maud is clammy: wet with rain and sweating too. She sits and feels the fold of flesh where her stomach lops over itself, all the gritty sweat stuck there in a line across her abdomen. An unbearable wave of discomfort washes over her, and she thinks right then that she cannot stay inside her body a second longer. But a second later, she's still there. She always is. She rips open the Milky Way.

On *Baywatch* a little kid drowns. The wind outside is raging, rain still sheeting down. Halfway through her chocolate coating the power goes out. The TV dies: zip, just like that. The dryer stops. The fan peters out slowly. Then there is just the rain.

Maud bites into the Milky Way. She can't see. The caramel is tough and stubborn and she can hear the spit smacking inside her head. Nougat slips against her fingers; she sucks at it. Suddenly the Milky Way is gone. She gropes for the empty wrapper and

licks the melted chocolate, expertly searching out the paper crev-
ices with her tongue, panicked, like she has to get it all, right now.

Seconds later there's a knock on the door, and Maud immediately crumples the wrapper and balls it in her hand below the
table. She wipes her mouth against the shoulder of her shirt.

"Anyone home?"

Maud wipes her mouth again.

The door opens; someone leans in.

"Anyone home?" the voice says again.

"Who are you?" Maud asks.

"Cyrus? . . ." he says, his voice rising to cue her memory. "I've
got candles in the bar if you want to wait it out inside?"

There's a long pause.

"I'm the bartender," he says.

"Um, sure, OK." Maud fumbles and stands up, gripping the
edge of the table. Suddenly she feels like she's so tall she'll bust
through the roof. Everything is moving incredibly quickly. Way
too quickly. Like rolling downhill, snowballing. Maud hurtles toward the door, thousands of miles away. She's like a meteor ca-
reening through space. She lets go of the Milky Way wrapper.
She follows Cyrus into the rain.

They tear across the parking lot and enter the hotel dripping.
Cyrus ushers Maud into the bar. Candles flicker in red glass orbs
at tables where students huddle, eating popcorn from plastic
bowls. They laugh. They lick their fingers.

"Come sit," Cyrus says, swiping the water from his arms in
quick strokes.

Maud pulls herself up on one of the red leather stools.

"Frog grog?"

"What?"

"Can I make you a drink?" Cyrus asks, whisking down a glass
from the rack above him and balancing it on his palm like a circus
performer.

"Oh, no," Maud says quickly. "Thank you, no, though."

"You're having a frog grog," Cyrus says. He smiles. Then suddenly there is something tall and fluted and green on the counter.

Clinging to the rim of the glass is a rather drunken-looking rubber frog.

"Every drink comes with a frog. Collect ten, win a free T-shirt." Cyrus points to a shirt hanging over the register. "Cheers."

Maud eyes the drink. It doesn't look like there's cream in it. What the fuck, she thinks, I just ate a fucking Milky Way. A fucking pint of Ben and Jerry's. I'll drink *some*, she thinks, half, that's it. She draws up the grog and sucks hard at its straw. The frog jiggles.

The room flickers red, spinning fast. Maud's chair is up too high; the ground is too far away. She reaches for a popcorn bowl, and her arm is so long that by the time her fingers reach the dish the hand isn't hers anymore. She drains the rest of her grog. Foamy green ice pools sadly at the bottom of the glass. Cyrus whisks it away and procures another, identical to the first, frog and all.

"Don't forget your friend," he says, detaching the first frog and setting it down on the counter. It's all liquid, Maud tells herself, I'll pee it out. It's not like I'm sitting here eating french fries.

But the popcorn.

There are three frogs on the counter and one still clinging desperately to a bar glass when Maud scoots off her stool. The student throngs have grown thick, and Cyrus doesn't see her slip out. On a table by the door there is a bowl of mints; Maud grabs a handful. They are stale and crunchy, and she shoves them all into her mouth at once. Lots of people make themselves throw up when they've had too much too drink, Maud thinks. It's not good to have so much alcohol in your system. She careens toward the bathroom.

There's a line. Swarms of girls. The entire student population seems to have sought refuge from the storm here, and Maud can't do it with all of them in the bathroom. It'll take too long. Make too much noise. The smell. She is panicking. She cannot slow her brain down enough to think what to do. She leans against the wall to steady herself, then slides down it and slumps there between the phone booth and the vending machine. Looming huge, right in her face, is the second Milky Way, untouched. Maud looks around. She grabs it, rips open the wrapper. The chocolate is warm and soft, the nougat doughy. It catches in her throat. She eats it fast, in smacking bites, and shoves the empty wrapper deep into the ashtray sand.

She can't do it at home: Drew will be there. His class will be over or canceled in the blackout. If she says she is sick, he'll want to be there, hold her head, stroke her hair. She can't wait for the line to thin out; she has to do it while all the liquid is still in her. She tries to think of where she can go, mentally scans all the bathrooms she knows, in town, on campus. School buildings will all be locked. There is nowhere.

Maybe Drew is out. Maybe he stayed late with friends, had a beer after class. She can beat him back, make it into the bathroom, and lock the door. Do it in the shower. Maud lifts her hips from the floor, reaches into her jeans pocket. Six pennies and a nickel: she used her quarters on the Milky Way. Milky Ways. She pulls herself up, faces the chattering line. Curls and teeth blur before her. "Does someone have a quarter I can borrow?" she shouts blindly into the crowd. A few women rifle vaguely through their purses, then look up apologetically. Maud feels like a panhandler. She whirls around and plunges back into the bar, burrowing through people, sweat, and smoke. Cyrus is swamped; she cannot get close enough to get his attention. Maud wedges herself in against the bar. She shouts to Cyrus; he can't hear. On the countertop something flashes silver in the candlelight: a small pile of change left as a tip. Maud grabs at it, catching some, losing some. She ducks away, swallowed into the mass.

The bathroom line has grown. Maud slips into the phone booth, drops the quarter in, dials. Between rings, the quiet pounds. Don't be home, Drew. Don't be home. There is a click, midring. And a voice: "Hello?"

She cannot answer.

"Hello?" he says again.

Maud is breathing hard. Time wheels past. Her brain is flying; one fist slams at her thigh. Drew hangs on; she can just see him there, waiting, at the other end of the line. Hanging on and waiting are all he ever seems to do.

It's Cyrus who finds her, curled in the phone booth, head between her knees.

"Hey Froggy, how you doing?"

And she thinks, Jesus, this is getting pathetic: flirting with drunk girls in phone booths.

She looks up at him: there have been better nights.

"I'm off," he says.

"Oh," she says back.

He's kind of tall, Cyrus, big. His hair is pulled back in a short ponytail and he's got a big jaw, big lips, a large tongue. His skin is red, scrubbed out. His eyes are big: the better to see you with, my dear.

"I have candles at my house," he says.

Holy fuck, she thinks. I am drunk, stuffed into a phone booth, all I want in the world is to vomit my lungs out and this man is trying to pick me up.

"That was subtle," she says.

"You think?" he does a sheepish look for a second. "Suave, huh?"

Then his stance shifts and he lapses, for a moment, into realness. "It's just across the street," he says, laughing. "You could get out of your wet clothes."

Maud stares up and laughs: the man is already undressing her. He realizes this and laughs too.

"That wasn't very subtle at all, was it?"

"No," she says, teasing, but then she gets on the level for a minute as well. "Hey, actually, do you think maybe I could use your shower?" she asks. "What I would really love more than anything is to take a shower."

"My shower is your shower," he says, offering her a hand. "I even have clean towels."

Maud has to unscrew the metal screen on the drain with a dime she finds in Cyrus's medicine cabinet. It leaves a rusty circle on the shelf beside a bottle of Scope. The drain finally comes loose, pulling with it a tuft of slimed hair studded with chips of plaster. Maud sets the grate on the lip of the tub, the hair streaming down like a mildewed Rapunzel.

The grog comes up easily: green froth with flecks of white rice, like confetti. Maud reaches out of the shower and feels for the Scope: disinfectant. She swigs a mouthful, sloshes, spits, and watches the sparkling blue swirl down the open drain. When the blue is gone, her head is still swirling. She washes her hair with Pert, the only bottle in Cyrus's shower, as green as the Scope is blue. There's no conditioner, and the shampoo leaves her hair stiff and prickly. She fumbles to recap the drain, but the dime slips from her fingers, and she winds up twisting in the screws with her fingernail. Cyrus's towels are large and coarse, the grayish-blue hue of laundry done badly. Maud wraps herself in one and unlatches the bathroom door. Cyrus is lying back, smoking, one hand propped behind his head. He squints at her through smoke. He's taken off his shoes, and his long toes splay out before him like dead chickens.

"Hey Beautiful," he says. And Maud thinks, Oh Christ.

"Too many grogs?" he says. He's probably got girls yakking in his shower all the time.

It's then that Maud thinks she sees Cyrus pull his hand out from behind his head and pat the empty place on the bed beside him. But she is looking all around at once—the postered walls, littered floor, like the room of a teenage boy—and it's a gesture so slimy, so sleazy, that she thinks, He simply cannot have just patted the bed. She looks down at herself, standing there dripping, her pale, squishy flesh wrapped in his stained, scratchy towel, and she is revolted and doesn't know how he isn't revolted, but he hardly seems revolted, and then somehow she is sitting on the edge of the bed where the cigarette smoke mingles with the shower steam, saturating the air, and Cyrus reaches out a finger, traces the line of her chin into the line of her shoulder, collarbone, breastbone, breast. And the towel slips, and Maud scoots up onto the bed, looking away from his face, down at his arm. She draws with her finger, dizzy figure eights through the tangle of hairs, and there is more shifting, and some writhing, and the connections are lips crushing lips, his lips big against hers, large and wet. The grind of his hips on her hips, pelvis on pelvis, and then his voice, something more than their rasping, his voice saying something like, "Is it time?" And Maud thinks, Time for what? And then she knows and is busy thinking, Jesus, what a fucking line— and he is reaching away, out of the bed, and there is crinkling, and a condom, and then he is in her, and that is fine, she guesses, whatever. And then he's come, and that's it, and she doesn't realize until quite a few minutes later that she can unclench her body. And she thinks, It's OK. I'm empty, I got rid of the grogs. I'm empty. I'm OK.

After Twenty-Five Years, at the Palais Royale

My parents spend their twenty-fifth wedding anniversary in Paris among their oldest, dearest friends, couples they've known since my father's tenure at the Federal Reserve Bank, brilliant French bankers and their wives loaned each year to the Fed from the Banque de France. My parents, insatiable francophiles, befriended them all, and it is these friends who throw the party. *Vingt-cinq ans,* they say, *c'est incroyable!* My parents arrive in a taxi at the Michaud apartment in the Palais Royale. Their friends have gone on to illustrious careers; *three men sign their names on a franc note,* my mother tells me, *and all three changed your diaper once upon a time.* The apartment door opens and my parents are lifted inside, showered with kisses, these friends like a burst of silver confetti raining over my mother and father. They swoop my parents up in their joy—the *oohs*, the *aahs*, the *mon dieu, ma chère, c'est merveilleuse*! They clasp them at arm's length: my mother is stunning, no longer dyes her hair, wears a black sheath, her short silvered crop dazzling. My father has grown a snow-white beard, the razor far more delicate work than his trembling hands can manage these days. He is younger but looks years her senior, *like Saint Nick*, people say back home. Like Father Time. Like an old man. People stand to offer him seats on the subway. He gets in for half-price at the movies. He'll be fifty-five in June. Although he's tired (my father is always tired, side effects of the dopamine, selegiline, amantadine HCl), his eyes are wide, though often they're wide now, as if no sight to him is less than perplexing, everything leaves him overwhelmed. He is frozen smiling, dazzled and confused. All the long-ago familiar faces! The lives that were once his pop around him like flashbulbs, these pieces of the past, chips of glinting mica in the air, wine glasses, diamonds, teeth, refracting light in shards that do not resemble what they reflect, do not reassemble once they've come apart. An ear, *bien sûr*, the terror *pop!* of a cork, laughter like xylophones, glasses clinking, arms around them everywhere, Simone and Jean, and Georges and Pierette, André, Nanou, Laurent, Thomas . . . And there is my father, his hat still on his head, coat buttoned against the night, stiff and clutched, standing in the center, the center of these lives, standing so still that my mother turns to him, turns from the rush of friends to face her husband of twenty-five years, recognition striking her like fear, in her whole body, seized, *My Bear, what's wrong*? And he doesn't know necessarily what is wrong, everything, there is so much love, all this love, only tears are running down his cheeks faster than he understands, everything moving faster and slower, ahead or behind, over and around and people, words, flashes, silver everywhere, and in the middle, he is the eye. In the midst of it all, he is stranded. Everything's so fast it's still, he is still, unfathomably still, and alone.

Think
about
if
You
Want

When her daughter Miranda was twelve years old, Sheila Daum fell in love with Steven Stone, the orthodontist who'd cast Miranda's bite in plaster and entwined her mouth in a labyrinth of girders and cables. The braces bit and snagged the insides of Miranda's cheeks and left the skin there feeling like the shredded pork schwarma at the gyro stand by the 59th Street subway which Miranda passed on her way to and from Dr. Stone's office. Less than a year into the ritual orthodontic torture Sheila moved herself and Miranda from Manhattan into a Brooklyn townhouse with Steven and his two kids, who for reasons related to Steven's custody agreement had to live in Brooklyn until age eighteen within a twenty-block radius of their mother, Steven's ex-wife, Felice. For over a year, Steven and Sheila rented the three-story brownstone in Park Slope before they decided that it was time to buy. The market was right, they were together for the long haul, and it seemed like such a waste to keep sinking money into a landlord's pocket when they could be getting ahead on a mortgage at the same monthly rate. Neither of them were game for another marriage, per se. They'd done that. We, they said, leaning in for a kiss, have something better than marriage: unadulterated love and joint property holdings.

Six months after the papers were signed Sheila discovered Steven was having an affair with his ex-wife. And so when Steven and his kids moved back into a similar Park Slope brownstone that Felice had gotten in the divorce settlement five years earlier and seven blocks west, Sheila and Miranda were left alone in the newly renovated hollow house, once a whirring den of love and mismatched teenagers, now the awkwardly quiet home of a very depressed forty-six-year-old attorney and her sullenly resentful daughter. Miranda's braces had come off a few weeks before the break-up, but once Steven was gone, Sheila refused to allow Miranda to be fitted for a retainer, as if to let Miranda's teeth revert to their natural state of imperfect alignment was an essential step in the eradication of every last shred of evidence that a man named Steven Stone had ever existed.

About a year after the split, Sheila decided it was time to fill up the oversized house. She planned to rent the top floor, share the kitchen and entrance, and provide, hopefully, some distraction from the fiasco that was her life. During Miranda's junior year they took in a couple, triathletes who left after three months to train in Colorado. Then came a summer French exchange student who had the entire third floor to herself but slept every night at a boyfriend's in the Village and showed her face in Park Slope all of twice. Then one afternoon in early September Miranda called Sheila at work to say that the new English teacher at school had just moved from Oregon, and she and her boyfriend were living on a friend's couch while they looked for a place, and could Miranda bring her over to the house to check it out and maybe meet Sheila too if she could get home from the office at a reasonable time?

"Sweetie," Sheila said, "maybe think about if you really want your English teacher in your kitchen on Saturday morning?"

"Oh, I see," Miranda snapped. "My orthodontist's OK, but you've got to draw the line at my English teacher?"

"Miranda."

"She's not *my* teacher, anyway. She teaches eighth and ninth. Besides, she's like twenty-three. She's really cool."

"Oh well, if she's *cool* then by all means. You should've said so in the first place."

"We'll come back later tonight, if that's OK," Wing MacArdle said as Sheila and Miranda walked her to the door. She was taking the place, just had to trek back to collect her boyfriend, Alexander, way out in Williamsburg at the home of a person called Stoker with whom they'd been staying. Stoker, according to Wing, had a studio apartment, a pet python to whom he fed live rats once a month, and nothing in his kitchen cabinets but a jar of solidified Cremora. "I can't tell you what a relief this is," Wing said.

"Do you guys need any help moving?" Miranda asked, and Sheila had to turn around to make sure the person leaning in the kitchen door frame and offering—*offering*—to do something for someone else was in fact her own daughter.

"That's sweet," said Wing, who was casting about in her shoulder bag for change. "We've got so little stuff, though. I think we'll be fine."

"Oh to be young and nomadic!" Sheila cried, and Miranda shot her a look like Sheila'd just broken into song.

Wing laughed. "And all this time I thought we were just poverty-stricken!"

"And with what I fork over in tuition to that school . . ." Sheila said.

Wing, obviously schooled in the inclusion of teenagers, turned again to Miranda. "Have you always gone to Emmons?" she asked.

"Since seventh grade," Miranda told her. "Before that we still lived right in the City. I only started at Emmons when we had to move out here." Her tone was venomous. For Miranda, Brooklyn was to Manhattan as Purgatory was to Club Med.

"What does Alexander do?" Sheila asked.

"Good question," Wing paused. "Alex," she said, as though he were a student whose record she was trying to call to mind. "Well, at school he was in film studies . . . Let's just say that Alex is still on the job market . . ."

Sheila leapt in. "I didn't mean . . . I wasn't . . . I mean I'm not questioning your ability, I'm not asking because of the rent, I was just curious."

"Oh no, no, no, I didn't take it that way at all," Wing assured her. "Alex, he's just, let me put it this way: I set up this teaching job for myself from school last year. But in Alex's field . . . He came out to New York right after graduation—I still had credits to finish up in the summer session—Alex came out in June to find a job and a place for us to live." She smiled and gave a little nod by way of punctuation. "Let's just say he's been about as effective on the job market as he was with housing." Wing looked to Miranda. "You solved one of our problems—maybe you've got a hot lead on a job for Alex too?"

"I'm on the case," Miranda said, resolving to check the classifieds.

Alexander Horlick was a brooding boy with dark, narrow eyes and exquisite cheekbones. He spoke little, preferred to stand in the corners of rooms, and tried to be touching Wing at every available opportunity. That first night, while Wing stuck a few things in the fridge (milk, margarine, a loaf of cheap sliced bread), Alex went to look at the upstairs. Miranda leaned in the entranceway as usual, as if to fully cross the threshold was more trouble than she was willing to take. She looked at her mom like she knew exactly what Sheila thought of Alex: she thought he was a loser. But Sheila, who was about as adamant as her daughter when it came to being defiant, was loathe to fulfil Miranda's expectations. Wing shut the refrigerator door, and as she passed by, Sheila slid an arm through hers, a maternal gesture, drawing Wing in. "He's *gorgeous!*" Sheila whispered, her mouth exaggerated. And this was how it would be: Wing as second daughter, Alex as the perennially present *she could do so much better and god knows what she sees there but she says he makes her happy* beau. As if on cue, Miranda strode from the kitchen and began to drag herself up the staircase with such laborious effort she might have weighed four hundred pounds, and Sheila and Wing were left in the kitchen, arms linked, smiling awkwardly after Miranda under the glare of the ticking fluorescent light.

Alex had enough left in a dwindling trust fund to keep up with his share of the rent and groceries and still maintain a near-perpetual high, and it wasn't that Sheila minded her house smelling suddenly as savory as it had twenty years before, what bugged her was that Alex never offered to share. When, once in awhile, Sheila worked at home for the day, she had to focus on the appraisal of court briefs, enduring the saintly green waft of smoke that permeated the house. Periodically, Alex himself emerged from the third-floor den for sustenance. He fed the way Steven's son, Ben, had at age thirteen: that same kind of bottomless, adolescent skinny that made it incomprehensible to imagine where all that food went once it got inside. On his way to the fridge, Alex passed Sheila's desk, sock-footed, and always gave a quick spasm of a military nod in her direction. This made her nervous and edgy. Alex, Sheila thought, was like every man she'd ever fallen for. He was like Steven Stone: good-looking, aloof, judgmental. They were men who operated like one-man "in crowds," men who had the power—to whom she *gave* the power, for Christ's sake, she was embarrassingly complicit, she knew—to decide who was "it" and who was not. Not that their lives looked particularly fun and exciting (couch potato stoner, philandering orthodontist), but it was through their sheer remove that they could make you feel like you were being left out of things you weren't sure you'd have wanted to be part of in the first place.

——— ———

One Sunday morning that fall, Sheila and Wing sat at the kitchen table with coffee and the *Times*, waiting for Miranda to return from the bagel place. Alex, who hadn't once seated himself for a meal with them, padded into the kitchen as usual for his snack, gave them each his little nod, and then turned to go, spoon in one hand, raspberry Dannon yogurt in the other. At the door he paused and turned back around. The women looked up from their papers, and all three were still for a moment until Alex did an odd little flat-footed jump in the air, turned on his woolen heel, and accompanied himself up the stairs with a jubilantly whistled chorus of the Skippy jingle. From the landing he called back to them, his voice a deadpan mockery of glee: "Happy! Happy! Joy! Joy!" And then he ducked back into the recesses of the upstairs.

Sheila turned to Wing, her face scrunched up in bewilderment.

"*Ren and Stimpy*," Wing explained, then realized that wasn't quite enough of an explanation for someone like Sheila. "From a TV . . . his favorite TV show . . . it's got rabbits, or mice, or something . . ."

There was something in Wing's tone—disapproval, or frustration—that emboldened Sheila. The words were out of her mouth before she could edit herself. "What exactly do you see in him?" she asked.

Wing didn't seem surprised by the question. Sheila guessed it probably wasn't an uncommon one. "He's different than he seems," Wing said.

"So was Ted Bundy," Sheila said, reaching for her coffee.

But Wing had her defenses down. "He's horribly insecure. Really really really shy. He's self-conscious to a degree that's literally debilitating . . ."

"Which is why he's not supporting both of you as a J. Crew model?" Sheila said.

Wing looked a little confused, like she thought that not at all an obvious thing to think about Alex, and Sheila could see her tucking it away in her mental store of curious things she might take the time to ponder one day. "His work . . . What he was doing in film—in theory—really it's excellent. Bergman's influence— the early work especially—on David Lynch . . . ?" Wing offered, but it sounded as though she'd said it so many times it didn't matter whether she believed it or not.

"Well," Sheila said, for she felt she had to say something, "you know what they say about still waters . . ."

The front door clicked open, then shut with a bang, and Miranda stepped into the kitchen waving a sack of bagels. Wing smiled; all that had been said seemed forgotten and not even in need of forgiving. She dipped a knife into the tub of cream cheese and brandished it toward Miranda. "And you know what they say about the early bird . . ."

Miranda, for her part, was accepted early-decision at Brown University. She'd been notified in December, which meant she was pretty much home free until graduation, barring any drastic fluctuations in her academic conduct. Miranda's school friends were all filing standard applications and wouldn't know anything until March or April, which left Miranda a lot of free time and no one with whom to spend it. Sheila usually didn't get home until seven in the evening, and Wing stayed at school until about the same time, advising the drama club, grading papers, and just staying on top of her teaching load. Thus, it was Alex, reigning sloth-king of the third floor, with whom Miranda spent the afternoons of her senior year.

"Does it bother you?" Sheila asked Wing one evening when they were still at the kitchen table finishing a bottle of not-terrible red wine. Miranda was upstairs with Alex watching TV. "If you minded having Miranda up there all the time you'd say something, wouldn't you?"

"I think the question should be whether you mind Miranda being up there all the time under the questionable influence of my great American stoner-boy?"

Sheila wiped a finger through the spaghetti sauce on her plate and sucked it clean. "I think I'm declaring myself officially through with having a say about who does or does not have an influence on my daughter. It's good training for next year. Ha! There's a job for Alex! Professional college preparation for parents. He could get people to pay him to come live in their houses and corrupt their children and let them grow gradually accustomed to being impotent in their kids' lives."

"I think," Wing laughed, "that you may be the only parent in America who'd actually go for a scheme like that."

"*Would* go for it—I *am* going for it!"

When Alex himself tromped down to the kitchen that evening for a microwave veggie pocket, he was quite obviously stoned out of his tree. He programmed the microwave, stepped out of its nuke-ray path, and leaned back against the counter to wait for the buzzer. His face was flushed, his eyes two slanted lines with dots of dark iris glimmering out from between the folded lids like polished gemstones. He also had a shining, domed pimple beneath his left eye which, for Sheila, made for a heartening interruption on his customarily flawless face.

"Are you up there getting my teenage daughter stoned on marijuana?" Sheila inquired.

Alex nodded his military nod. "Yes ma'am," he said.

"Good boy," said Sheila.

The microwave went *ding*. Alex flung open the door and removed the steaming pastry, joggling it between his hands.

"Paper towel?" Wing offered, holding one out before him like a fireman's net. He tossed it on.

"My savior," he said, collecting his dinner and pausing to lean in and plant a kiss on Wing's forehead.

Sheila had stood up; she moved across the room, opened a cabinet, and started fumbling through it. Unearthing a bag of pizza-flavor Goldfish, she held them out toward Alex. He reached for them with one hand and with the other placed his hot veggie pocket over his heart. Sheila tugged open the fridge. "Take some OJ too," she said.

"I am deeply moved," Alex said, looking at Sheila like she was breaking his heart. "A mother's concern for her child's munchies." He accepted the juice and backed out of the kitchen, bowing all the way.

Wing spoke first once Alex was out of earshot. She looked tired. "Have you ever been with someone so long you have a hard time remembering why?" she asked.

Sheila's laugh was a horse-snort. "What are you, my dear? Twenty-three?" She sat back down at the table. There was still some wine in her glass.

"Don't you tease me . . ."

They both laughed.

"I don't know that I ever know why I'm with them in the first place," Sheila said. "Maybe if I'd starting asking myself that question twenty years ago . . ."

Wing went on, her voice was not miserable, just intent. "I get afraid I'm wasting time," she said.

"I'd imagine cohabitating with Alex would make you feel like the most productive go-get-'em person on the planet . . ." Sheila stood and carried her plate to the sink.

"His sloth is infectious."

"No kidding. Check out my daughter." Sheila reached for Wing's plate.

"But to bail on Alex now would be like kicking him when he's down."

Sheila wondered, briefly, what Alex might be like when he was up. She turned on the water and squeezed some Joy into a sponge.

"I get accused of going yuppie, getting suddenly obsessed with money, being a fair-weather girlfriend . . . Sometimes," Wing said, laughing at herself a bit, "sometimes I think I wish that I'd get home from school one day and find him in bed with Miranda, or with you . . ."

"Oh please," Sheila cut in.

"It'd be a *reason*."

"But it's *not* going to happen." Sheila was emphatic.

"I know," Wing said, disappointed, resigned to Alex's fidelity.

"Need I point out that finding a *philandering* guy isn't usually the problem? I know quite an accomplished one, if you're in the market . . ." Sheila put on a Yente voice: "And wealthy too, an orthodontist . . ."

Wing laughed, but her heart wasn't in it. "But you *wanted* Steven," she said. "You wanted him to be faithful. God, I don't even know what I'm saying. I think at this point I'd be so thrilled to see Alex show a sign of life, I wouldn't care if he was fucking the cat!"

"You don't have a cat," Sheila reminded her.

"Well maybe we should get one!"

"Just don't put that down when they ask you at the ASPCA why you've decided to adopt a pet."

"What? *Sex toy*. You think that's inappropriate somehow?" Wing looked tired of even her own sarcasm. "Honestly, I think

I'm just a wimp. I don't know how to get out. He's a sweetheart. He's never been anything but good to me. How do you end a relationship like that?"

"You're settling . . ." Sheila began.

"Yeah, but when you've been settling for four years how do you suddenly turn around and say, OK Alex, I'm tired of settling?"

"You turn around and say, OK Alex, I'm tired of settling."

"It'd be so much easier if he'd do something really offensive!" Wing cried. "Like with you and Steven: he cheats, he gets kicked out."

Sheila turned away from the sink and faced Wing. The water was still running, and suds trickled down Sheila's forearms. "Oh but that's the difference," she said, so bitterly that Wing was taken aback.

"I'm sorry," Wing said. "I shouldn't bring up . . ."

"No no no," Sheila waved off the apology, sending out a little spatter of dishwater. Wing smiled a little, but the moment wasn't broken. Sheila stepped over and pulled out a chair. The running water forgotten, she sat. "You could kick Alex out. Who cares what's the reason? It's not enough of a reason that he lies around all day baking his brain?" She poked a long wet finger toward Wing. "If you want Alex to leave, you'll ask Alex to leave. You'll tell him to leave." She tapped at the air with her finger. She wanted to drill this in. "You have that in you," she said. "It's in you."

Wing blushed, a gracious blush, the modest acceptance of a compliment she was honored to receive.

Sheila leaned in, her face not a foot from Wing's, her breath warm with wine. "I didn't kick Steven out," Sheila whispered. She put a soap-sticky hand on Wing's forearm. The water faucet ran in the background like white noise. "I was so far from kicking him out." The tears rose in her eyes as if to spite her. "I asked the fucking bastard to stay. That's how sad . . . that's how pathetic, you don't even know . . . I begged that fucking bastard asshole to stay . . ."

It registered on Wing's face like disappointment, which she tried to cover and turned the look into something like pity, which was all wrong too, but nothing seemed right. And the truth of that suddenly didn't matter so much to Sheila, the truth of who she was, who she had been. Even though the truth was turning the look on Wing's face to something like disdain, it wasn't disdain for Sheila, necessarily, but for herself, for a future Wing. Like the road divided clearly before her: the Wings she might be. And in Sheila now Wing would have a tangible image of the Wing she'd be ashamed of. And that was OK, Sheila thought. If it made Wing take the other road, it was OK.

Sheila spoke as if she were posing Wing with a dare. "You can do it," Sheila said. "Walk upstairs, turn off his friggin' television, and say *Alex, we need to talk.*"

Wing laughed weakly; she looked miserable. "Yeah," she said, pondering the image of that confrontation: a ludicrous, pink-bubble fantasy.

"I'm serious," Sheila said.

Wing's smile was flighty and resigned. "I know, I know, but not . . . I mean, I've got to teach tomorrow . . . Anyway, Miranda's up there . . ."

Sheila was facing Wing with a conviction that, without fail, deserted her in the presence of nearly all men. "There'll always be an excuse you can make." She paused. She looked Wing straight in the eye. "Just do it," Sheila said.

Wing laughed for real this time. "What is this? A Nike ad?"

But Sheila wasn't in the mood; she had no intention of letting this dissolve into jokes. "It's your *life*," she said.

Wing sobered to attention.

"Don't do what I did," Sheila said. "Don't act like it doesn't matter."

Wing looked for a moment like she couldn't decide whether to be offended by Sheila's insistence or to seize the fever of her conviction and run with it, march herself upstairs and say what she'd been at least three years overdue in saying. Sheila wasn't going to back down; it even seemed clear that if Wing didn't do it, things between her and Sheila would never be the same. Sheila would withdraw, and the things Wing was coming to count on, those things wouldn't be there in the same way. This was one of those moments—Sheila had *created* one of those moments!—in life when a clear choice is put before you and you can see enough of the future to know that it's time you decide who the person is you'll be. And so it happened in a momentary retrospect like that—Wing looking back on herself from an imagined future and knowing which Wing she'd have to refuse to be. In nervousness her lips cracked again into a smile, with a question in her eyes to Sheila. She was at the edge. She needed one last nudge.

"*Alex, I'm tired of settling,*" Sheila said firmly.

Wing pushed out her chair. She seemed frazzled for a moment, like her brain had hit a snag it couldn't work through. She gestured toward the staircase. "Miranda . . ." she said.

Sheila stood and strode to the stairs. She craned her head up into the darkness. "Miiiraaaandaaaaa," she called, her voice lilting, giddy. She sang out again: "Miiiiiraaaandaaaaa!" Then she noticed the water faucet still running and practically skipped to the sink to shut it off.

They waited a minute in silence, but Miranda didn't appear. Finally Sheila started waving Wing up the stairs. "Just go," she said. "Just go. Send her down when you get there."

"OK," Wing said. And she went.

Sheila leaned back against the sink. She was tired. She wished there was just one more glass of wine, but the bottle was empty. She'd get Miranda to help with the dishes. She yawned and raised a hand to cover her mouth. Her fingers smelled of Joy, and she held them there beneath her nostrils until she was heady with lemon. She closed her eyes.

The feet on the stairs were too springy to be Miranda's. Sheila opened her eyes to Wing in the stairway threshold, one hand on either wall, leaning into the kitchen light. The posture was young, a little sheepish. She spoke before Sheila could. "They're stoned beyond coherent thought," she laughed, as if to admit the light and futile irony of her thwarted mission and to chuckle it off. "You want to come up for *Moonlighting*?" Wing asked, then hung in the stairway like Miranda would, awaiting a response.

Sheila's first instinct was to be angry, to fix Wing with a disappointed glare, point a finger up the stairs saying, *you march yourself right back around, young lady, and don't come down until you've done what you set out to do.* But she couldn't even say things like that to Miranda anymore, let alone to this girl she'd known only a few months, this girl who lived in Sheila's house with her stoned-out boyfriend, this girl who was almost a stranger, this girl she really didn't know at all.

Sheila shut her eyes again, and the world was milky cobalt and orange inside with flares and shadows of light. She rubbed one eye. "Yeah," she said. "Yeah, I'll just set some of these dishes to soak," said Sheila. "I'll come up in a minute."

Wing turned to bound back up the stairs, then looked back at Sheila, like she wanted to say something, meant to say something, like thank you, maybe, only she didn't, just smiled again, a smile in which Sheila thought she saw apology, and appreciation, and desire, and resignation all at once, and a thousand other emotions Wing probably hadn't yet lived long enough to understand. The smile was far too old for Wing's face, and then far too young as well. Wing turned again and climbed the stairs two at a time.

Sheila resumed the dishes. The road—it seemed suddenly very clear—did not diverge. Wing would no more leave Alex than Alex would leave Wing, no more than Sheila would have left Steven. Miranda would go off to Brown and do whatever Miranda would do at Brown, and Sheila and Wing and Alex would stay here in the brownstone in Park Slope. And Alex would smoke pot and watch movies and think about the theoretical implications of the zoom shot, while Sheila took the subway into Manhattan each morning and back each night, and Wing taught *Lord of the Flies* to children like Miranda who would grow up and do whatever they were going to do, and at night they'd sit around the kitchen table amidst salad dressing spills and reheated pasta, relishing those little pockets of red-wine time to step back a little and think about the rest of it all before they fed themselves through the cycle once again, waiting, always waiting for something to happen to change what they were. For the world to tilt, to quiver, to buckle beneath their feet and deposit them, blinking and afraid, into lives other than their own.

The
Animal's
Best
Interest

---

        * Sylvie is a healthy, fourteen-year-old, tiger-striped female with huge green eyes who has wanted nothing more than a lap since her owner died last spring. She's seeking a calm, gentle homebody, preferably female, who enjoys yarn play and can provide her with the finer things in life such as Fancy Feast Gourmet Cat Food, for which Sylvie has quite a discriminating palate.

It is one of my duties at the Lane County Animal Shelter to update the Adopt-a-Pet list we publish in the county's weekly community bulletin. The woman who did it before me was a predoctoral statistician at the university, and she kept it simple: color, sex, age, major deformities. But in the two years I've been here, we've seen a significant decline in our euthanasia rate, and though not everyone is convinced I am the cause, they don't argue anymore with my Pet Personals. Adoptions are up, and that's all the county really concerns itself with.

> *Phineas is a small, ten-month-old tabby who lost an eye in a childhood encounter with a raccoon. Quite sweet and somewhat shy, he'd like to live in a home with another cat or a whole brood who can help him rebuild his self-confidence. He'd like to meet a nice girl to share meaningful conversation and possible cuddling somewhere down the line, but as an activist for population control, Phineas has been neutered, for he does not feel that he could in any conscience bring another litter into this world.

Cheryl and I have already taken in three cats since we got to town, and that's in addition to Sid the Siamese and Bebe, Cheryl's ancient Newfoundland whose mostly inert yet breathing body the four cats like to use as a bed. The four of them'll be sprawled out across that big gallump like that's what she was intended for all along, and Bebe either doesn't mind or is so senile by now that she doesn't even notice. We know Bebe's going to go one day, and we try to talk about what we'll do then, but it upsets Cheryl too much, and she ends up saying, "When the time comes, Christine, you will pick out a lovely old dog from the shelter and you will bring it home and I will hate and resent it at first because it is not Bebe, and then I will eventually love it beyond all rationality because it will love me and we both know that I am powerless to turn my back on love." This is true. When we first met Cheryl didn't look at me twice, and I fell crazy in love with her, insinuated myself into her life by every possible human means and eventually got her to fall in love with me too. Thus, we both now know that's one way love can work. Cheryl says that I am more like a cat than a person sometimes: that for a human being to truly love another human being she has to hate her also, that love and hate go hand in hand like that. Cheryl both loves and hates me, which she says means she would stay with me forever. I, like a cat, she says, seem to be capable only of *loving* Cheryl, which is what has her convinced that I am capable of leaving, of finding someone else to love. But I have a different theory.

I think there are two different kinds of people: those whose natural state is alone, and those for whom solitude is like swimming underwater: you can only do it for so long before you simply have to come up for air. I fall into the latter group, not by choice but by the same virtue that I am a human being and not a fish. I have often wondered what it would be like to experience solitude as a norm. I imagine unbelievable freedom: to be able to move to Tibet, live in a teepee, whistle show tunes in the middle of the night, eat herring and onions in bed, and fall asleep without brushing your teeth. And it's fascinating to imagine, but so are sword swallowing and bungie jumping, and they're simply not things I'll do by choice during my time on this earth. I know that I would not leave Cheryl unless I had somewhere else to go, which means someone else to go to. And while I'm with Cheryl I'm not playing any other fields.

According to Cheryl's love/hate theory, she would never leave me, and according to my two-kinds-of-people theory, that's true, because she's not a loner either. And though she thinks I might leave her—for Tibet, for the teepee, for bad breath and Sondheim at 3 A.M.—because I don't hate her enough to really love her, I know that as a natural coupler, not a loner, I'll be sticking around. I tell her, Look at animals. It's not the loving, devoted, faithful cats who leave; it's their owners: dropping little Muffin off at the dump because she barfs on the carpet too often, letting Rover out of the family van at the side of the highway as they speed off to a new life in a new town in a new apartment complex that doesn't allow dogs. Too bad, out you go, Spot, out you go. I sometimes think about how many people would actually have pets if my personal ads worked the other way around: *Family with three terror-age children seeks masochistic cat for ritual torture.* Or *Flighty, itinerant couple looking to adopt cat for a very short period of time and then ditch it back at the shelter when they decide to rejoin the Phish tour.* The thing that kills me—and that's because it hits me where I live—is that the animals, they still go with those folks. And for the hour or the week or the years they're kept, they'll love those people unconditionally—pure, unadulterated, unselfish love. And inevitably, it's the people who let them down.

Take Arlene, for example. I'd been here a few months the first time Sniffles came in—*Sniffles*! I swear to god! There should be laws!—and it was her mother who brought him.

"He's my daughter's cat," she said, petting him mechanically on the head, as if someone had instructed her in the display of affection. She had the moves but not the soul. "My daughter's going into the hospital." She announced that bit of information like it was a personal challenge to me. She had on a dark velour sweatsuit-type thing over which Sniff—a white Himalayan fluff-ball—was shedding mercilessly. The woman would have made a pretty good stray herself: bony and shrunken, with deep circles under a pair of buggy blue eyes. "My husband's allergic," she told me, and then all of a sudden her defenses just seemed to drop away—so fast it was eerie, like watching a multiple-personality movie-of-the-week where some woman slips from Gretchen-the-Wicked-Bitch to Sissie-the-Pathetic-and-Deprived in a matter of seconds. She said, "This seemed like the only option. We don't know what else to do . . . ," then trailed off, waiting, as they all do, for some kind of reassurance from me. They want me to tell them they're not bad people, that I can absolve them of all guilt, and that really it's just a fine and peachy thing for them to adopt a pet and discard it again when they redo the living room and Fluffy no longer fits in with the color scheme. But this woman really did look like she'd been to hell and not made it all the way back. I'm a softie when it comes down to it. I scooped Sniff out of her thin, gangly arms.

"Hello there, Big Boy," I cooed into that flat fuzzy face, those gorgeous blue eyes. "Welcome to the Lane County Hotel. We'll let you take a nice hot flea bath, freshen you up after your trip, and then I'll show you to your suite. We serve a complimentary continental breakfast at eight, and quiet hours should be posted on the back of your door." With a free hand I pulled out the log book. "And under what name will the gentleman be registering today?"

The woman looked at me like I was possessed, then, total dead-pan, she said, "Sniffles," and she and I had a little bonding moment. The way it came out of her mouth, I knew what she thought of the name, and I raised my eyebrows to agree. She closed her eyes then, for just a second, but deliberately, on an intake of breath, like she was counting in her head to keep from flying off the handle, the way they teach you in Control Your Anger workshops. She opened her eyes slowly. "My daughter," she said, and it was a statement which alone was meant to explain everything—Sniffles, the hospital, the gray-black sacks beneath this woman's sleepless eyes.

> *Sniff is an independent three-year-old Himalayan male who, following the ill health of his previous owner, needs a stable and understanding home. He's been very influenced by EST and Gestalt therapy and feels ready to engage in a spiritual and/or physical relationship with like-minded feline, M or F. Please send photos and/or fur samples. Neatness a plus.*

Sometimes I worry that my ads get a little suggestive, but what can I say? Sex sells. And we do a background check prior to all adoptions, so we know we're not sending our kitties home with some sick fuck who wants pussy and doesn't know how else to get it.

No one adopted Sniff. We were somewhat overrun with kittens at the time, and that's what was moving. People came in to ooh and coo over the one-pound little skimps, and the adult cats just sat in their cages staring out dully from behind the bars, not a glimmer of life, no show of adoptability. It was like they knew it just wasn't worth expending the energy.

It was mid-December when the girl herself came in. Arlene. The wind chill was dipping us into record lows, and everyone and their grandmother was bringing in the family of strays that had been living under their porch since summer, feeding on table scraps, *but now with the snow . . .* et cetera, et cetera. Suffice it to say we were full to capacity and beyond, plus there was an insidious upper-respiratory thing going around the cat room, and we couldn't get any of them healthy before the germs just came right back around again. I wanted to get cats out of that room.

Arlene came in piled to Nanook proportions in a white parka that looked like it had been trimmed in Sniff-fur. She was padded down but had a belt cinched around the waist of that Twinkie-foam coat, which made her look like a number 8, and when she reached to her face to pull back some scarves so she could speak, I had a distinct vision of the grim reaper, as if she'd unveil herself to reveal there was nothing there at all.

She did have a head, it turned out, though it made me sick to look at it. It was shrunken, set back there in the recesses of that white furry hood, morbid. She tugged off a pair of knitted Guatemalan mittens and held her blue claws by her mouth as she spoke. "Um," she said, then "um" again, and it turned out she couldn't put a word into the air before she'd ummed like that for a full ten minutes, and then had to apologize halfway to heaven when she was done. "Um," she said again, and I settled my chin in my hand and waited for her to conjure up some alternate syllable. "Um . . . I . . . I've been . . . last month . . ." She took a breath. "Do you have a white cat here? Like a month ago, a white Himalayan, Sniffles . . . my mother brought . . ."

"Cat room's down the hall on the right," I told her.

Her face seemed to brighten, at least the bones shifted in an upward direction. "He's here?" she pipped, infinitely excited, as if her long-lost love had just arrived at her deathbed.

I nodded, pointed her down the hall, and began to compile the requisite paperwork.

Sometimes when I call the Pet Personal updates into the community bulletin I think I should put one in the human Personals for myself, just to see. *Christine is an even-tempered, short-haired brunette who seeks a stable, safe, loving home. She doesn't like to be left alone, is still playful and active at thirty-one, and wants to explore an intense relationship to see if she's capable of loving someone enough to hate them. Women only, please.* But I scan the Personals people place in the bulletin, and they're all pathetic, and I think, I love Cheryl. The Classifieds that break my heart open: *Free black lab puppies to good home.* And *FOUND by City Park last weekend, tabby male, no tags, yellow collar.* I think maybe we should just adopt another cat. There's too much hatred in the world as it is.

Arlene, when she wasn't in the hospital, lived with her parents in the neighborhood, such as it is. East Third Street dead-ends at the shelter, which backs on the County Sewage Treatment Center. On our block there are two "adult" "book" stores; a Christian Science reading room; Ball-o-Yarn, the pet supply/knitting supply shop; and a gas-station-turned-barbeque-joint-turned-dairy-mart where middle-school kids hang out in the afternoon playing Asteroids. Arlene might have been anywhere between fifteen and twenty-eight or -nine; it was impossible to guess. I don't think she was in school; I wasn't even sure what exactly was wrong with her—cancer, I guessed, maybe even AIDS, something serious—until she started in with the walks and I started putting it all together. The temperature stayed below zero for a good two weeks, but I'd see her out in it every single day. My desk looked onto the street, and I know she did three separate walking sessions each day, morning, midday and late afternoon, up and down that block, thirty, sixty, ninety laps. Just back and forth on dead-end East Third, corner to corner, bundled into that white snowball coat. And no matter how blackened and sooted and dog-urine-stained the banks of sidewalk snow became, Arlene's coat was always so white it practically glowed. In the winter sunlight she floated past the shelter windows, across my field of vision again and again and again, like some strange and deathly luminous apparition patrolling our little block.

Mid-January the mother was back, Sniffles under her arm like a bundle of laundry. She handed him over to me first thing, and that poor cat just looked like he was saying, *Here we go again.*

"She can't take care of herself, let alone something else," the mother announced, as if this dialogue had simply been on pause since the last time we'd seen each other two months before. "Don't let her take this animal back," she instructed me, and she was livid; there was fire in those icy-blue bug eyes, and I wondered how I'd react if it were my daughter killing herself by slow starvation. If I'd look as hateful as Arlene's mother did right then.

She truly appeared as if she hated her own daughter. But then her eyes welled up like her heart was going to plop out onto the counter and I thought, It's a fine line between love and hate, and maybe Cheryl's right that it's only the people for whom you feel one that you're capable of feeling the other. "I think," the woman was saying, "if she . . . I . . . when . . . oh god . . ." She slapped at her face as if to break her own emotional state. "Just please," she said, "find someone else to take this cat. Or just don't give it back to her." Her voice was starting to grow threatening again. "It's just going to be like this as long as she's alive," she spat. And here was this woman, standing beneath a SPAY—IT'S THE HUMANE THING poster discussing her anorexic child's imminent death, and I wondered if that end loomed for her a little like relief.

"Come on, Big Boy," I breathed into Sniff's coat of fuzz. "Welcome back."

———————

Another month: in strolls Arlene. It was mid-February, and the weather had mellowed a bit. She still had her hood drawn up but was minus the seventy-five scarves and mufflers. "Um," she said, pulling off a mitten and panting some tepid breath at her finger bones.

"Sniffles," I said in lieu of a greeting.

Her face washed in a sort of relief I didn't expect, as if she was taking me on as an ally in all this: the war with her mother over Sniffles.

"I can't give him to you," I said.

She froze for a second, but only for a second. "If there's some time limit on claiming them, I'll pay the adoption fee . . ." she said.

"We have standards potential adopters have to meet before we'll release an animal into their custody," I told her.

"He's my cat," she said.

"It hardly seems in the county's best interest—which is the animal's best interest—to place a cat in the home of someone with a history of abandonment."

"It is not abandonment," she hissed. "*I* don't bring him in here. You have a problem with people using this place as a kennel, take it up with my parents." She steadied herself against the counter, and I found myself doubting her ability to lift Sniff up at that point, not to mention carry him home.

I reached for the log book, flipped it open, and started reading aloud Sniff's record, which, I realized, was Arlene's hospitalization record nearly date for date. I looked up and could see the water rising in her eyes. I didn't actually want to make her cry; I had the sense that to lose even one tear's worth of anything from her body could put her over the edge at that point, and I didn't want Arlene dead there on the floor of the shelter, a chorus of *mews* and *arfs* heralding her way into the Great Beyond.

"Honey," I said, trying my best now to sound gentle, "we've got to know we're putting these animals in stable homes." But my tone was souring even as I spoke. "Do you think about what it does to that cat to get shuttled around this way? Do you stop to consider what the effects of your actions might be on him?"

She looked at me quizzically for a second, any trace of tears retreated back up into her ducts, and I thought of a movie strip, played backward and speeded up—snow rising from the ground to the sky, people growing smaller instead of bigger as their lives went on, Arlene slithering backward out through the door she'd just come in, back out into the snow to continue on her walk, scurrying backward up and down East Third like a leaf getting sucked into a vacuum.

I filled out the papers, doctored the books, and brought Sniff home with me that night. Once you've got four, it's hard to come up with a sound argument against a fifth. Sniff does well with the others too. They're all cats who've had to do a lot of accommodating in their lives. Sid the Siamese was part of a show cat's litter, and he got ditched by the breeder for a slight coloring irregularity that disqualified him from pure-bred competition. Swanson crawled out of a dumpster at the Golden Corral and into our hearts. Gertie and Alice were from the shelter here, two old goats—one blind, one missing a paw. No one was going to take them, so we did, and they're just the sweetest ladies in the world. Sniff joined the brood and the circle opened up to make room for him, like a new member at AA. Everyone slides on over, they drag out another chair, pour the coffee, *Hi, my name is Sniff and I've been abandoned.*

Next day, Arlene's back, as expected. "He's my cat," she said. "You can't refuse to let me take him home."

I just looked at her, blank as a slate. "And you're looking for . . . ?"

Her eyes narrowed in disbelief and her head tilted like a marionette's.

"A cat?" I reached for the log book. "What'd you say the name was you were looking for?"

"Sniffles," she said.

"Quite a name," I said.

"Sniffles," she told me again, the absurdity of that name absolutely lost on her.

I flipped pages. "Sniffles, Sniffles, Sniffles, oh, here!" I looked up at her. "Oh honey," I said, "I'm sorry. Sniffles, right here. It looks like he's been adopted. Last week, in fact. A real nice family. I remember. Really nice." I smiled apologetically.

"Adopted?" she said, incredulous.

"Maybe you'd be interested in something a little lower maintenance?" I offered. "Snakes make super pets, and you've only got to feed them once a week . . ." But I let it go. Arlene was crying. Then she mumbled something I couldn't hear, hands at her face, and she walked out that door for the last time.

For another week that February Arlene continued her foot patrols of East Third Street. She never came in the shelter again, never even looked my way, just passed by, back and forth, thirty, sixty, ninety times a day. And then at the end of the week she disappeared. I imagined her with the same look on her face that Sniff had when her mother carried him into the shelter that last time: *here we go again,* the anorexic getting shuttled off to another hospital, another IV shoved up her arm, another IV ripped out of her arm. Promises of ten pounds made. Promises, as always, broken. I never saw her again, and for all I know she is no longer alive. That seems most likely, I think, though it makes me kind of queasy to think of her dead, to imagine that she has succeeded at that, if nothing else.

Sniff is a good cat—docile, aloof, independent to the point of oblivion, with the purr of a steamroller and the sleeping habits of a narcoleptic. He plays well with the others when he's in a playful mood. Otherwise, he spends a lot of time by himself, tucked into a windowseat or up on a staircase, just watching the world go by. It's funny, but I worry about Sniff in a way I have not over any of the other four, or any cat I've kept company with in my life thus far. I wonder what kind of cat he is, Sniff, at heart and by nature. I worry that he gives himself away indiscriminately: went from Arlene to the shelter to me and Cheryl without so much as a sneeze or a hearty piss on some nice rug to say, *I've had it up to here with this nomadic life.* The thing is, I worry that I'll come home from the shelter one day and find him gone, wandered off with any partially warm-bodied stranger bearing a can of Friskies Buffet or dangling a scrap of string in front of his nose. But more than that, I fear that he'll just go on his own. That'll he'll get bored or restless and pull up stakes, or even that he'll just follow a butterfly down the road and keep on going. I am afraid that his disappearance would devastate me, inexplicably, irrationally. I think that I do not know what I would do if Sniff were to pick himself up and move along. I don't think it matters whether he loves just to love or loves enough to hate too. That's Cheryl's theory of the way things work, and I've decided I don't agree. Mine is the only theory that seems to make sense to me, and I guess that's pretty self-justifying, but what can I do? The thing is, I think Sniff is a loner. Me and Cheryl and Sid and Swanson and Gertie and Alice and Bebe—we're couplers, groupies, communal souls, and we'll stick with the brood. It's the safe place to be. But Sniff— I think Sniff's a loner. Like Arlene, maybe. Unlike us, at least. And I think maybe I'm jealous of that kind of personal freedom, envious of a body that can just take off running. It's a weightless abandon, so foreign that I almost can't even be envious. I can almost only just be afraid and a little bit awed at the same time.

Out of the Girls' Room and into the Night

Silver Tarkington went on a blind date to the Chilton School senior prom with a boy named Barry Gorda, who was the best friend of Jarrett, who was the boyfriend of Fernanda Albion, who was the daughter of the family friends with whom Silver happened to be staying for that particular weekend in June. Silver had to fly in from Houston for an early freshman orientation at NYU that coincided with the weekend of Fernanda's prom, and when Silver learned that Fernanda was finding her a date for said prom she was less than thrilled. She'd suffered through her own prom back in Texas a few weeks earlier and couldn't muster an ounce of enthusiasm at the prospect of slogging through another one. Besides, she'd broken the heel of one dyed-to-match pump and lost the other somewhere between the booming Houston country club and the sandtrap just past the third tee, where she'd smoked a joint with Cyril Houser while her own date puked peach schnapps into an azalea bush across the fairway. Plus, the fact that Fernanda had to import a girl from two thousand miles away to be Barry Gorda's prom date didn't exactly recommend him as a real winner. Nonetheless, Silver bought a fresh pair of hose, borrowed some shoes, raked on the requisite mascara, and squeezed herself back into the shimmery-sage snip of a dress that had seemed quite reckless and inspired back in Houston but here at a New York dance club amidst a group of eighteen year olds who appeared to be dressed less for a prom than for a haute couture funeral, she felt sort of like an oxidized Statue of Liberty: a trifle absurd and worse for wear.

Barry Gorda threw big parties when his folks left for weekends in the Hamptons, had love handles that bulged over his cummerbund, and was known affectionately as the Cheese.

"The *Cheese*?" Silver whispered to Fernanda. They were at their table watching Barry jog out onto the dance floor to entertain a group of break-dancing white boys who clustered around him chanting "CHEESE. CHEESE. CHEESE. CHEESE."

"Barry *Gouda*," Fernanda explained from beneath a well-arched eyebrow.

"Clever," said Silver flatly.

"Oh, they're quite a creative bunch, our boys."

Silver gave a little snort. She and Fernanda—estranged since age nine when the Albions had moved from Houston to Manhattan—were hitting it off again famously. Markedly less impressive was Jarrett, Fernanda's boyfriend of three years who made Silver think of a St. Bernard in tails. He was headed for Tulane in the fall, Fernanda for Hampshire College, and Silver figured any attempt to do a long-distance thing would last about three days before Fernanda hooked up with some multiply-pierced multimedia performance artist and sent Jarrett running to the Louisiana Tri-Delts for consolation.

"And what's the Cheese doing with himself next year?" Silver asked.

"Last I heard, moving to Amsterdam."

"Where prostitution's legal?"

"Drugs too," Fernanda added.

"Lovely."

Fernanda's voice was suddenly less confident. She faced Silver. "Do you totally hate me for setting you two up?"

Silver smiled reassuringly. "Please just don't phrase it that way—it sounds like you thought we'd really hit it off."

"Well he certainly seems to have taken a liking to you," Fernanda teased, but it was quite plainly and painfully the truth of the situation.

"I'm sure I've done something in my life to warrant a little penance," Silver said. "I'm thinking of this date as a sort of community service."

"OK," Fernanda said suddenly, her tone abruptly new, and she reached out and laid her hand on Silver's forearm. Her face washed over in a sort of eerie film. "Don't turn around, OK? Just sit there and pretend we're having a normal conversation."

"We're not?" Silver asked.

"What?" Fernanda's gaze was distant, but like she was trying to demonstrate to someone far away that she was focused very intently on Silver. Silver didn't turn around. She had the distinct sense that Fernanda might slap her if she tried. "Approaching from behind you," Fernanda said, "is someone we'd like to see spend as little time at our table as possible. If you think of anything that'll get me, or him, out of here, do it. Ready, two, one, we have touchdown."

Something had indeed landed beside Silver in Barry Gorda's empty chair. It spoke as if to announce itself: "Fernanda Albion."

Silver looked him straight on. "I thought *she* was Fernanda Albion?" she said, forking a thumb toward her friend. The guy didn't seem to notice or care.

"Smith Parker Hewitt," Fernanda said, stony as anything, drawn out and slow.

"What's that, a law firm?" Silver clucked, to no discernible response.

"Silver Tarkington," Fernanda said, lifting her chin in Silver's general direction.

"Is this *The Name Game*?" Silver said.

"You don't go to Chilton do you?" asked the man. He had a nice retro-looking shirt under his tux jacket. He looked old, maybe forty, and was not handsome but attractive. A sort of Neander-thal John F. Kennedy.

"Is it required that we all answer questions with questions?" Silver asked.

"That depends on what game we're playing, doesn't it?" he answered, still staring straight at Fernanda.

"Oh, OK, I get it," Silver said. "It's like Kazaam, right? You can't look at the person you're talking to?"

Suddenly Mr. Ape-Kennedy snapped out of whatever trance he'd been in, scooped a handful of peanuts from a dish on the table, and turned to Silver, all chatty-casual and peanut-popping smiles. Fernanda leaned toward Silver, yet spoke in a voice that anyone could hear. "Mr. Hewitt teaches Science at Chilton."

"Please," he said, extending a hand to Silver, "call me Smith."

Fernanda clapped her hand over both of Silver's and with extraordinary insistence held them to the table. "Call him Mr. Hewitt," she said. "Don't take any chances."

"It's so hard, really," Mr. Hewitt said at Silver, as though they'd been exchanging confidences all evening. "Even during social time," he swept a hand vaguely at the dancing crowd, "the students still insist on enforcing that dichotomy, reinscribing the gap between teacher and student, putting us at a surname's distance."

Fernanda snorted and recrossed her legs. "As if," she said, just as Jarrett lumbered up behind her. It was like she could smell him coming—not surprising, Silver could too: Polo cologne and tequila shots sucked back in a bathroom stall—and Fernanda practically jumped on him as he slid into the chair beside her. It was more affection than she'd shown him all night, and he slurped at her gratefully, like a long-neglected housepet.

"And you are . . . ?" Mr. Smith Parker Hewitt asked Silver.

"Confused," she said.

"You're a teenager," he funnelled another handful of peanuts into his mouth. "What do you expect?"

Silver pulled at a curl of her hair and inspected it for split ends.

"Confused?" Mr. Hewitt waved his hand right in front of her face, like a hypnotist checking to see how far under his patient had gone.

"Silver," she said.

"What?"

"Silver," she said again.

"Hi ho," he said. "What is this, word association?"

"My name," she told him.

"Silver?"

She nodded once, put out a hand to say, *enough, OK?*

Mr. Hewitt, to his credit, moved graciously on. "Here with . . . ?" he cued.

Silver turned toward the dance floor to point out her date and raised her hand at the exact moment that Barry Gorda happened to finish a floor spin and look up to see if Silver had caught his killer move. Mistaking her raised hand as a signal to *him*, he climbed to his feet, gave a little nod to the guys (*my woman calls*), and made his way toward the table.

"The Cheese?" Mr. Hewitt said with an unmistakable note of amusement.

"Blind date," Silver said, wishing she could lie well enough to pull off being madly in love with Barry Gorda. She couldn't. "I'm a friend of Fernanda's," she explained, at which they both turned again to Fernanda, who was thoroughly engrossed in picking the strawberries off an extra piece of shortcake at the table and looked like she'd forgotten completely that she was at her senior prom. She had the air of someone standing naked before an open refrigerator at 3 A.M. nibbling leftovers. Mr. Hewitt had the distinct air of someone who'd rolled out of bed behind her.

Barry arrived at the table frazzled to find his seat occupied by a Chemistry teacher and hovered awkwardly behind Silver and Mr. Hewitt. He said, "Hi," but no one was paying attention, so he just kept on standing there doing a little stationary sway-dance, trying to figure out how to reclaim his rightful place at the table. He flicked out his left hand and knocked Mr. Hewitt on the shoulder. "They didn't give you peanuts at the chaperones' table, Mr. H?"

Mr. Hewitt glanced up at Barry, seemingly unaware that he was eating peanuts at all. "Huh?" he said.

The song in the air ended, *Red Red Wine* giving way to a different beat which Barry's body seemed to recognize. With his right hand he knocked Silver on the shoulder like he was a pinball flipper. "Wanna dance?" he asked, twitching toward the crowd.

Silver seized the moment. She yanked Fernanda's arm. "Hey,

you guys, Barry wants us all to come dance." Barry pulled Silver from her chair; Silver, Fernanda; Fernanda grabbed Jarrett; and they flew onto the dance floor like a little chain of cartoon animals, airborne as a kite tail in their haste. Mr. Hewitt was left to his salted peanuts.

Everyone was dancing; Billy Idol roused even the most defiantly sedate promster. The four squeezed into the crowd and made a tight circle which felt to Silver like a doubles boxing match since someone had obviously tipped the boys off that if all dance techniques failed, they could do Rocky moves and no one would know the difference. Silver tried not to look at Barry or Jarrett, feigning instead what she hoped looked like a sort of music-infused trance, her energy concentrated in a white-girl overbite to let the world know she'd been transported by the song, but really, it was just not the kind of music that would inspire such blissed-out possession, and when Barry and Jarrett and the few hundred other sweaty teenagers joined in on the musical bridges like depraved football fans screaming "HEY HEY WHAT GET LAID GET FUCKED," it was simply impossible for Silver to maintain any sort of detached oblivion to the scene around her. It was all beginning to feel like her worst nightmare of a frat party—every reason she was getting the fuck out of Texas and coming to New York, where things were supposed to be different but, apparently, were not. Silver wanted *off* the dance floor.

Amid the frenzied, bouncing mob, Silver tried to catch Fernanda's eye but kept catching Barry's instead and then having to pretend she hadn't. Finally she just stepped across the circle and put her face to Fernanda's ear. "Bathroom," she shouted and then got mopped in the face by a carwash of thick, drenched-with-sweat hair as Fernanda nodded *yes* and stole Silver away from the crowd.

The ladies' room was not much roomier. A scantily ventilated cave crammed full of girls in bad dresses, it was the hang-out spot of the uncool, the dateless, and the dowdy, and it seemed to Silver that it was probably the place she most belonged at this entire affair: in the bathroom she saw the first outfits all night that bore even the tiniest twinge of color. These wallpaper girls were friendly, at least, smiling *hey* to Fernanda and introducing themselves to Silver right off the bat, like they were welcoming her into the clubhouse. Silver and Fernanda found a spot at the corner sink by the towel dispenser, and Fernanda pulled out a handful of paper towels and started blotting her face. Silver stuck her wrists under the faucet, looked in the mirror at Fernanda behind her, and wondered if it would be tactless to just demand an explanation about Mr. Hewitt. Fernanda read her thoughts.

"Oh," she said. "So Mr. . . ." and then she waved her hand to say, *yes I mean Hewitt, but there are too many ears here so I'll not use his name.* Silver turned off the water and Fernanda handed her a wad of fresh towels. "Jesus," Fernanda sighed, "it all goes so far back," and her voice was low, so Silver moved in closer to hear as Fernanda hoisted herself up to sit on the bank of sinks. "OK," she said again, "so I've been totally hot for him since like eighth grade. We had him for Life Science, or whatever you learn in eighth grade, and, I mean, you saw him—he's such a little hottie." Fernanda scowled then, as if it just made her crazy to admit how damned attractive she found him. "And I know everyone has the crush-on-the-teacher thing, whatever, but it wasn't like that. There was a *thing* with us. *Between* us, you know? We flirted. But not like teacher-and-student flirting, you know?" And though Silver wasn't sure she did know how else exactly a Neanderthal science teacher might flirt with a thirteen year old, she nodded anyway.

Fernanda lowered her voice conspiratorially. "Anyway, it goes on like that forever, Jarrett and whatever other guys in my life notwithstanding. And of course it gets more intense, you know, as time goes on, as I get older. It's like: once you've slept with *someone,* then the idea of sleeping with another someone just isn't such a big deal. And then once I'd slept with a couple people, you know, it was just like, OK, I want to sleep with Mr. Hewitt. Which is what it's all been about with him since fucking eighth grade."

Silver did a heavy-lidded blink, trying to convey shock. "You didn't."

"Ugh—I did." Fernanda's face broke in a guilty smile. "Three weeks ago," she confided, like this was gossip about someone else she was spreading, not her own life turning into tabloid before her very eyes. "Barry had a party. Jarrett was away with his folks at some family wedding something. Smith—Mr. Hewitt—he lives like a block away from Barry." Silver must have looked kind of revolted then, because all of a sudden Fernanda started trying to justify everything. "He's not total skeeze," she said. "It's not like he comes to high school parties on a regular basis."

Silver was skeptical.

"No, no, I swear. He doesn't even come to Barry's ever. He just came that night. He knew Jarrett was away."

Silver was barely hearing the details at this point; her brain was still trying to make its way around the original fact. When she spoke she could read her own lips in the mirror behind Fernanda's head. "You slept with your Chemistry teacher."

"Ugh," Fernanda grunted, like she'd heard all the admonishments before. "I know, I know, I know . . . But the thing is that that's not it."

"What *else* did you do?" Silver said, unable to imagine at that moment what else one *could* do.

"It's not what we *did*," Fernanda said, and Silver's relief was nearly palpable. "It's just, he won't leave it there, you know? You'd think it would be the other way around," Fernanda went on, "older guy fucks younger girl and then blows her off while she gets stupid and moony and decides she's in love, and he's the one, and yadda yadda yadda. And, you know: whatever. It was fine. It was sex. Whatever. But him—he's totally *gone*." Fernanda paused, as if to let that sink in, but Silver didn't want to infer anything about what "gone" meant until Fernanda clarified her terms. There were a lot of ways one could interpret "gone." The whole thing was a bad TV movie. Definitely one set in Texas.

"He calls my house," Fernanda said. "I had to tell my folks I was on the fucking *prom committee* and he was the advisor! He leaves letters in my locker, and they're all like: he's in love with me, he wants to be with me, I shouldn't go away to college . . ."

"He said that?" Silver asked, incredulous.

"In so many words," Fernanda said. "And it's like *he's* reassuring *me*—like I'm going to think he's bailing and he wants me to know that he's seriously in love with me. Like this is all completely his *real life*." She paused, almost out of breath. "I mean, what do I *do* with that?" she asked, and it was an earnest question, like she thought Silver might actually have a response.

The bathroom door swung open again with a blast of music

that made Silver feel like she'd had a wad of cotton yanked out of her ears. " . . . *like no one else, ooh, ooh, she drives me crazy, I can't help myself, ooh, ooh . . .*" Some girl on her way into the bathroom had stopped in the threshold talking to someone in the hall, the door propped open on her taffeta hip. Suddenly Fernanda's expression went tight, eyes narrowed to charcoal slits. Outside, Mr. Hewitt stood with one shoulder resting lightly against the opposite wall, ostensibly engaged in conversation with the girl in the doorway, but his stare was trained directly past her and into the bathroom. Fernanda shook out her hair, gave him the cool angle of her profile, threw back her head and laughed and Silver thought: what you *do* is stop doing *that*.

In the mirror behind Fernanda, Silver could see the row of toilet stalls, a steady stream of girls in black trotting in and out, the metal hinge doors swinging open and shut, all of it flipping past like a game you can't quite stay on top of, a round of Three-Card Monty where everything's moving far too fast. And these girls—all of them, with their sly come-hither stares, their *you want me you come get me* looks, or that dead-on frozen glare that says *in your dreams, asshole*—they turn away then, out of the girls' room and into the night, and what they know, or don't know—and maybe that's the crux and the tragedy of it all right there—is that they may be saying *you piece of shit bastard you think you can fuck me*. But at the same time, they're saying *I'll let you*. In the same breath they're saying *you can*.

The Iowa Short Fiction Award and John Simmons Short Fiction Award Winners

1999
House Fires, Nancy Reisman
Judge: Marilynne Robinson

1999
Out of the Girls' Room and into the Night, Thisbe Nissen
Judge: Marilynne Robinson

1998
Friendly Fire, Kathryn Chetkovich
Judge: Stuart Dybek

1998
The River of Lost Voices: Stories from Guatemala, Mark Brazaitis
Judge: Stuart Dybek

1997
Thank You for Being Concerned and Sensitive, Jim Henry
Judge: Ann Beattie

1997
Within the Lighted City, Lisa Lenzo
Judge: Ann Beattie

1996
Hints of His Mortality, David Borofka
Judge: Oscar Hijuelos

1996
Western Electric, Don Zancanella
Judge: Oscar Hijuelos

1995
Listening to Mozart, Charles Wyatt
Judge: Ethan Canin

1995
May You Live in Interesting Times, Tereze Glück
Judge: Ethan Canin

1994
The Good Doctor, Susan Onthank Mates
Judge: Joy Williams

1994
Igloo among Palms, Rod Val Moore
Judge: Joy Williams

1993
Happiness, Ann Harleman
Judge: Francine Prose

1993
Macauley's Thumb, Lex Williford
Judge: Francine Prose

1993
Where Love Leaves Us, Renée Manfredi
Judge: Francine Prose

1992
My Body to You, Elizabeth Searle
Judge: James Salter

1992
Imaginary Men, Enid Shomer
Judge: James Salter

1991
The Ant Generator,
Elizabeth Harris
Judge: Marilynne Robinson

1991
Traps, Sondra Spatt Olsen
Judge: Marilynne Robinson

1990
A Hole in the Language,
Marly Swick
Judge: Jayne Anne Phillips

1989
Lent: The Slow Fast,
Starkey Flythe, Jr.
Judge: Gail Godwin

1989
Line of Fall, Miles Wilson
Judge: Gail Godwin

1988
The Long White,
Sharon Dilworth
Judge: Robert Stone

1988
The Venus Tree,
Michael Pritchett
Judge: Robert Stone

1987
Fruit of the Month, Abby Frucht
Judge: Alison Lurie

1987
Star Game, Lucia Nevai
Judge: Alison Lurie

1986
Eminent Domain, Dan O'Brien
Judge: Iowa Writers' Workshop

1986
Resurrectionists,
Russell Working
Judge: Tobias Wolff

1985
Dancing in the Movies,
Robert Boswell
Judge: Tim O'Brien

1984
Old Wives' Tales,
Susan M. Dodd
Judge: Frederick Busch

1983
Heart Failure, Ivy Goodman
Judge: Alice Adams

1982
Shiny Objects, Dianne Benedict
Judge: Raymond Carver

1981
The Phototropic Woman,
Annabel Thomas
Judge: Doris Grumbach

1980
Impossible Appetites,
James Fetler
Judge: Francine du Plessix Gray

1979
Fly Away Home, Mary Hedin
Judge: John Gardner

1978
A Nest of Hooks, Lon Otto
Judge: Stanley Elkin

1977
The Women in the Mirror,
Pat Carr
Judge: Leonard Michaels

1976
The Black Velvet Girl,
C. E. Poverman
Judge: Donald Barthelme

1975
Harry Belten and the
Mendelssohn Violin
Concerto, Barry Targan
Judge: George P. Garrett

1974
After the First Death There Is
No Other, Natalie L. M. Petesch
Judge: William H. Gass

1973
The Itinerary of Beggars,
H. E. Francis
Judge: John Hawkes

1972
The Burning and Other Stories,
Jack Cady
Judge: Joyce Carol Oates

1971
Old Morals, Small
Continents, Darker Times,
Philip F. O'Connor
Judge: George P. Elliott

1970
The Beach Umbrella,
Cyrus Colter
Judges: Vance Bourjaily and
Kurt Vonnegut, Jr.

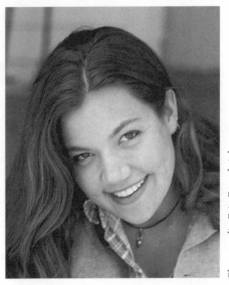

Photo credit: Erin Ergenbright

Thisbe Nissen received her MFA from the Iowa Writers' Workshop in 1997; she is currently a James Michener–Paul Engle Fellow at the University of Iowa. Her stories have appeared in *Story* and *Seventeen Magazine*. She lives in West Liberty, Iowa.